More or Less Reckless

Anne Marshall

BALBOA.PRESS
A DIVISION OF HAY HOUSE

Copyright © 2021 Anne Marshall.

All rights reserved. No part of this book may be used or reproduced by any means, graphic, electronic, or mechanical, including photocopying, recording, taping or by any information storage retrieval system without the written permission of the author except in the case of brief quotations embodied in critical articles and reviews.

Balboa Press books may be ordered through booksellers or by contacting:

Balboa Press
A Division of Hay House
1663 Liberty Drive
Bloomington, IN 47403
www.balboapress.com
844-682-1282

Because of the dynamic nature of the Internet, any web addresses or links contained in this book may have changed since publication and may no longer be valid. The views expressed in this work are solely those of the author and do not necessarily reflect the views of the publisher, and the publisher hereby disclaims any responsibility for them.

The author of this book does not dispense medical advice or prescribe the use of any technique as a form of treatment for physical, emotional, or medical problems without the advice of a physician, either directly or indirectly. The intent of the author is only to offer information of a general nature to help you in your quest for emotional and spiritual well-being. In the event you use any of the information in this book for yourself, which is your constitutional right, the author and the publisher assume no responsibility for your actions.

Any people depicted in stock imagery provided by Getty Images are models, and such images are being used for illustrative purposes only.
Certain stock imagery © Getty Images.

Print information available on the last page.

ISBN: 978-1-9822-6328-7 (sc)
ISBN: 978-1-9822-6330-0 (hc)
ISBN: 978-1-9822-6329-4 (e)

Library of Congress Control Number: 2021902140

Balboa Press rev. date: 03/31/2021

Contents

The Players You Met in Reckless vii
Flying High 1
Recalling the Usual Suspects 5
The Plan 10
The Best Gifts 13
Milan Fashion Week 17
Favours for Favours 21
I Can't Wait to Meet You 26
I'll Be There For You 29
Club Secrets 34
Don't Cry for Me Argentina 38
Take Me Home, Country Roads 45
You've Got A Friend 57
Ticket to Paradise 59
What a Wonderful World It Would Be 70
Water, Water Everywhere 73
The Art of the Game 84
Weekend in Wales 89
We Are Family 91
On Top of the World 95
Destiny, At Last 98
Welcome Home 110
Crazy, So Crazy….Why Not? 112
And Yet Another Second Chance 117

Home Stretch	127
You've Got A Friend	131
Easy to Forget	134
I'm Dreaming of a White Christmas	136
Moral Dilemma	138
Reflections on the Beach	142
Lavender	150
Have You Ever Seen the Rain	153
Rescue Me, Please	157
My Heroes Have Always Been Cowboys	166
(When Did You Fall) Out of Love	172
When We Were Young	179
Don't Give Up On Me	193
Broadway for the Soul	197
Getting By With a Little Help From My Friends	198
Audrey	200
Sam, The Professor	203
Dermot	204
Father Dominic	206
Giselle	208
Grace	210
Henry	212
Philippe	214
Sebastian	216
Love Me Like You Do	218
Wedding Bells	220
Save My Soul	224
Moonlight Sonata	226
Can't Stop the Rain	228
Someone Like You	229
Sebastian	233
End of a Chapter	237
I Want To Know Where Love Is	241
Stand By Me	243
Truly, Madly, Deeply	246
About The Author	253

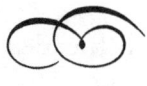 The Players You 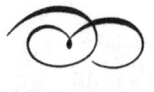 Met in Reckless

Madison (Maddy) Davis - free spirit Canadian flees to London for a year, finds love and heartbreak. She has blue eyes and dimples.

Sebastian Walker - reserved, widower, Design Architect, Chair of CityScapes Committee (urban redevelopment), falls in love with Maddy, described as tall, brooding and handsome, proper English gentleman

Belle & George - unacknowledged parents of Sebastian, truth is revealed on George's deathbed

Davi Singh (Daveesh) - Sebastian's driver, lover of Grace, friend of Maddy

Grace - owner of coffeeshop, emigrated from Trinidad, first friend Maddy made in London

Audrey - agoraphobic neighbour, becomes friends with Maddy, works with Maddy on renovations and interior projects

The Buttons - Jimmy and Jemma, orphaned children found by Maddy, adopted by Audrey and her husband Jeffrey, affectionately called The Buttons (cute as…)

Lambert - long time, trusted assistant to Sebastian, adores Maddy

Philippe - best friend and schoolmate of Sebastian, French winemaker

Henry - orphaned student, assigned to Sebastian for mentoring, attends boarding school, called to Australia by aging grandfather

Roderick (Rod) Frampton - solicitor, childhood friend of Sebastian, Council colleague of Maddy

Michael Riley (Mick O'Riley) - rogue financier/investor, befriended Maddy, sailed with Henry, presumed dead when his boat exploded

Sam Brown - (the Professor) Owner of Decades Nightclub, friend of Maddy, Davi's night school teacher, musician

Christian Gerhart - Manager of Deutsche Bank London, colleague of Sebastian, CityScapes Committee member, living in London while his family resides in Hamburg

Maria Aeschbach - practical Swiss representative on the CityScapes Committee with Sebastian and Christian, limited social skills

Mr Simpson - owner and collector of the vintage bookstore, friend of Maddy

Esme and Gordon - next door neighbours in London, retired couple

Preston Chase McAllen - (PC) wealthy Texas rancher, larger than life, Maddy negotiates the resolution of his gambling debt. Adores Maddy

Dermot Matthews - U.S. Ambassador in London, friend of Maddy

Deirdre Putnam-Fontaine - old friend of Sebastian, London socialite

The Contessa - owner of the Villa in Italy, believed Sebastian would be her adopted son and heir, sold the Villa to Maddy prior to her death

Giselle Gemil - French hotelier, befriends Maddy, begins relationship with Philippe

Sorento The Italian Designer - besotted with Maddy and her handling of his gambling debt, his *Azules Line* inspired by Maddy's eyes

Father Dom - village priest in Italy near Villa Contessa, befriends Maddy and Sebastian

Dag Andreson - world traveller and adventure personality, ranch owner in Canada, Maddy's life partner for 20 years

The Club - social club for gentlemen in Central London, UK, scene of many dinners

The Beach house - located on the coast, gifted to Maddy by George after she completed renovations in the old, unused cottage

Bellmere - family home in Maida Vale area of London, with garden apartment

Friends are forever

 # Flying High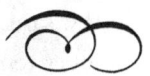

The aircraft was spinning, spinning faster and faster, falling towards the ground. The crowd was running beside the fence, waiting for the crash. The sirens were deafening as the firetrucks raced to the end of the runway, chasing the ambulance. He ran towards the field, blindly, angry at himself for allowing her to go, screaming her name, hoping she would hear his voice and not die in the inevitable crash...he sat up in the bed, his breathing raspy, as if he had been running a long distance. He rubbed his eyes, willing the dream to be over.

Beside him, Maddy was sleeping peacefully, one arm up over her head and one leg bent over the duvet - she looked like a Highland dancer. Sebastian leaned over and tenderly tucked her hair behind her ear. He watched her sleep for a moment or two, overcome by his absolute love for her. He wanted to hold her and protect her despite her reckless and independent behaviour...but, on the other hand, she was so lovable. He laid back on the pillow and closed his eyes. Maddy turned towards him, her arm across his chest, her cheek on his shoulder, her leg across his thigh. He kissed her forehead and fell into a deep sleep.

Earlier that day at Salisbury Hall, north of London.........
The roar of airplanes, the approving applause of the crowd, the smiles on the faces of the children - the airshow demanded your attention and admiration. Maddy looked over at Sebastian who was clearly enjoying being in the centre of the impeccable vintage aircraft collection. The British did love their history.

"Maddy, dare to come for a fly?" Sir Charles shouted over the crowd, hitching up his trousers and motioning towards the display.

Maddy shrugged and nodded, admiring his mint condition Tiger Moth. The 1930's classic biplane was the pride of the Flying Club. Sir Charles and his cronies had lovingly restored the wartime training aircraft. He handed her the goggles and helped her climb into the front cockpit.

Sebastian was leery, knowing it was too late to suggest it might not be the safest thing to do, especially with Sir Charles, who had just left the beer tent. Maddy, of course, was always up for a dare and this would appeal to her.

Sebastian held his breath as he watched Sir Charles and Maddy roll out onto the runway. She waved, her smile bright, pulling her goggles over her head. With relief, he saw her adjust the headset as well - at least they would have communication access to the tower.

The Tiger Moth rolled a few times, to the delight of the crowd and then it appeared to stall. Sebastian looked over at the radio centre; the operator was motioning for help...gesturing for someone to come to the booth. Normally the traffic would be directed by the tower but the vintage aircraft were being followed by the Vintage Aircraft Club members.

When he reached the booth he realized something was wrong - the operator had removed his headset and was explaining his dilemma to one of the older Club members. Heads were shaking; not a good sign.

"What's going on?" Sebastian hoped he sounded calm and reasoned.

"Sebastian, good fellow, it sounds as though Sir Charles has passed out, either from a heart attack or vertigo. His passenger is asking us to 'talk her down'. If it were only that easy..." The older man smirked. "We seem to be having difficulty finding anyone who is current. We don't fly it much, we just polish it. Heeheehee."

Sebastian searched the crowd for someone, anyone, who might know anything about the aircraft. Deirdre Fontaine's father, Rhys Putnam, had often told tales of the landing mishaps with the Tiger Moth during the war, no brakes, no flaps, no training...it was a pilot's dream to land her.

"Sir, can you talk Maddy into landing the Tiger Moth? I'm sure she's had flying experience and if anyone would try to land, it would be Maddy."

The older man was pleased to be asked, although he was rusty. He also saw the look on Sebastian's face and realized he must step up.

He grabbed the headset from the radio operator and took a deep breath. "Maddy, do you copy? It's Rhys Putnam, I'm going to try to get you and the biplane down safely." His voice was gaining confidence as he spoke.

"Roger, I copy. I'm maintaining altitude at 2300 feet; my speed is consistent at 150 rpm and I just found out how sensitive the stick and rudder pedals are…I don't see a brake or flaps so I imagine I want a great deal of runway and could you please ask for a medical team for Sir Charles. Thank you. Roger. Out.

The old man chuckled, looked over at Sebastian, "She's as cool as a cucumber and she's certainly got everything under control." He turned back to the radio control, "Maddy, here's what I need you to do…"

Sebastian watched the aircraft and listened to Rhys Putnam give detailed instruction over the radio. The aircraft was flying, everything seemed under control - there was no need to alarm the crowd and yet, Putnam looked over at Sebastian and shook his head. "I fear we've seen the last of the old Tiger Moth but I hope we are able to recover the passenger and pilot."

Not exactly what Sebastian wanted to hear.

When Maddy touched down on the runway, the wheels bounced lightly before the taildragger rolled to a stop - she was greeted by firetrucks, an ambulance and security vehicles. She stepped out of the aircraft onto the wing, unaware of the roar of applause from the crowd. Several arms stretched up to help her down. A reporter snapped photos while the medical team shouted instructions as it was difficult to remove the heavy weight of Sir Charles from the cockpit. An Airport Security Team surrounded Maddy, corralling her into the waiting car. At the gate Maddy slipped away, finding an anxious Sebastian and an excited Mr Putnam waiting for her.

"Well done, my dear." Mr Putnam was clearly pleased with their joint effort.

"Thank you for the wonderful instruction - your baby is intact and ready for the hanger. I hope Sir Charles will be okay." She hugged him, unaware that he was blushing.

She turned to Sebastian who was patiently waiting to wrap his arms around her.

"Well done, my darling. My heart only stopped twice." He whispered in her ear. What else could he say? She had been wonderful and the vintage aircraft was back on the ground, without a scratch. It was hard to imagine anyone handling the landing so efficiently, with a few verbal instructions. More or less reckless, but very Maddy.

"Have you seen enough of vintage aircraft for now? I'm ready for a drink." Maddy looked up at Sebastian, her eyes bright. "I'm sorry about giving you a fright but I wouldn't have gone up if I didn't think I could get down." Any conversation on safety or taking chances would have to wait.

"Indeed."

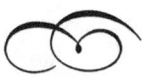 Recalling the Usual Suspects

The walls of the garden apartment were covered with charts and photos, like an investigation room - the photos and names on the chart were familiar and there seemed to be a storyline. Sebastian stood in the centre of the room scanning the flow chart, wondering what Maddy was up to now.

He found he was captivated with the connections. He placed his attache case on the table and walked over to the first chart when Maddy appeared at the door, carrying a box of photos and notes.

"What have we here, my darling?" Sebastian asked as he continued to follow the woollen strings between the photos.

Maddy kissed his cheek and stood with her hands on her hips.

"This is for Belle - she keeps asking me the same questions and she sometimes forgets who is who so I'm making a memory wall for her - she can follow the connections and hopefully recognize the faces."

Sebastian looked over at Maddy and shook his head. "What a daunting task. Good for you. How can I assist?"

"Let me walk you through it - you can fill in the blanks or make corrections. Fair enough?"

Sebastian nodded and followed Maddy to the first frame, amazed at the scope of affiliations.

"When did you start on this?" He asked as he watched her maneuver through the boxes on the floor.

"I got the idea this morning after speaking with Belle. Your mother was frustrated and I promised to see her on Wednesday with something to help her remember. I had to scurry to find photos and names. You can help me fill in the blanks, if you don't mind. Let's go…"

"Your grandparents are first…can you believe I didn't know their names. Here's a marker - please fill in. Next I have the two sisters, Belle and Serena. George, the love of Belle's life, as a young man, so handsome. I have several shots of George - here's a good father/son photo of you two. I can't decide - they're both good." She held up black and white prints.

Sebastian stopped for a moment, touched by the photos, remembering how he had grown up believing George was a favourite uncle, always with his aunt Belle. It was Maddy who had figured out Belle and George were his parents…too late, as it were. George had passed away the same day. George had left his beach cottage to Maddy, as she had redesigned and modernized the little cottage. Maddy had taken George to his hospital appointments and walked with him on the beach whenever possible. They had a lovely relationship - George often commented on lucky he was to have found a daughter in Maddy.

"Here is The Contessa in Italy with a photo of the villa where the sisters spent their summers. Here is the man your aunt married and here is your baby picture…so cute. Imagine how disappointed the Contessa was to believe you would be left with her when Belle returned to England, only to lose you when Belle wouldn't part with you. It was a risky ruse to return with a child, advising everyone you were her nephew and her sister had passed away. Your grandparents were so proper and concerned that people would see Belle and George together, they forbid any association. I would go crazy if someone told me I couldn't be with you."

She turned quickly, falling into Sebastian.

He kissed the top of her head and waited for her to continue, not wanting to dwell on any thought of being without Maddy.

Here's Belle's friend, Janet - she was at the Villa in Italy that summer - she had a son, Robert, who grew up with you as your grandparents forced George to marry Janet - no one ever knew who the father was - Belle said Janet was head over heels with the local baker but he denied any involvement so we'll never know. I only have one photo of you and Robert on the beach with George…do you think I should include this? I wouldn't want Belle to be sad about Janet and the stories of her suicide. Robert has not stayed in touch but she may have some good memories…" Maddy stopped to pick up another photo.

Sebastian let her continue, not wanting to break her train of thought.

"This is the only archive photo of the Vicar and Belle on their wedding day. Sad. He was so much older. I found the obituary - it was such a short marriage. Aren't these photos of you at school absolutely wonderful?" She smiled and continued. "I'm so glad I found the photos of Belle visiting you on parents day."

Sebastian smiled as he recalled the crazy school visits with Belle.

"Is this really your best friend Philippe? Hardly any photos of just the two of you - this will have to do until he sends me a better shot. Look at this - a great photo of you with a baby tiger…too sweet. I found several photos of your wedding day - you choose the one you like best. Oh dear, I was searching for your graduation picture…here it is." Maddy held up a copy and then handed him his framed diploma.

"You were so handsome…what happened?" She laughed and he spun her around in an embrace.

"Where did you find these photos? I didn't know they existed."

"Mr Simpson, from the bookstore, searched through yearbooks and archives for me and Belle thought there were albums in the storage area… not a great place to go hunting, unless you love spiders. Look at this - is this Stefan, your son?"

Sebastian nodded and held the photo for a moment before handing it back for placement on the board. Maddy stopped and asked if he was hungry or needed a drink, wanting to give him time with his memories.

Stephan was only a tyke when the accident happened. Sebastian and Philippe married French girls, best friends, who preferred to live in France with their little boys. Returning from a late night party their car hit a tree and all four were killed. Sebastian had been in London, at the office, when he got the call. It was a sad memory.

He shook his head and gestured for her to continue.

"I had to add your trusty assistant Lambert here - he was happy to provide a photo of the two of you. Nice. Here's your driver Daveesh, who we now call Davi, Belle may not recall that…he looks so proud in his uniform standing beside the car, doesn't he? You'll have to add the names of your friends and girlfriends on this panel...don't worry, I'll be fair." Maddy smiled at him.

"Now I have photos of you with Christian and Maria, your City Scapes Committee members. Belle knows them as the banker, here's Christian... and Maria, the bossy woman from Switzerland, here she is...she really has turned around, don't you think?"

Sebastian nodded, mesmerized by the effort Maddy had put into the boards.

"This next panel is mine...I arrive and meet Grace at the coffeeshop, who then meets Davi. Sam, owner of Decades Nightclub, affectionately known as the Professor...previously Davi's night school teacher, is right here. Our neighbour Audrey from across the boulevard goes here...with her husband Jeffrey and the children, the beautiful Buttons, of course." She paused to contemplate how much space she would need. "Here's Gordon and Esme from across the garden from us, they were neighbours of your grandparents and Belle would remember them. I'm not sure if Belle would know Preston aka PC from Texas and here's Giselle who I think is getting to know Philippe very well." She winked.

"I dedicated a panel for the Garden Show...just look at the gowns Belle has worn over the years." Maddy crossed her arms, admiring the vintage photos.

Sebastian smiled as he recalled the vision of Belle and Maddy arriving at the grand staircase of the Garden Show Ball. The first dance with Maddy had been exhilarating...he could almost feel the freedom of waltzing with her across the floor, her complete trust in him as he held her in his arms. He blinked, reluctant to leave the memory as he heard Maddy continue.

"Ahh, here is Henry - do you think he should have his own board or panel? We have so many photos of him with Belle and George at the beach."

Henry had lost his parents at an early age; his father had gone to school with Sebastian and Philippe so the Headmaster had requested they take Henry on in a mentorship program - to give him a male perspective and a sense of business. Maddy had taken Henry under her wing and introduced him to baking; exposed him to serving the homeless at the Mission; included him in their outings and assisting with his various school projects. She introduced him to her friend Michael Riley and sailing...

which became a passion with him. She was devastated when he was called away to Australia to be with his estranged grandfather.

Maddy stopped and looked at the photos, all the memories of that first year flooding back - the joy at meeting Sebastian, the heartbreak, the reunion, the dancing, the lovemaking, the losses, their makeshift, but never legalized, wedding in the hospital, the honeymoon and the secrets - finally revealed. How could you possibly show that first year on an inanimate space? Henry was gone - his relatives in Australia insisting he come home - what was to become of him?

She wiped a tear from her cheek and realized Sebastian was watching her. His tender look melted her heart, as it always did. He reached for her and they embraced, both lost in their thoughts of that first year of discovery.

How had sophisticated yet reserved, confirmed bachelor, once widowed Sebastian fallen so completely in love with reckless, free-spirited Maddy? At some point you just have to believe it was meant to be.

 # The Plan

Sebastian walked into the house, taking in the view of the gardens, pausing to watch the sun dancing through the glass walls, noting the warmth of the room - the feeling of home. He could hear Maddy's voice in the garden. It was comforting to arrive home and find her there - especially after having thought about her throughout the day.

"Here you are." He leaned over and kissed her cheek. "Isn't it a little chilly to be sitting out here?"

"Oh Sebastian, I'm so glad you're home. I have so much to discuss with you." Maddy touched his hand and smiled up at him.

"I'll get us a drink, shall I?" he asked as he moved towards the house.

"I'll move in and we can sit by the fire. How was your day?" Maddy gathered her papers and shivered, suddenly realizing she was chilled.

Drinks in hand, sitting on the sofa, Maddy wrapped in Sebastian's arms, they sat in silence for a moment, enjoying each others company.

"Maddy, why don't you set up an office in my building? We could travel to work each day, have lunch and spend more time together." It was not the first time Sebastian had mentioned the idea.

Maddy didn't respond immediately. She turned and looked up at him. "Sebastian, I so look forward to your coming home; you have a work life with luncheons and appointments and it might be distracting having me there…I'd be looking for any excuse to come by your office and wrap my arms around you. Thank you, it's a lovely thought but I'm fine working from here. Audrey and I meet at job sites now and I do a fair amount of running around during the day. Mr Simpson would miss me, I'm sure."

"So Mr Simpson takes precedent over me...I understand." Sebastian tried to sound hurt but he understood Maddy loved her freedom.

She touched his cheek and smiled at him. "I have a project we can work on together...I've been dying to tell you about it. Is now a good time?"

Sebastian nodded and waited for Maddy to begin.

"Maria, your Swiss committee member, always complains about hotels and how travel is not fun so I suggested we look at a Women Only Club where women could go and be treated like they were important and meet other women. It occurred to me the Villa Contessa, your inheritance property in Italy, was ideal for a getaway and I wondered if you would be amenable to converting the main house. Giselle would love to manage the project - she is expecting a huge settlement from her husband - he wants a divorce so he can marry his secretary and the children want to stay in Dubai so she has no ties or inclination to stay working but she would like to invest and own a part of something. The girls from the Spa down the street aren't doing so well and they worry about their Visa expiring so they would run the Spa part of things. Father Dom is keen to have meditation and other courses available in the village. Maria was able to get financial backing with a ten year return on investment...pretty reasonable, I thought."

Maddy took a breath. "All I need now is a fantastic plan that makes the most of the gardens, the view and the privacy allowed by the walls. The kitchen needs to have a working area for teaching and with 10 or 12 rooms, each with a full washroom, we can sell it to intimate groups as well as singles. Once or twice a year we offer a couples retreat but for all intents and purposes it's a retreat for women. What do you think?" She watched his face for signs of enthusiasm.

Sebastian was once again overwhelmed with her 'total package' approach to selling him an idea. He threw back his head and laughed.

"You've given this a lot of thought. My role is what, exactly?"

"You re-conceptualize the interior so it's elegant but rustic. Giselle and I can manage the finishing points and do whatever you suggest to make it simply wonderful." She was motioning with her hands and her enthusiasm was delightful to see.

"So, if I understand correctly, I am allowed to design and lead the project from a building angle? Is that what you want to do with the villa?

I thought you loved it just the way it was." He was sure Maddy wanted to return to the villa and live in the village.

"Sebastian, it's your villa, but you don't seem inclined to visit much so I'm trying to make it a special place, hopefully it's profitable as well. It's too beautiful not to share. Is that okay? Would you rather we didn't touch it? I'm sorry, I should have asked you first, before I got excited about the possibility and the influx of money. I guess it was rash to assume you would be excited about reinventing your birthplace." Maddy's face clouded over with the realization she had gone too far.

Sebastian rubbed her cheek, feeling rather shabby for letting her think he was less than enthusiastic about her plan. "Maddy, the villa is ours and I can't think of a better way to make use of the land and your friendships than creating a haven for others to enjoy. Father Dom will be excited to have the vineyards cared for and the village busy with enterprise. Bravo. Just give me your specs and I will do my best to design something simple, yet elegant. When would you like to get started?"

Maddy brightened and jumped up from the sofa. "I have the notes here and I want to get started as soon as possible. We'll be in Milan for the fashion show so we can head to the villa right after the show. Audrey and PC will be with us and they are anxious to see the sight. I think PC also wants to invest. Oh thank you Sebastian." Maddy threw her arms around his neck and kissed him. "It's going to be just amazing."

"Indeed." Sebastian whispered into her hair.

 # The Best Gifts

"Maddy, Harvey Gold and his son Ephrom, from New York City are arriving today after five weeks in Asia, they seemed desperate to have some friendly company tonight. You remember them, I'm sure, from the night of dancing at The Starlight…they fondly remember you. Harvey invited us to dinner - does that work for you?" Sebastian called from the car on his way to his last appointment of the day.

"Of course, but please invite them here for dinner - we can have a casual evening and I know just what to serve homesick New Yorkers. I need a few hours…is 6 p.m. okay?" Maddy was already planning where to get all the ingredients she needed for the meal.

"I'm sure they'll be fine with whatever you suggest. Are you sure you don't want to go out? I must say I'm looking forward to staying home. Thank you, that's a great suggestion. Anything I can do?"

"You can ask Davi to pick up some cream soda pop from Sainsbury's on Tottenham Road - he knows which one I mean. They have lots of soda flavours. I only need four cans to make it real. You are in charge of wine. Will I see you before 6 p.m.?"

"I'll be home as soon as we get done at the Council office. Just call if you need anything else. Thanks again Maddy, I look forward to the surprise." Sebastian sat back, smiling, wondering what Maddy had in mind - it was sure to be wonderfully fun and clever. He hoped it wasn't tacos.

Harvey Gold was delighted to be asked to the house. He had known Sebastian for many years and yet they had never crossed the line of personal vs business acquaintance, not until Maddy came along. He arrived at Bellmere House with a bouquet of fresh flowers, a gift for Maddy and a rare bottle of Scotch whisky for Sebastian. He looked tired and older than Maddy remembered. He said he wasn't enjoying the travel as much, especially since his wife had passed away. He was considering retirement but his children were having too much fun to settle down and take over the company. He apologized for Ephrom, who had made arrangements to meet his old school chums.

Maddy served pastrami on rye with a selection of mustard, coleslaw and chips from the corner chip shop (Mr Sanjay had delivered them just as they sat down to eat so they were hot and irresistible). Dill pickles and cream soda completed the meal. Harvey Gold was delighted with the menu and the thought. Sebastian had to admit he hadn't seen anyone so effusive in their praise for a simple meal and he himself enjoyed the sandwich, which Maddy piled high with meat.

"You have made my day, my lovely girl. This is the best meal I've had in weeks - my favourite. Thank you. How did you know? It's perfect." Harvey Gold said over and over, between big bites and sips of cream soda. "Ephrom will be disappointed he opted to meet his old university buddies instead of joining us."

"I'm glad you're enjoying it. When I'm in New York or Montreal I go straight to the Deli and get my fix. I thought maybe this was comfort food for you too. Save room for dessert - I have the best cheesecake ever." Maddy was pleased her scrambling around for pastrami and rye bread and pickles had resulted in an authentic food offer. Grace had, of course, baked the cheesecake…complete with a lovely black cherry topping.

"Maddy, I hope you don't mind, I took the liberty of choosing this gift from one of my suppliers. My wife always said every woman should have them. I bought some for Rachel, my daughter, when she turned eighteen. She cut them off the string and added them to her aquarium. My wife cried. You know Rachel is my daughter and I love her but I don't always like her. I think the only thing in her life she wanted and didn't get was Sebastian…lucky Sebastian." Harvey laughed a hearty laugh and wiped his eyes.

"These are for you Maddy." He handed her a lovely velvet case with the most lustrous pearls Maddy had ever seen. She looked up in shock.

"They're magnificent. I can't accept this, it's too extravagant." Maddy was overwhelmed with the gift.

"No, you must accept them. You said you were wearing borrowed pearls when I met you at The Starlight - you should have your own. Please, I chose them for you. I want you to have them. Think of them as a fair exchange for a lovely night of dancing with an old fool and for the best meal I've had in weeks. Maybe when you wear them you'll think fondly of me." Harvey had leaned forward, touching Maddy's hand, pleading with her to take the gift.

"May I?" He stood and offered to fasten the clasp.

"Thank you. I'm honoured and of course, I will think of you whenever I wear them. Let me have a look at them in the mirror." She stood and kissed his cheek. He was touched by the gesture.

As Maddy left the table to see the image of the pearls on her neck Harvey looked over at Sebastian. "I hope you don't mind Sebastian, but I remembered the hurt on her face when she came back to the table after Rachel had interrupted your dance and I felt I had to make her smile when she thought of us."

Sebastian looked away, recalling the night clearly. He had been dancing with Maddy and had just learned that Rachel had gone to his house to find him - she had been shocked to see his gardener dancing with her father...

"Thank you Harvey. I almost lost her that night. I appreciate the thought and Maddy is obviously pleased with the gift. Thank you." He realized he was whispering.

Maddy returned to the table, cheesecake in hand and the conversation continued in a lively manner. Maddy invited Harvey to play the piano and he was happy to entertain for the next hour.

When Harvey had gone, effusive with invitations to visit in New York, Maddy and Sebastian sat by the fire listening to a recording of a new band Maddy had discovered at Decades.

"Maddy, I wish I had bought you the pearls. I never know what to get you and Lambert is always searching through magazines or retail catalogues to see what's new and what you might like. What would you like to have?" Sebastian realized he spent hours wondering what he could give Maddy to make her happy. She seemed to buy things on a whim, yet they were perfect for the person she gifted them to. She didn't buy much for herself. The pearls would have been a lovely gift, although he wouldn't have had the confidence to get the right length or hue.

"Sebastian, we've been through this before. I don't want things from you but what I love the most, what I cherish, is when you to come home after work - you always look so happy to be home; you kiss me when you meet me, regardless of who is around; you put your hand on my back when we walk into a room and it makes me feel secure and loved; you hold my hand when we walk somewhere…those are wonderful gifts that make me feel loved. What more could I want? What more could I possibly need?" She snuggled her head into his chest and at that moment he felt as though a veil of happiness had been tossed over him. He held her tight, afraid to let go. If his touch and tenderness made her happy he would never stop.

Maddy stood slowly and put her hand out to him - she smiled and he felt bewitched.

"Let's go to bed." She said in a husky voice.

He took her hand and followed her up the stairs.

Milan Fashion Week

Audrey was beside herself with excitement; the Texan - PC, his daughter Jessica and son-in-law Riley, Maddy and Sebastian were in the limo enroute to the fashion show at the *Case di Sorento*. Maddy was stunning in her Sorento ensemble; PC's daughter Jessica, also wore a Sorento original and Audrey herself had purchased a large silk scarf with a peacock feather graphic - she had never owned anything so vivid and so blue. Why was everyone else so calm…they were seated in the front row and Audrey felt eyes on her, people were wondering who they were, why they were seated in front, near the family. Audrey felt like standing up and shouting "we're here because my friend saved his bacon." She realized she didn't know the story of how Sorento and Maddy became so close…it seemed to be the sort of thing you would tell your best friend. All Maddy had said was that she did him a favour once.

Maddy was summoned to the back room and the lights were dimmed. The background music was Vivaldi, the crowd hushed and the room was filled with stars - sparkling stars everywhere.

Suddenly the music was upbeat and modern, the stars still swirling. It was magical and everyone seemed captivated with the stars, the music and the anticipation of what was about to happen.

The models began walking down the runway, all in blue, the lighting changed to looked like rippling water…it looked as though the models were making their way through the water. Audrey held her breath - the effect was so beautiful. She had never seen anything so spectacular.

The music changed to a song by Lou Rawls and there was Maddy strolling down the runway in her simple blue dress, stopping to take a call on her mobile, moving naturally down the long runway towards the designer, who was sitting at a table enjoying a cappuccino - when had the table been added? How did he get to the end of the runway? When Maddy reached him, she leaned on the chair, air kissed his cheek and then they walked together up the runway, stopping to wave to the crowd. Sorento took his bows, to his appreciative crowd, and the lights starting flashing blue hues.

The models and Sorento were arranged at the entrance to the runway, looking as though they were posing for a painting. Maddy walked onto the staging area, took a selfie with the group and motioned for the audience to acknowledge the orchestra and then the models and finally Sorento, who walked towards her, took her hands in his and bowing, kissed her hand. He applauded Maddy and then air kissed his wife, sitting in the front row. The crowd stood and applauded the collection and the designer…his *Azules* Collection sure to be a hit. The designs were being shown in Madrid in the next month so the name was fitting…azules was blue in Spanish… Sorento hoped to expand to this new market.

The cocktail reception with the models and family was loud and frenzied as everyone expressed pleasure with the show. Audrey and Sebastian exchanged looks as they watched Maddy circulate through the crowd, clearly not intimidated by the event. PC and his daughter were standing back, not sure of the protocol - Maddy introduced them to the buyers, explaining how fond of the designs Jessica was - suggesting she could assist with American retailers.

"Does it bother you that Maddy walks into situations as though she belongs in that world?" Audrey asked Sebastian.

"Not at all. That's who she is…I wouldn't be comfortable but she certainly has no issues with new experiences." Sebastian wondered why Audrey would ask such a question.

The group had decided to dine together after the show, feeling Sorento and his family should revel in their success alone. Sebastian had to admit it was exciting but he hoped they were done with the fashion show business… remembering his own part on the runway waiting for Maddy in the lovely wedding dress. He wondered if she regretted not having a big wedding but when she smiled at him across the table he knew she was not one to regret anything.

The next day the group made their way to the villa. Father Dom was pleased to see Maddy and Sebastian and welcomed the group to an outdoor luncheon in the gardens, as per Maddy's instructions. Audrey was quiet as she took in the grounds, the buildings, the village, the friends Maddy had told her about. She could see the vision Maddy had described - she could feel the relaxing calm of the village.

"Well, what do you think?" Maddy was beside her, breaking her reveille.

"It's wonderful. I wish I was a part of the renovation plan. I guess Giselle will take that on now. What a life you have Maddy. These people are so happy to have you back here. I'm jealous that you have so many friends." Audrey hung her head.

"But you're my bestie." Maddy hugged her. They stood side by side watching the interaction at the table laden with platters of food. Father Dom approached them, asking if everything was to her liking. Maddy took his arm and said she couldn't imagine life without him. He looked embarrassed but pleased. Audrey thought Father Dom was too handsome for his own good. She would have to watch him.

"Maddy, you realize these people don't speak English, right?" Audrey looked concerned. Maddy laughed, amused. They were in Italy after all.

After lunch Maddy asked Sebastian to outline his design concept for the new enterprise. He was businesslike in his approach to the flow of guest traffic and the mechanics of the design, careful to mention how the vision notes from Maddy had influenced his plan. He had a large kitchen, ten guest rooms, a living area for he and Maddy, a suite for the manager - Giselle, dining areas indoors and outdoors, a dance studio/yoga/meditation room (located in the Contessa's former bedroom) and an art studio in the attic. The vineyard plan was presented by Father Dom, who had consulted with Sebastian's oldest friend, Philippe, who had his own winery in France. A local farmer spoke about his cheese making skills and his wife claimed her green olives and focaccia bread were the best in the village. Everyone wanted to be involved.

PC and his son-in-law were anxious to invest as Jessica thought she would like to take cooking classes here with her friends.

Someone asked what they would call the venue…is it still to be the Villa Contessa? Sebastian cleared his throat and suggested they name the villa after Maddy and call it *Villa Mirage*. Maddy was shocked but the crowd applauded and Sebastian showed his rendering of a logo incorporating the name and the sketch of the Villa.

Audrey watched the crowd applaud and wondered how the name applied to Maddy…she seemed to be the only one who didn't know the story. Shouldn't your best friend know these things? Giselle seemed very friendly with Maddy. Everyone seemed rather chummy. Audrey felt Maddy was slipping away from her.

When they were alone in their room Maddy asked Sebastian about the name - why he had chosen it. She had thought he would want to name it after his son Stefan. Sebastian explained that he had been touched by her story of Paris and her first lover…he thought the name her lover had given her, *Mirage*, was perfect because he was so happy he could imagine the man not believing she was real to him. Maddy had tears in her eyes when he kissed her.

Favours for Favours

Sebastian heard a phone ringing and thought he was dreaming - it was dark in the room and yet the ringing continued. Maddy moved her head from his chest and reached out, her hand searching for the phone. "Hello?" Her voice was thick with sleep. She sat up, listening to the caller, Dag, her ex, shouting into the phone.

"Dag, is Scotty there with you? Let me talk to Scotty. Dag, stop talking. Hand the phone over to Scotty, please." Maddy was calm and wide awake now.

"Dag, why are you still talking? Please hand the phone over to Scotty. I need to talk to Scotty." There was a pause as she listened. "Because Dag, you don't always give me the whole story. Please, I'm begging you to pass the phone to Scotty. If you don't let me speak to Scotty I will hang up and you can fix this problem on your own." Maddy was running her hand through her hair, impatiently.

"Ah, Scotty, tell me what's going on. Is it really as bad as Dag thinks it is?" Maddy sat on the edge of the bed, listening, one hand stroking Sebastian on the arm, letting him know she was fine. She stood up and moved out of the room, hoping Sebastian would go back to sleep.

When Maddy returned to bed she reached for Sebastian and sighed. He pulled her close, knowing she would tell him what was happening when she was ready. He closed his eyes, held her, taking in the scent of her, wondering why Dag would call her in the middle of the night. Wondering why Dag would call her at all. Maddy had left Dag - why would he expect her to help him? Sebastian fell asleep holding her close.

The next morning Maddy was busy with phone calls and emphatic instructions. Dag and his friends were on a motorcycle tour and one of the American lads had brought a young lady into his hotel room in Casablanca. It turned out she was underage although she had met the men in a late night bar. Her uncle had followed them back to the room, breaking down the door, finding them in bed together. The police arrested the man and he was being held in the local jail. The tour was on hold until his release. Dag had never dealt with the authorities or with conflict - Maddy had always handled everything for him. In desperation he had called her for help, knowing she would somehow solve the problem...she always had.

Maddy had called her friend Dermot, aka Ambassador Matthews, at the American Embassy, for assistance, and he was able to contact his counterpart in Morocco to plead the case and release the American. The tour was leaving Casablanca in the next hour or so. Dermot was pleased he could help Maddy as he needed a favour himself.

Dermot, as he insisted they call him, had been tasked with visiting the D-Day sites as a civilian, reporting on the status of the American presence versus the British and Canadian sites. He had asked Maddy to accompany him as she was familiar with the area and naturally, she had suggested Sebastian would be an asset from the British perspective and his knowledge of the battles.

Sebastian looked out the car window, wondering how it was he had agreed to a road trip with the Ambassador. Maddy had been very persuasive and here they were on the Normandy Coast in France, travelling as friends, no official car or driver, visiting World War II sites.

The threesome stood at Pegasus Bridge, with Maddy as their enthusiastic guide - both men caught up in the historical significance of the area. The Canadian Museum at Courselles-sur-Mer on Juno Beach was a wonderful start to their mission - Maddy proudly showed them the dunes and the columns of benefactors after they had completed a tour of the museum. They ate lunch in silence as they processed the information Maddy had shared with them. She had insisted they try the moules (mussels).

Driving west along the north coast and reliving the events of D-Day was proving to be an emotional history lesson for both men. As they settled into the quaint hotel Maddy had booked in Bayeux both Dermot and Sebastian realized they wanted to learn more about the plans for D-Day and what had occurred. They found seats at the bar and traced the events of the day on the map over pints of beer. Maddy announced she was taking a 'lovely hot bath' before dinner and left the men at the bar. She smiled as she watched them deep in strategy discussions. They may just become friends after all, she thought, hopefully.

Dermot placed his empty stein on the bar and looked over at Sebastian.

"We might as well deal with the elephant in the room."

Sebastian looked back at him, unsure what was next.

"I got the message loud and clear that Maddy was only interested in you - Sam, the Professor, was pretty clear about leaving her alone - he basically said he would beat the crap out of me if I tried anything with her…can you believe that?" Dermot laughed.

"Maddy was the first person to talk to me as if I was just a guy…she told me what to say, what not to say, made me laugh and then told me off - all in the first ten minutes of meeting her…she's quite a force but I am clear, oh so clear, as to her feelings for you and my role as her friend, nothing more, although she would be dynamite in the political ring." Dermot was still smiling. "I don't know why you don't marry her." Dermot was serious.

"We are married, actually." Sebastian looked up from the drink he had been nursing.

"I don't think vows made in a hospital ward make it legal….do you?"

Sebastian sat quietly, contemplating the weight of the question. He decided not to respond, unsure why Dermot would be interested.

The bartender asked if they needed another drink, thankfully changing the subject.

"Not for me, I better freshen up for dinner." Dermot stood and moved away. "Dinner at 8 p.m. I believe Maddy said." He looked at his watch, bowed slightly and left the room.

Sebastian signed for the drinks and walked slowly to the room. His mind churning with the possibility that Maddy might not want to be married to him...how could he be so naive? How could he not have taken care of this? Would she want to marry him now? He leaned against the wall, his knees weak. He couldn't imagine not having Maddy in his life, in his bed, in his arms. He opened the door and heard soft music, the mirror steamed from the bath. He knocked on the open bathroom door and was pleased to hear Maddy invite him. She looked lovely sitting in the bubbles, her hair piled high with wet tendrils framing her rosy face. He smiled at her and realized he could not live without her. She smiled back at him as he shed his clothing and stepped into the bath.

Dinner was enjoyable and served as a planning session for the next day. Sebastian and Dermot were willing participants in the plan - anxious to see the suggested 360 theatre and make their notes. The group agreed the Canadians, British and Americans had done a fine job of keeping the war memories alive.

Maddy and Sebastian finally returned to their room and met under the covers.

"Thank you for being such a good sport about this weekend. I think you are rather enjoying seeing the sites you've read about in history books." Maddy whispered as she snuggled into his arms.

"Indeed." Sebastian whispered in response. He wanted to tell her he was no longer offended by the assertive behaviour of the American; that he was becoming used to sharing her with others; that he always wanted to do this journey but had never had the opportunity to enjoy the experience; that he wanted to marry her again, this time with witnesses...there was no need to speak as Maddy had fallen asleep in his arms. For a moment he wished he was in her dreams and then he slept, the sleep of a man who is holding his dream

Dermot proclaimed the weekend a great success, praising Maddy for her guidance and her organizational skills. He joked he would hire her in a flash if only she was American. He remarked he might be the only person he knew who had seen the famous Bayeux Tapestry, depicting the battle of Hastings.

His report would outline several shortfalls and suggestions for increasing the profile of the American memorial centre on the coast.

Maddy had innocently asked each venue for sales figures and visitor counts - she had done all the work.

As they were saying their goodbyes in London, Dermot asked if the couple would join him, as honoured guests, for the annual Thanksgiving Dinner at the Embassy. Maddy was surprised when Sebastian accepted with a firm nod.

"Indeed."

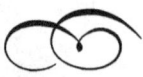 # I Can't Wait to Meet You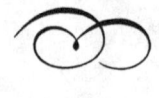

"Grace has been very tired and moody lately. Do you think she is having second thoughts about the wedding?" Davi asked Maddy as they were driving into the city. The wedding was six months away, delayed as the coffee shop renovations took priority. Davi was one course away from his business school graduation but his heart was in the kitchen at the coffee shop - he was enjoying testing pastry recipes and preparing lovely cakes for special events. Soon Sebastian would lose his driver.

"I'm stopping by this afternoon so I can check on Grace - she has been short on the telephone. Is she feeling okay? She seems happy enough with the growth in business and the staffing - she loves your Auntie and Uncle and I think she enjoys having you around as well." Maddy smiled at him.

Davi smiled back and knew that Maddy would find the answers - she was the best person to ask if you needed help with something. He respected her approach to fixing things - she had been brilliant with the professor at school, taking over his class and making him realize the students were all entrepreneurial in their own neighbourhoods.

"Oh, Davi, Sebastian is going to the Club with Christian so he won't need you to be at the office before your night school. Good luck with your presentation tonight. I can get off here......it's a short walk from here. Ta ta." Maddy stepped out the car and Davi drove on, smiling at how cheerful Maddy made each day.

"Hello you." Maddy greeted Grace, her first friend in London, as she came through the door. Grace removed her apron and leaned over to hug Maddy.

"Chai?" Grace asked as she wiped the counter.

"Absolutely. Let me get it. You sit down. You don't look so good. Are you alright?" Maddy was concerned - Grace was usually so vibrant - her clothes vivid and her features bright. Today she looked wan and tired.

"I'm not at my best, that's for certain. I'll have a peppermint tea, if you please." She smiled a weak smile as Maddy prepared their drinks and sat beside her.

"Grace. How long have you known?" Maddy asked her friend, rubbing her tummy.

"Oh Maddy, how did you know?" Grace was crying, tears of happiness and relief.

"When I hugged you I just knew. Your face is plumper and your body temperature is near boiling. I'm so happy for you. How far along are you?" Maddy was clearly delighted.

"I haven't told a soul - I'm safely past the first trimester. I'm terrified - what will Auntie and Uncle think? What if Davi isn't ready for this? I couldn't even talk to you about it - the wedding plans have been so overwhelming I just couldn't drop this news into the mix. Whatever shall I do Maddy?"

"Congratulations Mama. Let's have a little reception with baby cookies and announce the news…after we, well after you, tell Davi. I'm assuming the father is Davi."

Grace threw her apron at Maddy. "Of course Davi is the father. Who else could it be?"

"Just wanted to be sure. I'm so happy for you. Don't you worry about how everyone will react…they will be tickled. The wedding was getting so big and out of control - this is perfect. Why not have a small ceremony and celebrate the baby when he/she arrives? I think you were dreading the wedding - you wanted to think about it, plan it and cook for it but you didn't want it for you and Davi. Am I right?" Maddy recalled the dreamy look Grace had thinking about the wedding plans and how she had recently made comments on how much happier they would be eloping.

The idea of marriage was far more appealing than having a wedding. Problem solved…now to tell Davi.

Sitting on the sofa with her feet up, Grace looked relieved as Maddy ran down the list of invitees, menu and timing for the baby reception. She must tell Davi the news and confess her fear of having an elaborate wedding. Davi would understand, he was a humble person and he wanted her to be happy. Grace felt blessed to have Maddy and Davi in her life. Maddy knew how stressful a wedding could be and hoped she had not caused any unnecessary stress for Grace. They laughed as they worked their way down the wedding list and exchanged flowers for a crib, table centrepieces for a change table and the steel band for a baby monitor.

"I have to go but I'm so excited for you both. I won't say a word until Davi mentions it to me. Of course, I'm now officially an 'Aunt' and that means I get to help you through this. My first piece of advice - rest. I want you to be healthy when I call the midwife. Do you have a midwife? Are you going to the hospital or having the baby here?" Maddy's mind was racing.

"Let me tell Davi first and then we can think about all the other details. I don't know. I'm just beginning to get excited now that you know. Give me time to think about it." Grace laughed at Maddy's enthusiasm.

"You'll be a wonderful Aunt. Now go….take some brownies with you."

Grace was still chuckling as Maddy waved from the street.

I'll Be There For You

"Maddy, I have a gentleman interested in the house down the boulevard from Bellmere. He wants to see the property, but only if you show it. Are you available tomorrow morning? Please say yes." Lambert was more enthusiastic than usual.

"Any idea who it might be?" Maddy was intrigued.

"Can't tell you but he was most adamant about you showing the property. Don't you think it's time it was sold?" Lambert had been waiting for the listing for some time as Maddy and Audrey completed the interior decorating and modernizing.

"Okay, but what if he's a kidnapper or a sicko?" Maddy was laughing.

"That's not funny - shall I have backup ready?" Lambert was considering the possibilities…how would he deal with Sebastian if anything happened to Maddy on a call he made…it was too risky.

"Listen, forget it. I'll wait for the callback and let the weirdo know it's not going to work out. Lost sale but safe you."

"Don't be silly. I'll meet him at 10 a.m. Wish me luck with the sale." Maddy placed the phone in her pocket, wondering why someone had requested she show the property and how they would know her. She wondered if she should discuss this with Sebastian - no point in worrying him with something so trivial.

The next morning Maddy walked across the boulevard to the property and waited patiently for the prospective buyer. A black limo slowly approached the drive. The driver stepped out and held the door open, motioning for Maddy to enter the limo. Maddy smiled and shook her head. It seemed irrational to expect someone to step into a limo without knowing who you were sitting with.

She stepped closer and put her hand out, motioning for the keys - at least they couldn't drive off if they pushed her in.

"Madison, please join me. You are safe and Albert will not drive off but he will give you the keys, if that makes you feel better." The voice of an older man, amusement in the tone.

"Do I know you?" Maddy asked cautiously.

"We met a long time ago, you were a child and you were left alone in the park. I'm Carl - we went for pizza. You were precocious. I have made a lifetime of watching over you. I don't have long so we need to talk. Please join me." The amusement had disappeared.

Maddy took the car keys and stepped into the back seat, curiosity getting the better of her. She sat across from an elderly man with dark glasses and waited patiently for him to speak. He adjusted the blanket on his knees and began.

"Madison, I apologize for the cloak and dagger approach but it was necessary to meet like this. I don't believe anyone has followed either of us, however, a public meeting is not prudent. You might remember a weekend in New England, you were a child and you were left alone in the square at the park. I thought you were lost and I was enchanted with your smile so I waited with you until the 'black eyed man' came back to take you to dinner. Do you remember?" He waited, watching her search her memories for the moments in time.

"That was a long time ago…I remember the 'black eyed man', he was supposed to look after me but he kept leaving me alone. It was okay, I knew he would be back - my father said he was strange so I shouldn't worry." Maddy smiled.

"He was a hired killer."

"You were kind and I invited you to join us for pizza. You got a call during dinner and I thought you were a police officer…I remember the waitress laughing when I told her you had to go solve a murder."

"Madison, I have a confession. I was a lowly reporter at the time, following the police radio emergencies, hoping for a big story. You inspired me to keep hunting the bad guys, writing about crime. I spent the rest of my life ensuring you were safe; all the while chasing and writing about the worst people. People who are rotten to the core. Someone had to protect you." His words sounded sorrowful.

"Why would I need protecting? Why weren't we friends? Why didn't we meet again?" Maddy was curious.

"You had moved on - I was just an onlooker, I had no right to you or your life. Your father was a great friend; I knew he would want you to be safe. We trusted each other although we were working for different causes. He trusted me with his savings, knowing he would have no pension to leave you. He was never able to explain who he really was to you."

"I was fine. I got by..." Maddy looked away. "Why bring this up now?"

"You were looked after by Paul Boursalin and the rest of his team but you should have had a comfortable life, given what they did and how they used you."

"I'm not sure I understand..." Maddy was confused, "I had a good life."

"Madison, nevertheless, I have been successful because your father helped me with contacts. Any wealth I may have has been deposited to an account in Switzerland, along with the items your father entrusted me with."

"I've been given a month to live...I don't have a family...you were my inspiration, at a low time in my life. I watched you in the restaurant after your lover Paul's funeral - Les Deux Magots, I believe. The look of shock when you saw the bill was priceless - I couldn't let you pay for your homage to a great man...I paid your bill and left the restaurant before you saw me....if you had looked at me I would have taken you home...I knew that. I couldn't stand that you were abandoned again. I had to let you go." He paused.

"The work transfer to South America was difficult but you were immediately captivated by that Amazon man and I believed he would take care of you..." The old man touched his forehead with his hand; he was tiring.

"Madison, go to this address, here is the key and the number you need to access my things - they are yours now. Do what you will with them. Your father gave me whatever he had. I put it away for you. It's not much, I'm sorry to say. I dreamt for so long you would be alone in the world, ready to meet me and make my last days happy...but you see, I am a fool.

A lonely old fool who has watched your life enfold without ever making a move to let you know I was here for you. You were my moonbeam. I want to die knowing you are looked after, knowing you are loved and you are happy. I hope you can understand my …"

They were interrupted by the squeal of tires and a male voice calling for Maddy. Sebastian rushed to the door of the limo and frantically looked for Maddy.

"Maddy, are you alright? I'm here…" Sebastian tried to sound relieved and in charge of his emotions.

"I'm fine, really I am. I'm visiting with an old acquaintance. We won't be much longer." Maddy was surprised but relieved to see Sebastian. She knew her time with the older gentleman was limited.

"I see your *Knight in Shining Amour* has come to rescue you from a foolish old man. Go to him. I think he means to look after you. That's a relief to me." The old man sighed and coughed into his glove.

Maddy leaned forward and kissed his cheek.

"I wish I had known you were there for me. I would have enjoyed your friendship."

The old man tried to smile, his features contorted. "Kind of you to say. Good bye Madison." The driver cleared his throat, his hand out to assist Maddy. It was time to go. Maddy started to climb out of the vehicle and suddenly turned back.

"How did my father die? They said it was a heart condition but I know he was fit."

The old man hesitated and then turned his head towards the front of the car. "Someone called a hit. It was such a waste. Sad, but true." He coughed again and the driver handed him a steroid puffer, moving the blanket up over his knees.

Maddy stood outside the limo, deep in thought. She leaned in, unable to stop herself.

"Was it my mother? Did my mother call the hit?"

"Madison, when hurt we do what we must to protect ourselves. Just remember that. Good bye."

Maddy retreated, feeling overwhelmed with the answer. She turned to Albert, the driver, and asked if he would be in touch with news. She didn't want the old man to be alone in his death. She owed him that much.

Albert looked amused as Maddy handed him the keys, wistfully looking back at the man in the limo.

As she walked into the arms of Sebastian she remembered the scene in the park, oh so long ago…Carl, the old man was Carl. She smiled as she recalled how handsome, how kind and how worldly he had seemed to her.

"Thank you for coming for me. How did you know I was here?" Maddy looked up at Sebastian as the limo disappeared around the corner.

"I heard Lambert fretting about leaving you alone with a crazy old man - where else would I be? Are you alright?" He asked tenderly.

"Maddy, you know this was another reckless endeavour on your part… what if you had been in danger? What if something happened to you?"

"I'm fine, no need to worry or wonder about danger, I'm fine." Maddy turned away, a smile on her lips.

"You think this is amusing, don't you?" Sebastian felt his jaw tighten.

Maddy turned towards him, her face lit up with a broad smile. "It was kinda hot. You know, my *Knight in Shining Armour* appearing and all."

Sebastian tried to look stern but he laughed at her complete lack of fear; her chin out and her eyes full of mischief. How he loved her, his thoughts of danger cancelled out by her suggestive look. He wrapped his arms around her and kissed her with all the passion he felt for her.

"Will you come to Switzerland with me someday? Apparently my past awaits me there." Maddy's face was now clouded over, wondering just what awaited her.

Sebastian nodded. "Of course. I know so little of your life."

Maddy smiled at him. "I know so little of my life."

"Are you alright?" He asked, realizing she was shaken by the meeting.

She nodded, touched by his concern. Someday they would make the trip. Someday she would be brave enough to know what awaited.

"I don't know about you, but I could use a drink." Sebastian sighed, straightening his tie and then pulling down on his shirt cuffs."

"I know just the place…come with me." Maddy reached for his hand.

"Indeed."

 # Club Secrets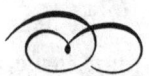

Maddy walked into The Club, hoping Sebastian was already at the table. The day had been hectic with appointments and she was looking forward to having a quiet drink with him. She wondered why he wanted to meet here rather than at home but as she scanned the room she recalled he wanted her to meet someone who could assist with her hospital fundraiser. She took a deep breath and walked into the room. She waved at Jason, the bartender and smiled as he pushed her drink across the bar. They exchanged a few pleasantries before a Club member appeared at the bar. The man was stroking his beard and staring at Maddy. She felt uncomfortable with his gaze and turned to walk away.

"Don't leave. I can see you are sexually frustrated and looking for someone to ease your pain." The words made Maddy shiver with disgust.

"I can talk you into an orgasm. It's what I do." He laughed a wicked laugh.

Maddy turned to go, not wanting to engage in a conversation.

"Don't walk away from me. You know you want what I have to offer."

"I'm sorry you can't find someone to have sex with, but I'm definitely not interested." Maddy whispered, not wanting to make a scene. She looked down the bar to see where Jason had gone.

"You feel sorry for me?" The man grabbed her arm, hurting her.

"You feel sorry for me? You women are all alike - you want it but you think you can insult me." He was sneering at her and his grip was getting stronger.

"Let go of my arm. Now." Maddy's tone was firm but her mind was racing and she felt fear competing with anger. She quickly raised her knee and connected with his groin.

The man stopped laughing his wicked laugh, a threatening laugh.

He twisted his hold on her arm as he bent over in agony. His left fist connected with her face and Maddy screamed with surprise.

The man uttered a litany of profanity as Maddy lashed out, scratching his face.

He punched her in the ribs, sending her down to the ground.

A crowd was gathering, wondering what was going on.

"She's crazy, stupid b……" his words were lost as he leaned over the bar in agony. "She attacked me."

"Seriously, that's the best you can do? You harass me and punch me and you say I attacked you." Maddy was indignant. She touched her face and winced.

Sebastian heard her voice as he entered the Club. He rushed to the bar area, pushing his way towards her.

"Maddy, what happened? Who hurt you?" Sebastian was clenching his fists.

"This degenerate started speaking to me, making lewd comments and grabbing my arm." She showed him her bruised arm.

"When I wasn't interested he hit me and when I fought back he punched me - I think I may have a few broken ribs." Maddy was gasping from the pain.

Sebastian stood, looked over and swung with such force, the sound of cracking bone echoing through the room, the man fell, sputtering about legal action. Sebastian rubbed his knuckles, surprised at the connection. "We don't hit women, we don't act like this in the Club, and we certainly don't condone your behaviour." His comments directed to the man on the floor.

Maddy looked around at the shocked faces of the members. No one came forward to assist Sebastian.

"Is this acceptable to the rest of you?" She was trying not to move or cry with the pain. "What if he attacked your daughters or one of their friends? Would you be more engaged? Isn't the Club supposed to be a safe place for your wives and family? Is this the first time this has happened? Am I the only one he's approached? Why didn't I know to avoid him? Please tell me no one knew he was lurking about in the Club." Maddy was feeling nauseous. "I'd like to call the police."

"Now Maddy, let's be reasonable," an elderly gentleman pleaded.

In the silence a small voice was heard. "He hurt me. I was afraid to say anything."

Another voice. "I didn't think my husband would believe me."

"I still have bruises where he forced me against the wall."

"We should have reported him but he's on the Club Executive, who would take our word over his? It's dreadfully unfair."

The men in the room shifted uncomfortably, hearing their wives respond.

Sebastian was beside Maddy on the floor, kneeling down, holding a cold cloth on her face. He looked up at the group and asked if an ambulance had been called. He turned to Maddy and asked if she would like to lay charges. Before she could reply a booming voice suggested she get medical attention first and any charges be handled by the Club Executive.

"Immediate resignation and banning him from the Club should make our wives feel relieved, don't you agree?"

Cries of "no, not good enough" and "how do you know he won't carry on elsewhere?" Came from the crowd. The women were now charged up and wanting some action, not just a sweep under the carpet.

As they debated the action to be taken, a stretcher appeared to transfer Maddy to the hospital. Sebastian held her hand as they left the Club. The women shouting well wishes and promising they would not be silent anymore.

Maddy looked up at Sebastian and smiled wanly. "Nice left hook, Rocky."

Sebastian squeezed her hand, not sure who Rocky was but pleased he had reacted. He couldn't imagine what kind of man would physically hurt a woman. He was concerned about Maddy and how she would recover from this incident. He should have been there to protect her...

The hospital confirmed broken ribs, no damage to the face, just a colourful bruise moving up her cheekbone. Maddy was released with instructions to rest. The doctor knew Maddy from her volunteer visits and suggested laying charges would be prudent to discourage a repeat performance by the man, no mention of gentleman, at the Club.

Several of the women from the Club visited her at home the next day, checking first with Sebastian to be sure a visit would not upset Maddy. He was pleased to know they had all gathered at the Police Station to make statements against the man. It seemed he had a record for other offences and all the charges had been dropped. The women believed he had paid out large sums of 'hush' money to cover the damages.

Sebastian left the women sitting by the fire and went upstairs to his office. He could hear their voices and eventually their laughter and goodbyes. Maddy was asleep when he came down to see if she needed anything. There were cards and packages on the table. She had made new friends. He covered her with the soft throw and sat beside her, patiently waiting for her to wake. It was a peaceful feeling, sitting here beside her, wanting to care for her, loving her.

He fell asleep, dreaming of Maddy.

Audrey looked over the cards and gifts with a critical eye. Why hadn't Maddy called her - Audrey would have been only too happy to watch over her - instead she was only now hearing about what happened and she was unnerved by the feeling of jealousy flowing through her. Maddy had shrugged off the visit by the ladies, explaining they were worried and needed to share their experience, which until now had been a secret.

Within the week the women had given their depositions and the man was charged with several harassment offences. The police assured the women they would not have to appear in trial court - after the incident at the Club several sources provided new evidence against the man. Mishandling of corporate funds, harassment, fraud and trader misconduct were amongst the charges.

The women at the Club had formed a bond - they met once a week for lunch - Maddy enjoyed their discussions on fashion, entertaining and the latest plays in town. She was part of their enclave now - part of the women's network. Sebastian was proud of her - it hadn't taken her long to be accepted in London.

Audrey was less than thrilled with Maddy's new status...she knew these women to be ruthless gossips, shallow and self-serving...not at all Maddy's cup of tea.

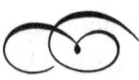 Don't Cry for Me Argentina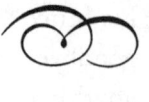

Sebastian saw his phone light up, from the corner of his eye, but he couldn't bring himself to pick up the phone, he was concentrating on the meeting. He and Maddy had been in Argentina for almost three months now and he was continually challenged by the antics of his local partners. There wasn't a day the partners didn't argue about safety issues, require *under the table* payments for permits or disagree on deadlines. He was torn - he could not leave the conference room or be distracted before they agreed on when the crew would actually break ground. Leaving the room would result in another strange change in direction. He was also angry with Maddy.

Just this morning, Maddy had casually mentioned he should offer the project for sale and return home. She said there was no shame in selling out and going home, especially if he wasn't happy with the arrangement. He had not responded to her - upset that she thought it was so simple; that he had failed; that he was complaining too much. He had walked out without kissing her goodbye. He wished he could go back to the bedroom and talk this out with her.

Loosening his tie, he walked out into the reception area. Lourdes, the reception/secretary for the group was anxious to see him.

"Señor Walker, your wife, she was here trying to reach you. She was calling and calling. She was *hangry* that she could not speak with you. She is gone with the Doctor to the mine in the mountains. She was *hangry, muy hangry.*" Lourdes was speaking quickly, motioning with her hands, pointing to the mountains. The flash floods and the relentless rain were unusual for this time of year, but the damage to roads and crops was devastating.

"Where is she now?" Sebastian stopped, trying to understand what Lourdes was telling him.

"The mine collapsed and the Doctor was hesitating to go alone. Señora Maddy knows the roads so she is driving. They are gone now. Why you didn't answer your phone?" Lourdes looked at him over her glasses with a chastising glare.

Sebastian sat on the plush chair near her desk and looked at his phone. He saw the messages pop up on the screen and then it registered. Maddy would have been trying to speak with him before she left for the mountains. It was folly to go up into the mountains with the roads washing away, the rain made it difficult to see and it was almost dark. Why hadn't he answered the blasted phone. He felt helpless as he realized there was nothing he could do - he was too late to stop her. He had left for work without kissing her, he always kissed her before he left for the day. He had walked out of the discussion, wanting to punish her for her glib suggestion of surrender. How he wished he could go back to the bedroom, kiss her and express his appreciation for her concern.

She would be driving in horrible conditions wondering why he was so *"hangry"*, as Lourdes said. How selfish on his part. He watched the rain for some time, stood up, feeling old and tired and slowly made his way to the car. He didn't remember the drive to their country cottage - couldn't see anything anyway. The rental cottage was cold and dark - no Maddy, no welcome.

He poured himself a drink, a large pour, and sat on the sofa, waiting to hear from Maddy, waiting to hear news, waiting…

Sebastian and his team had sold the projects in Argentina to a local design firm only a year ago. The contract had stipulated a joint effort with the UK office and Sebastian had agreed - Maddy was enthusiastic about living in Argentina for a year; learning the language and studying the tango. Now, sitting alone in the cottage, he wondered why he had ever agreed to this move. He had changed - he wasn't living his comfortable London life - he was a stranger in a foreign country and every day he felt Maddy slipping away from him.

The bright sun reflected off the hall mirror and woke him. He shook his head, wiped his eyes and realized the rain had stopped. He had fallen asleep on the sofa and his neck was stiff. He tried to stand but felt shaky. Finally he walked to the bedroom, shed his wrinkled clothes and stepped into the shower. He let the water wash away the tiredness of the last few weeks and hit the wall with his fist, angry at the situation. He had no connection to the mine or the young team believed to be at the mine but he tried to think how he could assist. He called the local office and they discouraged any involvement as the roads and weather made it impossible for any safe rescue.

Sebastian felt useless - his limited knowledge of the language and culture made him an outsider. Maddy had, as usual, embraced the people, the culture and the sense of neighbourhood - she belonged. The locals loved her for her joy of learning everything about the town, the customs, the tango, the food…she seemed to have an endless group of women in the cottage, cooking, sewing, making things for the market. He smiled as he recalled the happiness he felt when he walked into the room. His smile faded as he remembered falling asleep before Maddy said goodbye to her new friends. They had no time for love making or intimacy - there was always someone waiting for Maddy in the morning before he left for work - always someone including them in a winery reception or an outdoor asado - always an invitation to a christening or birthday celebration. He looked around the room, not sure how the stovetop coffee machine worked. Maddy always had coffee brewing.

Sebastian missed Maddy. What if she and the Doctor had car trouble or went off the road in the night; what if the mine site was too dangerous, what if they couldn't rescue or even find the young team of architects, sent up to the site to test the soil and the rock? What if Maddy didn't return from the mountain? How could he ever forgive himself for not taking her calls? Would he have dissuaded her from going? Could he have dissuaded her?

He wasn't sure how long he sat at the table, looking at the blank page in front of him. He rubbed his forehead and started to write, his pen struggling to keep up with his thoughts. He looked over at the laptop and laughed…why did writing feel so much better than typing…he must be getting old. He laughed out loud and headed for the office.

Lourdes, his receptionist, had not heard from Maddy or the Doctor and her clipped tones didn't disguise her feelings for his shortcomings yesterday. When she gingerly placed his coffee cup on his desk, without a word, Sebastian knew, without a doubt, she was on Maddy's side.

Don Diego and his cousins (everyone seemed to be related) arrived after lunch, as they usually did, exclaiming they were ready to discuss the brief Sebastian had left on the boardroom table. Sebastian stood, took a deep breath and walked into the room, closing the door behind him.

The next morning Lourdes burst into the office announcing the team had been found and they were on their way back - the ambulance was meeting them at the junction. Everyone was alive - dehydrated and filthy - but alive. They would be home any moment. She was breathless, pounding her chest, as though her own children were returning home safe.

Sebastian ran out of the office, leaving the car, he sprinted to the square, anxious to see Maddy. He stopped as he saw the Doctor chatting with the neighbours. Maddy was leaning against the ambulance, talking to the driver. She tapped the side of the vehicle, motioning him to drive on. She looked exhausted, her hair tangled, her clothing dirty. Sebastian wanted to hold her in his arms and kiss away the weariness. Before he could reach her, the Doctor stepped forward and wrapped his arms around her, stroking her hair, talking to her. She nodded and seemed to fall into his embrace. She shook her head and put her hands on his chest, refusing the bottle he offered. She bent over coughing, her body racking. Sebastian ran forward to catch her before she fell.

"Maddy, Maddy, thank God you're alright. I'm so sorry. We have a lot to talk about, but first, you need a warm bath, something to eat and some sleep. Come on, let's get you home." Sebastian picked her up in his arms, acknowledging the Doctor.

"She was so very brave and so very capable. We could not have found them without her…the roads were very bad…she wouldn't give up…be sure she gets some rest…she is exhausted and she won't take the sleeping draughts. I'll come by tomorrow." The Doctor called after them.

In their cottage Sebastian laid Maddy on the bed, slowly undressed her and covered her while he ran the bath water. When he returned to the bedroom she was asleep. He lay beside her, careful not to wake her. To his delight, she turned in her sleep and flung her arm across his chest. Oh, how he had missed her.

Maddy opened her eyes and was surprised to find she was draped across a familiar body. She was afraid to move, for fear of waking him. Sebastian stirred and gathered her up in his arms, kissing her neck, her cheek, her eyes and finally her lips. They made love as if it was the first time, tenderly and unselfishly. They lay side by side, holding hands, not wanting to break the spell.

"I missed you Maddy. I miss us." Sebastian whispered.

Maddy looked over, her blue eyes moist, her heart still pounding.

She blinked and smiled, a shy smile, not sure what to say, still smarting from the last time they had been in this room. He had been angry with her, hadn't taken her calls - what happens now, she wondered. As she wiped her eyes she realized her hands were caked in mud. She laughed as pieces of dried mud fell on the sheets.

They realized the bed was covered in reddish brown clay and as they shook the sheet the mud flew off onto the floor.

"I promised you a warm bath but I think a shower will take the rest of the mud off first. Come on, let's get you scrubbed off." Sebastian held out his hand, waiting for Maddy. She took his hand and stepped onto the floor. He pulled her close and holding her face in his hands, he kissed her again.

"Oh my darling, I was so worried. What you did was reckless and brave but it did give me sleepless nights. I'm so sorry for the way you left…can you forgive me for being such an eejit? I should have taken your calls…"

"Let's go home. You're not happy here. I'm sorry if I hurt your feelings but it's not worth selling your soul for money. You don't need the money. You need to be happy." Maddy hoped her words were not too late.

"I've offered the company for sale. You were right. I'm sorry I treated you so badly. When I heard you had gone to the mine I realized I could have stopped you - I could have saved us. I realized you were more important than my pride, my foolish pride. We're going home."

Maddy smiled at him and rested her head on his chest. Everything was going to be fine…she still needed time to process the last few days, but now the future was clear.

Sebastian understood she might need time alone so he dressed quickly and went out for coffee, chai and food. The sun was shining. She was home. She was safe and she was still in love with him. He had to believe everything was fine. Indeed.

The sale of the project was completed with unheard of efficiency. Sebastian was free of his South American partners and they were returning home, but first, Maddy had one last tourism guiding job to do for the local travel agency. She invited Sebastian along to experience Iguazu Falls and the ice fields near El Calafate - he could room with her. He was reluctant as he wanted to spend time alone with her but he agreed he should see the sights before venturing home. He would not be anxious to return to South America.

The tour group of twelve persons were a mix of couples from the United States, Australia, Spain and France. They were older, experienced travellers but they seemed to vie for Maddy's attention at every turn. They needed her recommendations for meals, her help in translating, her assistance in securing the right rooms and with photo taking. Maddy seemed only too willing to accommodate their demands and their whims. She was efficient as a guide - organized and caring.

Sebastian was not enjoying the group but he dared not add to her stress by voicing his opinions. He watched her handle the tourists with ease and he felt a surge of pride as she finessed difficult situations and left the group loving her.

"I think I just fell in love." The large man from Minnesota exclaimed, as he watched Maddy slowly make her rounds at the reception. He and Sebastian were standing at the bar, enjoying a whisky before dinner. As Maddy made her way towards him, smiling and radiating confidence, he understood why the travellers loved her - she looked irresistibly vulnerable and yet, indomitable. He couldn't help but smile at *Mr Minnesota*, Brian, he remembered.

Maddy had been reserved since the rescue. She was supportive of the sale and eager to get packed for the trip back to London. She assured Sebastian she had become so involved in the community just to pass the time as he had been so busy with his work. She gladly gave up her tango lessons, citing that if she had the opportunity to slide down someone's leg she wanted it to be his.

Sebastian offered her his hand as she neared, kissing her neck and whispering how lovely she looked. He wished they would soon be on their own. He hoped Maddy would be less business-like when they returned home and settled into…he couldn't remember what settled meant with Maddy. He chuckled and Maddy looked over, curious.

"Just thinking about how happy your friends will be to see you when you get back to London." He took her hand in his. He wasn't sure he should say anything more.

"Soon enough." She looked around the room, her eyes sad.

"Did you enjoy the day, Brian?" She asked the man at the bar.

"It was fantastic - better than you promised. My wife is talking to the children on her phone - she can't stop gushing. Great trip Maddy." He raised his glass. "Here's the Missus now. When do we eat?" He placed the glass on the bar and rubbed his hands together.

Maddy smiled. "We're all here, we can go in anytime. Shall we?" She looked at Sebastian, waiting for him to walk into the dining area. He placed his hand on the small of her back, a familiar move that made him feel very protective of her. Maddy looked back at him and gave him the smile; the smile that started at her lips, moved to her eyes and lit up her face; the smile that lit up his heart. Everything was fine between them. Just fine. Indeed.

Leaving Argentina was difficult for Maddy as her new acquaintances were relentless in their goodbyes - receptions, teas, luncheons and gifts were showered upon her. She had made such a favourable impression in her short time in the town. She was anxious to get Sebastian back to London - he seemed so disheartened.

Sebastian had completed the work necessary for the sale, releasing Lourdes and closing the office. He wasn't sure the project would ever begin. He was anxious to get home and continue his orderly life in London, his committee work and his comfortable routine. He also looked forward to spending more time with Maddy.

 Take Me Home, 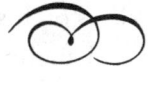 Country Roads

Maddy was asleep on the sofa in Sebastian's office when he opened the door. He walked over and sat on the adjacent chair, watching her. He was captivated by the look of innocence on her face. Maddy stirred and opened her eyes, smiling broadly as she looked up at him.

"I didn't think my meeting was that long?" Sebastian returned her smile. "I tried not to wake you."

Maddy sat up and stretched, admiring the skyline of London through the window. "I got here early and I started reading the Commission Report," she pulled the folder from under her leg.

"It's not very inspirational. I guess I fell asleep. What time is it? We don't want to be late for the awards ceremony."

Sebastian laughed and leaned forward to kiss her lightly on the cheek. "We have time. I haven't started the report but if it put you to sleep I'll hold off."

Maddy ran her fingers through her hair and looked under the sofa for her shoes. "I got here early because I had some sad news today and I wanted to, well, I hoped to convince you to travel with me."

Sebastian moved to his desk to refer to the calendar. "What news?"

"My friend, actually MaryJane was my assistant for ten years, anyway she was in a very bad car accident and they don't expect her to live past the weekend. I really want to go back and see her. Will you come with me, please. It's time you met my friends and they are anxious to meet you. I just wish it was a happier reason to get you all together. We should go tomorrow…do you need to see Ephrom or Harvey Gold in New York? We could add a quick stop if that makes it easier to justify." Maddy took a breath and waited to hear from Sebastian.

"This is important to you, we should go and of course it would be efficient and perhaps fun to include a New York visit as the drawings for the Gold family were approved and we will be expected within the month." He sat back as Maddy threw her arms around his neck and placed several kisses on his face. "Thank you, thank you, thank you."

Laughing, he called for Lambert to arrange their travels.

"We should go, we can walk over to the hotel and have a drink before the speeches begin. Ready?"

"Oh Sebastian, it will be so great for you to meet everyone and Harvey promised to walk the Brooklyn Bridge with us - I'm so excited…I get to show you my old stomping ground in Canada and we get time in New York City…how amazing is that?" Maddy spun around with her hands clasped.

"Amazing, indeed."

As they boarded the flight for Toronto Maddy received a text that her friend had passed away during the night. The injuries overtook her will to live and the arrangements were being finalized for the funeral on the weekend. Sebastian let Maddy deal with her grief, holding her hand, hoping she could feel his support - words were not necessary.

They spent the night in Toronto, meeting several of Maddy's friends for cocktails and a late dinner. Clearly they were delighted to see Maddy and meet Sebastian.

It was an interesting mix of people - some younger than Maddy, an older couple, a widower and a female artist. In some way or another Maddy had helped promote their work, travelled with them or done business with them. They shared their favourite stories, with laughter or tears and too soon the evening was over. He watched Maddy say her goodbyes, making everyone feel special. It was no wonder they loved her. Any concerns Sebastian may have had about being accepted by her friends were immediately put to rest as they clearly indicated if she was happy; they were happy.

The two hour ride north to the ranch where Maddy had lived for over 20 years with Dag, before they separated, provided Maddy the opportunity to introduce the players he would likely meet at the funeral. She gave him descriptions, who belonged with who, what they did and how they factored in the group of friends. He didn't ask if Dag would be there, but it seemed inevitable.

Sebastian wasn't prepared for the effusive greeting Maddy received from her friends. They were dealing with the loss of one of their own but they were clearly delighted their leader had returned. Sebastian stood beside Maddy for introductions and then sat at the back of the church, motioning to her he would be fine waiting for her there.

He watched Maddy walk up to greet the mourners with a touch, the brush of a cheek, a hug or grasping of hands. Everyone wanted to see her and be consoled. When Maddy came to sit beside him he wanted to tell her how well she had handled the crowd but several latecomers stole her attention.

The family had opted for a less formal celebration of life, more about friends and family than religion.

"Thank you all for being here to say goodbye to our mother." Two women stood to speak. "We were shocked by the terrible circumstances of our mom's death, it was a freak accident but when we were going through her things we found ourselves laughing and embracing her life as she would want us to do. Our first memory is of our mom storming out of the house on her way to get a job - her first job. She said she needed something to do - we were becoming too independent, dad stayed at work late and she was losing herself. We thought she was losing it alright. A few days later she arrived home wearing the most awful, brightly painted silk kimono and she was carrying a bag of takeout from the Chinese restaurant - we had never had takeout before and mom always wore solid colours so we were worried. She announced that she had a wonderful new job with a great boss who taught her that life was all about colour so she was shedding her black and white life for colour. Of course, her new boss was Maddy - our lives have not been the same since those two got together. In our house we called mom's boss *our mistress* - we all loved her but we weren't going to leave each other for her." There was great laughter and side comments as the group agreed.

Sebastian looked over at Maddy, she was smiling, remembering her friend and their journey together over the years. MaryJane had been a loyal and enthusiastic assistant to Maddy - they had laughed and cried through many tough times but their friendship was strong - they spoke everyday - sometimes just to check on each other. When Maddy left for London MaryJane was devastated...she felt abandoned but the calls continued and Maddy was able to maintain the connection.

Sebastian handed Maddy his handkerchief when he realized she didn't know the tears were streaming down her cheek. She smiled up at him, as she always did when he offered the gesture. She squeezed his hand, letting him know he was consoling her by just being there.

Following the service, which was emotionally draining, the group of friends met across the courtyard for the reception. They had planned dinner and a tribute at the local pub where they traditionally met through the years. Maddy and Sebastian were included in the invitation, of course, they proclaimed, refusing to hear any excuses.

Suddenly the group parted to make way for Dag, who was walking towards Maddy - a man with a mission. Maddy was speaking with one of the women when she realized there was a hush and everyone was motioning for her to turn around. Sebastian put his arm around her to show his support. Maddy turned as Dag arrived beside her.

"Maddy, I need to talk to you before you hear the poisoned version from your gang." He looked desperate. "Just give me a minute. Alone." He touched her arm and motioned away from the group.

"Maddy, you need to know that the kids, my lovely children, the same children you tried to warn me about, have sold the business to a foreign buyer who, I think, has a grow-op or golf course. They were seduced by the money and I know they never appreciated the value of having roots and history - you were right - they just want to go anywhere else but here. The money won't last long and they won't have any legacy but I can't fight that anymore. I'm leaving with my share. You know I always wanted to live somewhere warm, by the sea. I bought a dive school in the Maldives - money isn't important to me but I think I'll be happy there." He stopped talking and looked at her, holding her hands in his.

Maddy felt sad that the ranch was no longer in his family, he had loved telling the stories of the settlers and connecting his family history to the land.

She touched his face tenderly. "I'm sorry to hear the ranch will be sold but I hope you will be happy now. Just live for yourself, do what you want to do and live the life you want. I'm happy for you."

He smiled. "You're the only one who ever made me feel good about myself - you made me the action figure I always wanted to be. I'm sorry I couldn't love you in the way you needed to be loved. You look happy with your Englishman." He looked over at Sebastian.

"Maybe I didn't tell you what I needed." Maddy sighed.

"Did you tell him?" Dag motioned over to Sebastian.

Maddy felt her cheeks burn, "I didn't have to." She looked down at her hands.

"Well, if you ever want to go diving, come and see me. Best deal ever." He laughed and he looked like the younger version of Dag that Maddy remembered.

"I wish you could have met my friend Michael, he's an Irish sailor and he's alot like you - you two would have been great friends. Good luck Dag." Maddy blinked to stop the tears she knew were waiting to burst forth. There was so much to say but it was too late.

Dag kissed her cheek and turned to go. "Oh, Maddy, I almost forgot. These are the receipts for all the assets the auctioneer has taken. I put them in your name so you should see a substantial influx of cash pretty soon. I don't need the money and you never paid yourself what you were worth. Think well of me, will you." He winked and then he was gone.

Maddy leaned against the wall and willed herself not to cry but when Sebastian handed her his handkerchief she smiled through the tears.

"Thank you."

He wrapped her in his arms and asked if she wanted to go. This tender act made her sob. She felt warm and safe with Sebastian but saying goodbye to Dag, knowing he had lost his home, pained her. She had moved on and she loved Sebastian but she would always have fond memories of Dag and their volatile life together. She wiped her eyes and looked up at Sebastian. He was watching her with a look of trepidation - he was worried, scared and hopeful that Maddy still wanted to share her life with him.

"I'm sorry. I'm okay now. Let's go back to the hotel. The girls want to get together and the guys have invited you to go fishing with them…you really should go. We'll get together for dinner. I don't think we should miss it - I don't expect to be back here." As Maddy spoke she knew she wouldn't be back - it wasn't home - home was wherever she and Sebastian happened to be. She gave herself a shake, squared her shoulders, feeling confident and ready for whatever life offered. She squeezed Sebastian's hand - he was her future.

When Maddy and her friends arrived at the Pub the men were standing at the bar. Sebastian gasped when he saw Maddy with her shorter, very bouncy new haircut. The men whistled as she turned to pose for them. She did look lovely, he had to admit and he told her so when they embraced.

Her friends gathered around, anxious to assure Maddy she was loved and that Sebastian was welcome. There were toasts to MaryJane, toasts to Maddy and Sebastian, toasts to the future and of course, to the friendships that endure the test of time. The DJ was ready with their favourites and soon the dance floor was filled with friends having fun.

"I hope Dag didn't upset Maddy earlier today. He has a knack for pushing her buttons." The man they called Billy sat beside Sebastian, placing a drink in front of him. Best lager we have on tap. Cheers."

Sebastian nodded thanks and waited for Billy to continue.

"You know, we all worked at the ranch at some point. Maddy looks happy - I'm sure the girls have warned you what will happen if you ever make her unhappy…it's a tight group." He laughed at the image he hoped he had created.

They sat in silence for a moment. Then Billy continued.

"Those two worked together for so long - it was a pattern - Dag wanting to do something outlandish, Maddy setting it up and making sure he succeeded. They would fight over the details - Dag wasn't a detail guy - Maddy would book the tours and he would argue about crazy stuff, he would be yelling at her and throwing things - we were scared, scared for her and for ourselves. But Maddy would speak softly and tell him she would handle it. Several times she would do the skydive or the stunt herself, just to prove to him he could do it. She would tell him to go, get out of the office, go do something wildly immature and come back when you're ready to discuss the program. He would throw something and there would be a horrible crash, Maddy would cry out and we never knew if he hurt her or the furniture. She would calmly tell him to get out and come back with his tool kit to fix whatever he broke. He would storm out and we could hear Maddy on the phone, carrying on as if nothing had happened." Billy shook his head, reliving the memories. Sebastian watched Maddy with her friends on the dance floor, wondering why she stayed so long with someone so volatile.

"It was insane. Dag would return and we all held our breath, not knowing what to expect but he was contrite - he would walk in, sit down at her desk and say he was hungry.

"Italian or Thai?" he would ask. Maddy would say Thai. Dag would laugh and say "excellent, that's my girl. Let's go."

Maddy would remind him, in a calm voice, "not until you fix the bookcase and return the books" or whatever he had messed up. He would repair or clean up and then say "your chariot awaits madame, right this way." They would leave laughing and the fight would be forgotten. Maddy always won…he would do whatever she booked for him. We miss her but we don't miss the drama." Billy looked wistful.

"Why did she stay with him?" Sebastian asked cautiously.

"She's not a quitter. I think she felt she needed to take care of him. I guess she was right. As soon as she left his kids sold out. We all sold out - we rarely get together anymore." Billy lowered his head. "You know we watched Maddy grow up and Dag let her make most decisions. He's not good without her."

Sebastian nodded, he could relate.

MaryJane's husband Steve, approached Sebastian and asked if he would like a drink of the scotch whisky he and Maddy had brought as a gift. Sebastian nodded and the two men walked out to the parking lot. They climbed into a large farm truck and Steve poured them both a drink in plastic cups. As they sipped the Highland single malt, appreciating the smooth flavours, Sebastian wondered if Steve needed time away from his friends.

"I'm sorry for your loss. It seems insufficient to say the words." Sebastian looked over at the man who was grieving for his wife - he wasn't sure what else he could say.

"MJ left me long ago. She and Dag had a thing going for years. I never understood why Maddy befriended her, she must have known. It wasn't about sex, it was the drugs. I miss Maddy more than MJ - we all do. She was our…our guiding light, our 'go-to' person. When you needed help, you called Maddy. If you needed bridge financing, you called Maddy. If you needed to plan a party or fundraise, you called Maddy. She was our religion. We believed in her. We needed her. She bought my girls their prom dresses…they love her. She never shared any of our problems or talked about what she'd done…imagine a woman not yapping about how she helped you? You know, she never missed a birthday or anniversary, amazing. I wouldn't ever want to see her hurt or abandoned…" he paused. "You must think I'm a rambling fool." Steve smirked and looked out the front window of the truck.

"Maddy is special and she's fallen into the same role with her new friends in London. I'll take care of her. It's not a task, it's a labour of love." Sebastian responded quietly.

"How did you meet her?" Steve asked.

"We met in an art gallery and she told me off for staring at a very awful painting. I think I fell in love with her that night, but she frightened me. She was so confident. She changed my life - for the better. It's difficult to remember life without her." Sebastian smiled and finished his whisky.

Steve smiled back. "Thanks for the scotch. Thanks for looking after her. She deserves to be happy. I think she just wants a place to call home." He looked over at the pub door.

"We better go back in before they notice we're missing."

"Oh no, it's our group dance…we used to do these next songs together…you better come, you're one of us now. C'mon…no excuses." Steve motioned for Sebastian to join the friends on the dance floor. They walked towards the crowd and Maddy came to take Sebastian's hand. Everyone danced together, it was like being back at uni, Sebastian thought as he moved with the crowd. It was like a pagan ritual, everyone dancing, singing the words and bumping each other.

A country song came on and the group danced with choreographed steps, Maddy sometimes leading, others taking over. He stood back to watch - they were clearly familiar with the music and each other.

Maddy grabbed his hand as the song ended, leaning into him, seeming to anticipate the next song, a slow dance. She guessed right and as they danced, close, holding each other, he felt she was returning to him and his world.

"Are you happy you came to see your friends?" He whispered in her ear.

"I'm happy you came with me."

She looked up and gave him that smile, the smile that said *'it's time to go home, lover boy.'* He leaned in and kissed her neck, nibbling on her ear. It was time to go home. Indeed.

The next morning Maddy woke as the sun came up. She looked over at Sebastian who was sleeping soundly. She slipped out of the bed, careful not to wake him, and dressed.

"Good morning. Where are you off to?" Sebastian asked in a sleepy voice, rubbing his eyes.

"Sorry, I didn't want to wake you. I thought I would take a last ride around the ranch. Come with me. I'd love to show you the view from the hilltop." Maddy sat on the bed.

"Are you sure you wouldn't rather enjoy it alone?" He sat up.

"No, I'd like to share it with you. There are jeans and boots at the stables. Come on." Maddy leaned over and kissed him quickly.

Maddy and Sebastian were greeted by Tale, the groomsman, at the barn. He was brushing a horse, getting ready to saddle the horse for Maddy. "I knew you would want a last ride this morning Mrs Maddy. Look, Magic is happy to see you."

"Thank you Tale. I will ride Skylark today and let Sebastian take Magic." Maddy went to the stall and whispered good morning to the horse. She started brushing the horse, talking and scratching his ears and chin.

Tale smiled and nodded. "Are you Mr Maddy?" He asked Sebastian.

Sebastian laughed and shook his head. "Yes, it appears I am."

"She is a good lady. She helped my family when we came to Canada. She was my sponsor and she has been good to us. I was sorry to see her go." He looked up at Sebastian and motioned to the tack room. "You can change in there."

He could hear Maddy asking about Tale and his family as he changed. Tale was taking the horses with him to the Riding Academy for Girls across the highway when the ranch closed. Maddy was thrilled that he and the herd were looked after.

When Sebastian walked out to the hitching post Maddy whistled and touched her heart. "You were meant for blue jeans Cowboy. You look great."

Sebastian could feel his face redden at the compliment. "They seem to be fairly tight." He looked down at the jeans and his boots.

"A few minutes in the saddle will loosen everything...here's Magic, your new best friend." Maddy handed him the reins. "I never asked - you do ride, right?"

"I haven't been on a horse for years but isn't it the same as riding a bicycle?" He hoped he looked confident as he mounted Magic.

"Magic will take care of you. We'll take it slow. We have time."

Sebastian marvelled at the size of the property - the rolling hills, the views of the lake, the forested areas and the fields with grazing cows and horses. It was a lovely ranch - he understood her connection to the land.

They stopped on the hilltop and watched the sun wash over the fields, glistening off the water, highlighting the contours of the land.

"What a shame. This beautiful ranch will soon belong to someone from the city who has a big bankroll and no appreciation for the scenery or the fact it isn't developed. I hear they want to build a golf course here... makes me want to boycott golf." Maddy sighed. "It's beautiful, isn't it?" She looked over at Sebastian.

"It's lovely Maddy. I'm sorry to hear the family have let it go. Would you have liked to own it?"

"No, I had a wonderful time here and I have excellent memories of the rides I took over the years - but it's time to go. It's time to move on. Ready for some good old fashioned ranch-style breakfast? Come on Cowboy, let Magic take you home. Oh, and Sebastian, keep the jeans." They rode back to the stables, Maddy giving her horse the opportunity to gallop across the ridge. Sebastian took one last look at the view and followed - Magic did indeed take him home.

Sebastian woke and realized Maddy was not beside him. He sat up quickly, feeling a wave of panic - calling her name, wondering if she had second thoughts about leaving. The goodbyes had been emotionally draining and as they boarded their flight for New York he sensed she might not be ready to leave her friends at the ranch.

They had walked for hours in Manhattan, returning to the room for a most wonderful night of lovemaking. Now she was gone. He sat up and saw the note on the mirror.

Join me at the pool, top deck

He dressed quickly, chinos and a shirt, no shoes, not bothering to shave. He saw her in the pool, swimming lengths. The pool area was deserted, the sun was peaking through the tall buildings creating an orange glow to the deck area. A light breeze was moving the potted trees and the muted noise of traffic below added to the surreal scene before him.

He sat on the chaise near her towel, waiting for her. She finally stopped to rub her eyes and saw him. She swam to the edge of the pool and smiled up at him.

"Good morning. You looked so peaceful I couldn't wake you. I just didn't feel like walking without you. Come on in…it's really warm and lovely." She teased him with a spray of water.

"Good morning sir, may I get you something?" The pool attendant held his tray out as he bowed.

Sebastian reached in his pocket, pulled out a twenty dollar bill and held it out. "Do you think you could arrange for a chai tea and a bold roast from the Starbucks downstairs?"

"Yes sir, right away." The pool attendant ran off.

"That was very New York." Maddy laughed, "and very sexy."

Sebastian held out her towel, trying not to smile at her comment.

Maddy pushed herself up out of the pool and walked into the towel he held. They sat on the chaise together, watching the rays of the sun bathe the deck. Sebastian leaned back and Maddy sat between his legs. He reached for another towel and covered her legs. He could feel the damp towel against him but he had her in his arms and his clothes would dry. The pool attendant arrived with their drinks on his tray and presented them with great ceremony, happy with his tip as Sebastian waved the change away and added another bill.

"When do you have to be at your appointment?" Maddy asked, snuggling into him.

"Harvey and Ephrom suggested ten o'clock so we could meet you at noon at Bryant Park for lunch. Does that give you enough time to shop or do more exploring?" Sebastian knew she loved the city.

Maddy nodded. They had theatre tickets and a late dinner with friends planned. Tomorrow morning Harvey would join them to walk across the Brooklyn Bridge - he was embarrassed to admit he had never been to Brooklyn or crossed the bridge. Harvey had arranged a helicopter to take them to the Hamptons so they could spend the next two days together at the family estate. They would leave for London after the visit. But right now, watching the sunrise, holding the love of his life in his arms, Sebastian felt his world was complete.

As the plane ascended, taking them back to London, Sebastian and Maddy sat back, holding hands, lost in their own thoughts. Sebastian with a better sense of what life had been like for Maddy; Maddy wondering what life would be like moving forward.

You've Got A Friend

"We're off to the Council meeting. Won't be long. Shall I invite Rod for dinner with us?" Maddy kissed Sebastian on the cheek.

He responded by moving his arm around her hips, looking up over his glasses.

"I should be done by the time you get back. My deadline is 4 p.m. It's dreadfully tight but I think if I buckle down I can finish the costings and forward the document in time. I'll be ready with drinks when you return with Rod." He reached up to touch her cheek.

"I'm glad I'm not distracting you from your work. Later." Maddy blew him a kiss, grabbed the keys and left the cottage, whistling a ditty.

Maddy and Sebastian seemed to gravitate towards the beach cottage more and more throughout the summer. It was easy to make the transition, listening to the waves crashing on the rocks, being closer to Belle, and Maddy was always in demand for local projects. Rod, Sebastian's childhood friend, was pleased to have his friends nearby. He enjoyed their time together - of course he and Sebastian had a lot in common but he still had a soft spot in his heart for Maddy. Rod was frequently included in dinners, especially after Council meetings.

"That was a brilliant idea Rod. It looks as though we won and everyone is going to be happy with the result." Maddy and Rod arrived home in a celebratory mood with bags of groceries.

"Maddy, it was your idea - nice work congratulating me so everyone believed I thought of the amalgamation myself." Rod laughed. "That was smooth."

Sebastian was leaning back in his chair, having just pressed 'send' on his computer. Time to celebrate. He walked into the kitchen, pleased with himself and happy to see Maddy and Rod pouring the wine.

"It sounds like we all had a great afternoon. You two are looking particularly pleased with yourselves." He accepted the wine glass from Maddy. "Cheers to us." They clinked their glasses in a toast.

"I need a walk on the beach before we start into preparing the feast we have planned for dinner. Anyone interested?" Maddy had slipped out of her shoes and was walking towards the bedroom to change.

"Why not, it's a lovely day...we haven't had many lately. I never thought I'd complain about the weather, but here I am..." Rod shook his head and realized he was sounding just like the old men in the town.

Sebastian laughed and assured him it was his God-given right to express concern about the weather - they were British, after all.

The three friends walked along the beach in silence for some time, enjoying the sound of the waves, their company and the sunshine. When they turned back the conversation turned to Argentina and the challenges there. Rod was anxious to hear their impressions as he had imagined himself retiring to a new world, where wine was produced and he could learn a new language.

Maddy suggested he visit the Villa Mirage in Italy before he ventured to South America. Besides, she offered, we would be there and Sebastian would have someone to cheer on England in football.

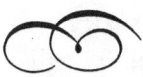 Ticket to Paradise

"Grace, I don't know what to think or what to do - you have to admit it's weird. Who gets a ticket to a south sea paradise with no explanation?" Maddy poured tea for Grace and herself and sat at the counter. Grace needed more sitting breaks now that her ankles were swollen and her belly bumped into the counter. Grace need not have worried about telling the family and Davi about her pregnancy - they were ecstatic and she looked radiant.

"Only you Maddy, only you would get a ticket to paradise and question why you got it or what you should do…you will go and you will send me a postcard and there will be a wonderful, crazy story attached to that ticket." Grace reached out to pat Maddy on the hand. "Why are you fretting? If I got the ticket, which I know would never happen, you would tell me to go and enjoy it, wouldn't you?"

Maddy smiled at her friend, knowing she was right but still feeling unsure about the reason or origin of the ticket.

"You know, it could be your Texas friend wanting to get your approval on his latest purchase, or some stranger you met on a plane who wants to dazzle you with his new hotel or maybe you won a lottery…" Grace was laughing.

"Look at you, giving me advice and making the decision harder to make." Maddy sipped her tea.

"I'm going to be a mom soon - I'm practising giving advice. You aren't the only one who can do that. Now go, get out of here and take that flight and remember every detail because I live my life vicariously through your crazy experiences. I have baking to do." Grace struggled to stand - holding her stomach she leaned over and kissed Maddy on the cheek. "Hurry home, this baby is not coming out until you get back."

Maddy watched Grace waddle back to the kitchen, smiling at her good fortune - having a friend like Grace was such a gift.

Sebastian sensed Maddy had something on her mind when he saw her enter The Club. Her brow was furrowed and she seemed preoccupied. When he saw her bite the inside of her cheek he knew for sure. He stood to greet her and she touched his face with her hand as they kissed.

"Jason, the bartender wanted you to try this new cocktail, it's called Paradise." Sebastian moved a bright blue cocktail with an umbrella and a skewer of fruit her way.

Maddy felt like laughing or crying, she wasn't sure which. How serendipitous…a blue cocktail called Paradise.

Sebastian waited for her to sip the drink, not wanting to rush her, she was usually so eager to try something new. The bartender always had Maddy give the new drinks a thumbs up or down before adding them to the menu. Unlike the Club members Maddy was always willing to try something different.

Maddy stared at the drink for a moment and then turned towards Sebastian. "Would you like to take a beach holiday with me? Somewhere far and exotic, where the water is this colour…"

Sebastian blinked and touched her hand. "Sounds interesting. If that's what you want, let's do it. When do you want to go?" He was playing along.

"Tuesday."

Sebastian cleared his throat and pulled at his tie knot. "That's sudden, indeed."

Maddy looked at him and blurted out, "I got a ticket in the mail today and I don't know who sent it, why they sent it or what I should do. Normally I would be thrilled and I would just go…but it was only one ticket and I do things with you now. You aren't travelling overnight without me, how can I go so far without you? Please come with me. It can't be dangerous or too crazy - the ticket has an open return. Who would send you a return ticket if they were going to hurt you?" Maddy shrugged.

Sebastian was processing the information, nodding his head, wondering who would send a single ticket, without any explanation. He might have been suspect a year or two ago but since meeting Maddy it seemed logical she would go and if she really wanted him to travel with her, he would go along. It was typical of Maddy's reckless approach to life.

"Well, it seems you are committed to going, regardless of anything I might say, so if you want me to share the adventure I best secure a seat on your flight. Shall we eat first?"

Maddy laughed and reached over the table to hug the man she loved.

"Excellent. I'm hungry. What shall we have?"

Later that evening, lying in bed with Maddy draped over him, he wondered just what awaited them in paradise. In his dream he and Maddy were walking on a long white beach with clear blue water lapping at their feet, cloudless skies above, a big ominous looking door ahead on the beach with a large padlock - the sun reflecting off the golden key Maddy had around her neck. The sign above the door read *'Enter Paradise at your Peril.'*

Audrey and Lambert came along to the airport to see Maddy and Sebastian off on their mystery flight. Audrey couldn't believe they were heading out without knowing precisely what they were doing or why, or who they were meeting. She hugged Maddy tight, not sure she should let her friend go at all. She shook hands with Sebastian and warned him to make sure the crazy lady didn't get into trouble. Sebastian nodded and sighed as they waved goodbye and boarded the plane for unknown paradise.

The flight was long and Sebastian was pleased he had brought work with him. Maddy read and watched movies, her hand resting on his thigh. It was a comforting gesture and he leaned over to kiss her cheek several times during the flight. They slept, they ate and finally they were landing; anticipating whatever was about to unfold.

The heat hit them like a warm blanket. The sun was so bright they had to shield their eyes to navigate the stairs on disembarking. The heat rose from the pavement, forcing them to quicken their steps into the terminal. They quickly passed through passport controls and security and gathered their luggage. Maddy headed for the door - Sebastian followed her, not sure where she thought she was going.

A tall, dark man was waving a sign covered in hearts with *Maddy* written across it. She waved and walked towards the sign.

"Greetings and welcome to our paradise. I am Jerome and I will see you safely to the hotel. Is this all your luggage?" His voice was deep and rich. Jerome recovered quickly when Maddy introduced Sebastian. He had not been expecting two passengers. He led them to an open-air jitney, loaded the luggage and drove off, singing a catchy tune and waving to the locals.

The hotel was part of a large resort complex. Jerome handed their luggage to the concierge and departed, refusing a tip. He bowed slightly and kissed Maddy's hand, wishing her a lovely stay.

Their suite was on the second floor with a large balcony overlooking the ocean. The white voile curtains moved with the breeze and the fresh flowers throughout the room gave one the impression you were sleeping outdoors. It was indeed paradise.

No notes, no welcome - just a property map with a big circle on the Palm Court Bar. Sebastian thought Maddy should go on her own, he would follow shortly. He didn't want to ruin any surprises. He loved the way she approached this cloak and dagger situation…she was fearless. He suddenly realized her biggest fear was how he would react when she told him of the situation. He sat on the bed, head in hands and wondered what had him so cautious, so reluctant to be open to possibilities. Maddy had changed him and he loved her for it, but he was still cautious and thoughtful in his actions.

He looked up as she walked past him in her bathing suit - he wasn't sure he should let her go out - he wanted her - all of her. He stood up to embrace her but she was pulling a coverup over her head and she was clearly anxious to get going.

"Ready?" She asked, barely able to contain her excitement.

"I was ready for you but I see you want to get out there and find whatever treasure awaits…you go ahead, I'll follow." Sebastian sighed and walked out to the balcony. The view of the Indian Ocean was stunning.

He watched as Maddy made her way along the path, greeting people, laughing with the staff, taking in the tropical scents and colours. An older man, perhaps a gardener, presented her with a flower for her hair. They had an animated conversation that ended with a hug from Maddy and a lovely smile from the old man.

As Maddy followed the path Sebastian saw dive tanks and guests returning flippers. He held his breath as he imagined Dag, her ex, having sent the ticket to lure her here. He hurried after her, ready to protect his love and he wasn't sure what was ahead, but, he had to be sure Maddy knew he was there for her.

Maddy ducked under the banyan tree and smiled as she saw the beach bar ahead. Green glass jars in nets adorned the posts, popular tunes floated out, a large blender sat on the counter and a colourful parrot or myna bird oversaw the bar from its perch - it was a perfect island bar. There were two men at the bar, huddled together in deep conversation. She noted the man on the left had long sun-bleached hair and a rather unkept beard while the other man seemed very muscular and clean cut. As she approached the bar stools the younger man turned to her and smiled.

Maddy stopped in her tracks. For a moment, just a moment, she felt she was imagining things. Could it be? Could it really be?

"Henry? Oh, my goodness, Henry." Maddy was running into the arms of the young man, laughing and crying at the same time.

Sebastian heard her cry out and ran towards the beach. He watched as Maddy and Henry embraced. Henry lifting Maddy off the ground and turning with her. The second man came forward and Maddy stood still, her hand over her mouth, not able to speak, her emotions so raw.

"Michael. You made this happen? Thank you. Thank you."

And then Maddy was in his arms. Michael held her, closing his eyes, wishing she would stay in his arms, come and sail with him, make his life complete. He held out an arm and Henry joined the embrace. They were laughing and touching foreheads and sincerely happy to be together. Sebastian could not help but feel he was intruding.

Maddy pulled away, her hands clasped in front of her, shaking her head. "Sebastian won't believe this…I'll get him." She turned and fell into his arms. "Sebastian, isn't this just the best surprise ever?"

Henry came forward to shake hands with Sebastian and Maddy was pleased to see them embrace.

Michael scowled; not sure he should stay now that Sebastian was here. He could not risk having good citizen, law abiding Sebastian Walker turn him in - his disappearance and eventual death had taken careful planning. For a moment he was disappointed that Maddy had brought Sebastian. She wouldn't have known what he had planned but he had been looking forward to some time alone with her - he missed his friend.

Maddy realized Sebastian would not expect to see Michael Riley in this tropical paradise, with Henry, his mentoring charge, the boy they had come to love - the boy who had been taken away from them without warning. She set about to calm things down and hear how this had come to pass. She ordered a pitcher of drinks, pulled a table over to the beach, under the palm tree. She motioned everyone over and sat down, barely containing her excitement. She held Henry's hand in hers and looked directly at Sebastian, suggesting the Captain, remain nameless, for his own safety. She would speak to Sebastian later about being discreet and never mentioning Michael - she hoped he would understand.

"Please tell us what's going on. We, that is I, hoped you were alive and enjoying your freedom, but this is beyond anything I imagined. Sebastian, we have been given a gift so let's think only of the future. The past is going to be explained to us right now." She reached out and touching his hand, she smiled at the Captain and asked him to please start.

Sebastian was shocked to see Michael Riley, his old schoolmate and former successful London socialite who had allegedly been blown up with his boat on the Thames. Maddy had not grieved as much as he had expected, she seemed to believe there was hope they would find Michael, her friend and sailing instructor to Henry. Sebastian had been assigned to mentor the young Henry, a student staying at the boarding school. He was orphaned at an early age, but his school fees had been paid - his distant relatives in Australia had demanded he return to Australia to see his grandfather - it had been sudden and Maddy had been devastated to lose Henry, who she had come to love and care for in the year she met Sebastian. It had been Maddy who worked on his projects, took him to galleries, encouraged him to cook and sail. Maddy and Henry and Michael had become quite close before Henry was sent away and Michael had disappeared in the accident.

"I guess I'll start, and the lad can fill in if I should leave anything on the table." The Captain began, looking at Maddy.

"I knew how distraught Mad was when the lad was called away. I felt guilty leaving myself, I couldn't implicate you Mad, so when I arrived in Melbourne and realized the boat needed some work, I left it at the harbour and ventured inland towards the sheep farm where the lad was supposed to be. I hitched a few rides and rode the buses, and then it rained, rained so hard I looked for shelter. Mad told me once that you could lose yourself in a library, so I went in and got myself dry. I did enjoy the place and the librarian was right friendly. She told me of a young English boy who came in for books - she said she kept a pile of damaged books for him as he lived out at the ranch and she felt sorry for him. So, I waited and soon the lad walked in for a new box of reading material. What's more impressive here Mad - that he wanted to read or that I went to a library?" He stopped to take a drink. He raised his glass to Maddy, who was laughing at him and encouraging him to continue. The Captain stopped for a moment to rub his eyes.

"Uncle Max, that's what I called him, came back to the ranch with me and stayed in the shed. By this time grandfather had passed away, I never did get to see him or talk to him, he was pretty much dead when I got there. The aunts needed a work hand so I was given chores and I must say I know a lot about sheep now. The old aunts were balmy as bats, but they did feed me. Although I may never eat lamb again." Henry looked out over the water, blinking his eyes to stop the tears. He did not want Maddy to see him cry.

The Captain continued, "the lad and I tended the sheep and stayed until it was time for shearing, always a good experience. In the meantime I visited the local authorities and reported the old aunts. They were taken to a care facility - they did not go easily. The ranch, if you can call it that, had been left to the boy and they were reluctant to leave the property they had lived on all their lives - they were also afraid to give it over to the lad. After a few drinks in the pub with the local officials we were able to secure ownership and put the ranch up for sale. The neighbour had been eyeing the land for years but he was always turned away, with rifle shot. The old aunts were crazy but crafty. The land isn't worth much but the boy has a slush fund, for his future. He didn't want to stay on the land, surprise to no one here." He stopped to take another drink, wiped his face with his sleeve and smiled at Maddy. "I think he missed you."

"I knew you were heartbroken when the lad left so it seemed like the right thing to do, take him with me - I needed an experienced first mate anyway." Sebastian felt a twinge of jealousy as he watched the two friends exchange a look of grateful love.

"How did you end up here?" Maddy asked, wanting to know how they had connected.

Henry was keen to respond. "We sailed into port farther south and we moored, set up fishing lines and waited to hook our dinner. A small inflatable boat came by and offered us fish. We invited the bloke to join us and he shared his catch with us. He drank a bit much and at one point he said Maddy would have been proud of how he had made a success of something he loved. He told us several times that Maddy would love this picture of him meeting strangers on the seas. Now, how many people know someone called Maddy? The more he talked about you the more we got excited about asking questions. Before he passed out, he told us Maddy had wanted him to meet an Irish sailor, imagine that. It was too much of a coincidence…" Henry paused and looked over at The Captain, motioning for him to continue.

"Yes, well, we got this big guy off the boat as soon as we could in the morning, bidding him goodbye and then we set about with our plan to let you know we were both alright. It was insane to think we could pull this off without being caught. It was a gamble that you would even come. We both wanted to see you, for different reasons…and here you are." He raised his glass in a toast to Maddy and then turned to Sebastian. "Sorry, you are now part of the clandestine operation, whether or not you care to be. My wife would be livid if she knew I wasn't really dead."

Sebastian looked at the faces around the table - Maddy was ecstatic; Henry was beaming, and the Captain looked lovesick. He cleared his throat and addressed the group.

"Listen, Maddy seemed to know you were alive, thriving somewhere exotic and she definitely missed Henry - so this was brilliant. We don't want to put you in any danger, but we should know what happens next."

The Captain nodded, "Fair enough. The lad can stay with me and sail the seas, or he can return to school with you but he has concerns - he can address those with you. As wonderful as this reunion has been for my soul I really should move on. I don't want to go back to London - I hope everything is settled and everyone has moved on without me. Maddy, I need to talk to you before I go. The lad needs to decide what to do so let's split up before it gets dark."

Maddy had been looking out at the water. She turned back to Henry and touched his hand. "You have a place at the school, and you will always have a life with us. I hope you will choose to come home with us." She moved away before they could see her tears.

The Captain shook Sebastian's hand. "Take care of her, will you?"

Sebastian nodded and wished him well. "She misses you. Be safe."

He turned to go. "Captain. Thank you." Sebastian pointed to Henry.

Maddy and The Captain walked down the beach in comfortable silence, enjoying the salt air, the waves and just being together.

"I hoped you were sailing and loving your freedom. Are you lonely? Are you okay? So many questions…how are we going to stay in touch? Do we need a code? I need to know you are well." Maddy stopped and placed her hand on his cheek.

"Ah, Blue Eyes, I'm loving being away from my fake life, the world is a beautiful place but, I do get lonely - I have my music and my books and I have my memories. You always told me to write my story, so I have started - you'll be the first to see the manuscript. Maybe you can publish for me. I need a new name…any thoughts?" He smiled at her tenderly, brushing her hair away from her eyes.

Maddy smiled and her eyes were moist with tears she had been holding back. "I would love to read your book and I'll get it published for you - I have a connection I never knew existed. You could be Declan or Dillon… what's the name of your new vessel?" Maddy had forgotten to ask earlier.

The Captain laughed and grabbed Maddy's hands in his, "Of course I called her *My Blue Madness*, what else would I call her? She's a beauty but she's not easy. Just like her namesake Godmother. Someday I'll sail into a port and take you away with me. It's our destiny, luv." The Captain embraced Maddy with a fierceness that frightened her - he had not had the opportunity to say goodbye before - he wanted her to believe in him.

"I hope there wasn't any pressure on you after the explosion. Francesca, my so-called wife, could be difficult. Listen, the lad should go home with you - he really needs a family. He's a great kiddo. Be well, my Muse."

He slipped away into the copse and was gone. Gone from her life, again. Maddy sat on the beach, counting the waves, counting her blessings, content with her life. Michael had reached out, he was fine, well, at least he was alive and free; Sebastian had come with her and Henry was back in their lives. How lucky she was.

Sebastian and Henry slowly approached Maddy on the beach, not wanting to disturb her reverie. They sat on either side of her, each placing an arm around her. The three of them sat like that for some time, peaceful and content to be in each other's company. Each of them lost in their own thoughts - Sebastian was replaying his conversation with Henry - Henry was envisioning his return to school and life with his new family - Maddy could hardly wait to get home with the men she loved and start their life together as a family.

As the sun set on the horizon, casting a pale pink hue across the sky, they watched a sailboat cross the sun, it seemed to be waving - not a goodbye but more like a good beginning.

Henry fell asleep watching television; he had been mesmerized changing channels and seeing the choices available. Maddy covered him with a light throw and turned the lights off. The moon on the water was providing enough light in their suite. She walked out to the balcony and stood looking out at the sea, torn between happiness for herself and sadness for her friend, sailing alone.

Sebastian wrapped his arms around her and looked out to sea with her, inhaling the scent of her hair, feeling closer to her than ever.

"What a day. I couldn't be happier. You?" Maddy whispered.

"It was a wonderful day, indeed. It was dangerous for some, sad for some and yet, here we are together, ready to build a future with Henry. He was worried you might not want to split your love between us, but I assured him you had a great capacity for loving, more than anyone I've ever known." He kissed her neck and she turned in his arms.

"Sebastian, I saw Henry and wanted him to come back with us, live with us, whatever it took, but I didn't ask you first…I'm sorry. I just thought we both missed him and we would want him to have a chance. We can be a family, of sorts. He needs your influence to balance my crazy, don't you agree?" She wanted to make a case for Henry - she wanted Sebastian to embrace the family idea.

"Stop, Maddy, no convincing required, of course I agree Henry should live with us if he wants to - he has a brilliant mind and he needs an education. I was worried he might want to stay on the boat - not a good future for a young man with such promise. It sounds like he needs some stability for awhile. We have a few days here before we return to reality so let's get to know each other again, enjoy the beach, have a vacation together before we have to face the future." He kissed her, leaving her breathless.

"Any idea how much I want you right now?" His voice was husky.

Maddy sighed and wrapped her arms around his neck, her legs around his hips. "I want you more."

"Indeed."

What a Wonderful World It Would Be

Davi and Grace were delighted to see Henry when the tanned crew returned home to Bellmere House. Henry was excited to meet the baby boy, cementing his role as Uncle as he comfortably held little Chance in his arms. True to her word, the baby arrived the day after Maddy returned home. Chance was a lovely baby.

In the garden at Bellmere Grace had prepared a welcome meal for the *usual suspects*, she called them. Christian and Lambert arrived to greet the boy who was now taller and muscular, bringing a bicycle with them. Audrey and the Buttons walked over to say hello before bedtime. The Buttons greeted Henry shyly, he had changed but so had they. It seemed everyone was getting taller. Jimmy showed Henry how to ride the bike and soon everyone was laughing as Jemma gave orders from her chair.

Henry told his story and answered their questions with the patience of an older, more mature teenager. He seemed at ease with the group. The Captain was never named or referred to - it was their secret. Maddy caught Sebastian's eye and smiled like a proud mother.

When the last well-wisher had gone home Henry asked if he could please go shopping with Maddy the next day. He had leafed through magazines on the airplane and realized his clothes were totally unsuitable for life in London. Maddy was thrilled to be asked. Sebastian suggested he might like a visit to his tailor and Henry was quite diplomatic in his refusal. He said he thought that, for the moment, Maddy would have a better sense of what a young man required in a casual wardrobe. His school uniform would cover most occasions.

Sebastian smiled, realizing they might have many such discussions now that Henry was back. He would defer to Maddy, of course, on matters of lifestyle. Maddy, as usual, offered an option so everyone felt engaged… she would take Henry shopping for a casual wardrobe but she pointed out that every young man needed a suit for those special occasions so they should also see the tailor - it was hard work keeping her men happy. Sebastian and Henry shook hands in agreement after Henry asked if Maddy could accompany them to provide a final approval on the styling. Sebastian nodded - his tailor was always happy to see Maddy and seemed delighted with her fashion sense.

Maddy had already contacted the headmaster, who was grateful to have both Henry and Maddy back in his realm. Henry would take the standard exams to see where he would best fit in - his time away had been spent reading history and keeping up his maths, thanks to the librarian. Maddy suggested the testing so he would not be bored returning to the same class as his former classmates. The headmaster shook his head and wondered what other changes she would suggest - he was looking forward to the challenge.

Christian arranged for an internship within the bank so Henry could catch up on his required work terms.

Henry asked to return to the Mission with Maddy, anxious to see if any of his old friends were still there. He was tall enough to work behind the food counter now - Maddy was pleased to see the self-assured young man welcome the residents with easy banter and familiar greetings. He looked very smart in his jeans and striped shirt - he had grown into a lovely young man.

Sebastian was spending more time with Henry, including him on projects and taking an interest in his homework. He showed Henry how to use the drafting applications on the computer and together they worked on a design required for council approval.

Maddy and Henry continued to visit art galleries and cook together. Mrs B, their semi-retired housekeeper, was thrilled with his skills and she had to admit he cooked a better lamb stew than she ever had. They settled into a comfortable routine, competing to bake the perfect scones and new desserts. The Buttons were in heaven - so many treats.

Henry seemed to be enjoying his return to school although he confessed to Maddy, he found the constant noise distracting. He had learned to appreciate the silence in the Outback house - his old aunts had not been much for conversation.

Maddy and Sebastian worried about Henry's ability to socialize but he was resilient. At Maddy's suggestion, after a few private lessons Henry found he enjoyed the sport of fencing - much to Sebastian's delight. Maddy smiled as the two of them practiced moves and talked strategy. It seemed their lives were settling into a happy, contented pattern.

Indeed.

Water, Water Everywhere

"Hello Sweetheart, you had a delivery this morning from a mysterious courier. You have to know I'm dying to see what it is. Hurry home. I have dinner. Missed you today." Maddy left the message and hurried towards the underground, hoping to be home before Sebastian.

Sebastian was sitting on a stool at the kitchen counter, nursing a drink, waiting for Maddy. He would open the package when she got home - he knew she was like a child at Christmas opening packages...he could wait.

Maddy arrived, laden with bags of groceries and books. She dropped the bags and threw her arms around his neck. Her welcome home greetings were always appreciated - Sebastian and Henry both looked forward to her enthusiastic welcomes.

"Henry is staying at school tonight - he has a group paper to write. He didn't want you to worry." Sebastian passed the message along.

Maddy sat beside him and rested her head on her hand, smiling, her eyes twinkling with mischief. She eyed the package and raised her eyebrows.

"Go ahead, open it." Sebastian moved the package over towards her.

Maddy rubbed her hands together and wiggled in her seat. She slowly opened the box, careful with the wrapping. She turned the box so Sebastian could flip up the cover, exposing the contents. He was enjoying watching her, smiling at her deliberate care. He looked over and she nodded for him to hurry. He lifted the cover and inside were several small carvings, a design portfolio, airline tickets, a colourful scarf and a letter addressed to Sebastian.

"Hmm. This is from a schoolmate I haven't seen for years. He is developing a resort area on a small island, off the coast of Africa. He needs a consult for the design and structural components of the project. He wants us to visit and make it a working holiday." Sebastian looked over at Maddy. She was clearly excited.

"I'm not sure I'm qualified to consult on an island project. I'll read the prospectus and decide if I can offer any assistance at all."

"It's a beautiful island, I looked it up this morning because the stamps were so stunning. Here, I printed some info for you. It's not far from Principe. It's not really ready for tourists yet but it would be fascinating, wouldn't it?" Maddy produced maps and printed aerial views. "Your friend would be lucky to have your opinion…smart guy." She leaned over and kissed his neck.

"Why aren't there any photos of the locals in the expensive material you have? I wonder if they are indigenous to the island. I couldn't find any info on inhabitants." Maddy asked as she watched him read through the materials.

"Skylar was always a dreamer, always scheming, not very sensible. He's done well with resort developments and he certainly seems to have enough financial backing for his latest projects. Let me read through this." Sebastian kissed Maddy on the cheek and began reading the material.

Maddy prepared the meal and sat beside him as Sebastian closed the document, looking thoughtful. He looked over at Maddy and smiled.

"It might be worth seeing the island, I'm not convinced the infrastructure would be sound."

He leaned over the casserole dish. "This looks interesting, smells great."

Maddy poured the wine and they ate, laughing at shared incidents of their day. Maddy reported on Grace and Chance, the baby was already enjoying the smells of the bakery and the many hands of regulars who insisted on holding him throughout the day. Belle was expecting them on the weekend. Audrey was debating letting the Buttons go to football camp - they were very athletic. The house down the boulevard had sold… over the asking price. The owners were delighted.

Sebastian listened to the report, smiling at the number of lives Maddy was involved with each day. He reached out for her hand and held it, hoping the love he felt was transferring into his touch.

As they crossed the tarmac, heading towards the private jet waiting to take them to the island, they chatted with the other members of the group. By the time they were seated Maddy had met all the passengers and knew why they were invited, what their skill set was and how they knew the developer. Sebastian was amused by her interest - she would have made a great intelligence officer, he thought. He smiled as he settled into his seat - there had been no doubt in Maddy's mind they would be going on this trip.

The flight was pleasant, the welcome gracious. Guests were invited to freshen up and meet at a reception in the main hall. Maddy took a swim, anxious to walk the beach and meet the locals. When she arrived at the door in her flowing white dress and sunhat, her cheeks pink from being out in the elements, the sun light creating a stunning silhouette, she was searching for Sebastian, unaware the crowd had stopped talking to watch her entrance.

Their host was quick to take her hand and introduce himself. He raised an eyebrow when Sebastian appeared at her side and kissed her, whispering in her ear. Maddy blushed and smiled, apologizing for her tardiness. She explained she couldn't resist the beach and assured her host the setting was indeed lovelier than the brochure.

Godfrey Skylar, their host, was a tall, slim man with dyed hair - Maddy described him to Sebastian as a man who oozed self-confidence and arrogance but seemed a bit shady. Sebastian laughed and responded that was how he had been perceived as a student. He told her Philippe would agree wholeheartedly with her assessment. He also told her she looked wonderful and he felt enormously proud to escort her into dinner. They shared an embrace and moved into the dining room.

Sebastian found Maddy on the beach the next morning, after his first meeting. She was surrounded by children playing a game of frisbee. There was gleeful laughter as the children learned how to throw and more laughter when they fell trying to catch the disk. Maddy had filled her luggage with beach toys, snorkel masks and flippers for the children - hoping there were local families in the community.

As he approached, the children grabbed Maddy by the hand and ran for the water. They bobbed in the waves and shouted for her attention as they showed her how they surfed the oncoming waves.

He waved and Maddy motioned him into the water. He sat on the hot sand, waiting for her to join him.

"I see you've been busy making new friends." He handed her a towel when she ran over to him.

"Aren't they lovely and energetic?" Maddy laughed and sat beside him. "How did your meeting go?"

"Thought provoking. The resort development is ambitious given the resources available but money doesn't seem to be an issue so I guess we'll have to work on the logistics." Sebastian looked concerned.

"I took a walk into the village this morning. Interesting. When you have time, I'd like to take you there and show you what I saw." Maddy waved at the children who were calling her back into the water.

"We should join the rest of the group for lunch around the pool. Here, I'll help you up. You might want to head for shade - you've had a great deal of sun." Sebastian wrapped her in a towel and kissed her.

As they walked towards the pool Maddy asked more questions and then told him of her morning adventure. The group seemed to be huddled under the umbrellas, tall drinks in hand, the women fanning themselves, the men loosening their shirts. Maddy wondered why they were dressed for London when they were on a tropical island. She suggested they should take a swim - the responses made her laugh. It seemed the group was worried about the sea creatures, swimming pool testing and sun blisters.

Sebastian watched as the staff welcomed Maddy by name, brought her a specific drink and spoke to her directly about the luncheon specials. She, in turn, announced what she would recommend for lunch. The group conceded that she should order for them.

Standing on the balcony, overlooking the beach, Maddy asked if her attendance was mandatory at every meal. Sebastian pondered this and although he enjoyed having her beside him - conversation was always livelier with Maddy, he guessed she had plans to visit the village again. He left it to her to decide when she would join him. He also reminded her the group would miss her as she guided them through the fresh fish and foreign vegetable buffets.

Maddy did not tell Sebastian she was uncomfortable around Godfrey Skylar. He insisted on sitting beside her at mealtime and he continuously touched her arm. He asked her opinion on the outcomes of each meeting, although she had not attended, and he ridiculed some of the ideas the team had put forward. When Maddy scolded him on his bad manners he laughed and declared he was charmed by her honesty.

Something seemed wrong with the development, Maddy confided in Sebastian. The village was in a sad state - no fresh drinking water; no sewage system; the perimeter of the village was a fortress with mounds of plastic and the streets had ditches flowing with the grey water from the resort. How could anyone treat their workforce like that? What future did the village have if this continued? Maddy was passionate about the situation and worried the team Skylar had assembled would not consider the village in their plans.

After a few days it was clear Skylar saw the development as his dynasty and himself, the absolute ruler of the resort and the island.

Maddy walked through the village with the children, meeting the families, studying their home life and their struggles. She offered to witch a well for fresh water, dismayed at the conditions - she had to explain dowsing as the village was concerned there were witches in the water. Dag had taught her how to take a forked branch and wait for the vibration to find the water. They had searched for water in several countries during their time together.

Sebastian was concerned that Maddy was spending too much time in the village - she had stopped asking him to walk with her - she was aggressive with Skylar, asking him about water, waste and recycling. He knew better than to suggest she leave it alone.

"Maddy, we are guests here. Perhaps you could be less passionate about the conditions and just enjoy the beach for the next day or so. We have to leave on Saturday - apparently air transport is being halted for a few weeks while the runway is being outfitted for night arrivals." Sebastian was cautious.

"Sebastian, this place is a mess. The garbage is stacked so high, the smell is disgusting; the water quality is poor and the recycling is dumped around the village. How can this development survive such abysmal conditions? How can the island people survive this? Aren't you concerned? Isn't anyone in your elite group concerned about the future? It isn't ethical..." Maddy was clearly upset and her words were intense. "I think there's a coup planned after our departure."

"It doesn't concern us. We'll report back and hope the waste management systems are in place for the future. Let it be..."

"I can't. The people in the village are real and they need our help - now - not after a report gets sent. I'm going to see how I can help the revolution." Maddy stuck her chin out, crossed her arms, daring him to stop her.

"Maddy, you are the most frustrating woman I have ever met. You are incorrigible." Sebastian sputtered.

"Is that good?" She asked, looking up at him with a mischievous look, her eyes dancing.

Sebastian could not resist the demure look or her innocent question.

"Yes, yes I suppose it is somewhat good." He smiled in defeat.

"Just promise me you'll be careful." He tried to sound stern.

"Of course. Don't worry. It's all under control." Maddy kissed his cheek quickly and walked away, turning to look back at him with a smile.

He watched her leave and although he was smiling, he felt a sense of dread. He knew something was happening, something he couldn't control, something that involved Maddy...he wondered if, or how, he was supposed to protect her. The hotel employees had been noticeably quiet the last few days - if Maddy had not mentioned a coup he might not be so sensitive to the changes in their level of hospitality.

Saturday morning and the sky was blue; the sun beating down and reflecting off the water; the guests anxious to leave the island...all of them for very different reasons. The engineer had mistaken the wife of the Catering consultant for his own in the dark, on the beach; the banker had determined the project was too risky for his portfolio; his wife was sunburned and quite ill; both of the investors had sampled too many cocktails and were still sleeping by the pool; Maddy had padded out at first light, leaving Sebastian to pack and continuously check his watch. Skylar had hoped to have his dream resort plans ratified by now. He was confused by the hesitation of the investors and builders. He had a solid plan to secure his future and now it seemed his group of 'so called friends' were letting him down.

In the village the digging continued - Maddy was convinced they would reach the underground water any moment...she was covered in mud, sweat running down her face, clumps of clay in her hair and on her clothing. You could feel the excitement in the air as each bucket was hauled up from the well.

When the shuttle bus arrived at the hotel Sebastian waited until the others had been seated, the luggage loaded, to ask the driver to drive through the village for Maddy. The driver was nervous, he had been told the guests must never see the village. He also knew Maddy was working with his neighbours to bring fresh water to the village. He shifted on his feet, looked around and then met Sebastian's eyes.

"I will go to the village, but we must hurry. It is forbidden. We cannot wait there. We must go to the airfield." The driver was whispering.

Sebastian looked over towards the beach, his voice quavering. "I understand, but I won't go without her."

The driver nodded and motioned for him to board the bus. There was no chatter on the shuttle, just a sense of relief to be leaving the island. So different from their arrival, when they had all been excited and anxious to be at a holiday resort.

As they pulled into the village the visitors were uninterested in their surroundings - those who dared look out the bus window, were shocked by the conditions - the makeshift living quarters, the piles of recycling, the windblown garbage spilling from torn plastic bags.

They watched in horror as a line of men, women and children passed a bucket back and forth, dumping the clay in a heap, over the garbage. At the end of the line they saw Maddy, covered in dirt, working with the locals. As she brushed her hair away from her face, she spread a wide strip of wet clay - she seemed unaware of the shuttle as she and the locals focused on the well.

Sebastian ran out to the line and called Maddy. "It's time to go. We have to get to the airfield. Now, Maddy. Please come with me." He begged.

Maddy looked up and smiled. "We're getting some wet clay; I can't go yet. I'll make my way there. You go ahead."

"I don't want to go without you…please come with me." Sebastian was pleading.

"I can't go now. I have to see this through….my whole life has been so ingenuous….I have a chance to make a difference, a real difference, right now, right here. Please don't take that away from me. I'll be on the flight, I promise." Tears stained Maddy's face.

"Maddy, why can't you just let things go? Why do you always need a cause?" His frustration apparent.

"You want me to be like the others? You want me to be like that?" She pointed to the shuttle bus.

Before he could respond, the driver grabbed his arm and urged him to board the bus. The locals were yelling, closing the circle around Maddy and the men at the well. The bus moved forward - the driver advising Sebastian to sit down. "We must go. It is not safe. I will come back for your wife, you have my promise. My people will not harm her."

By this time, the others in the bus were wondering what was happening.

"Why are you leaving Maddy?"

"What's going on here? We can't leave her here. Stop the bus…"

"Hey, what are you doing? Why are we going without her?"

"Is it possible to get more air in the back of the bus? It's a bit stuffy."

"Sebastian, you need to control your woman. She's endangering all of our lives."

Sebastian stood, tired of their voices…sorry he had even suggested Maddy be any different; she was reckless and courageous, which he loved, and now he needed to be supportive.

The driver held up his arm. "Sit down, I will get you safely to the airfield and then I will come back to the village. I suggest you not mention this at the airfield."

Sebastian looked back at the concerned faces and felt helpless.

"Maddy is helping the village find fresh water…she'll be fine. She'll be along before we take-off." He hoped he sounded more optimistic than he felt.

The airfield was surrounded by soldiers with automatic weapons. The plane, door open, stairs in place, sat at the end of the runway. The group was taken to the plane and invited to board. The passengers walked up the stairs slowly, taking note of the soldiers, the stillness in the air - unsure of what was happening.

"What about Maddy?" The banker asked, turning to Sebastian. "Can you trust the driver to go back and get her?"

Sebastian looked around the field and watched the driver throw the luggage from the shuttle to the airplane with a determined look.

He nodded, hoping he was not giving himself false hope.

The driver left the tarmac and the passengers settled in, nervously looking out the small windows. The heat wafted off the tarmac in waves, the plane was stuffy; the passengers were sticking to the leather seats.

A uniformed guard boarded the aircraft and demanded all phones and cameras be placed in the pillowcase he was carrying. The window shades were lowered, and the guests told to sit quietly, prepared for take-off. Several passengers questioned the process and were told to be quiet. Sebastian imagined he could smell their fear.

Moments later a limo pulled up to the terminal, a small open-air building. Skylar stepped out of the car; his white shirt stained with sweat. He surveyed the bank of soldiers and started yelling at his assistant. The passengers in the plane could not hear the conversation but it was clear from his tone he was demanding to know what was going on. The flight officer reported what he could see from the open door…speaking softly into the microphone.

A soldier appeared in an open-air jeep, his passenger guarded by two soldiers, their guns trained on her. Maddy held two jars in her arms, as if she were protecting them. The jeep stopped in front of Skylar, delivering their passenger. Skylar stood hands on hips, speaking to Maddy who was pushed out of the jeep onto the tarmac.

The passengers, hearing the exchange, exclaimed in shock, now frightened by the scenario in front of them, beyond the closed window shades. They could not make out the words but the raised voices were disconcerting.

Maddy was barefoot on the hot tarmac, Skylar amused by her hopping from foot to foot. He was holding his hand out and Maddy was shaking her head, guarding her glass jars. She started walking towards the airplane, Skylar yelling at her, Maddy shaking her head, continuing her walk. He was obviously angry; she was obviously determined.

The passengers, now sweaty and scared, slowly lifted the shades, trying to catch a glimpse of Maddy…holding their breath, as Skylar took the gun from the guard and aimed at Maddy. Maddy turned and walked backwards, almost taunting him to shoot. As she neared the stairs to the airplane, he trained the gun on her and pulled the trigger. Maddy winced and bent over, cradling the jars. She struggled to stand and with a cry she kept on walking. At that moment, a cacophony of gun shots could be heard as the soldiers aimed at Skylar. He lay on the tarmac riddled with bullets. A soldier appeared from under the plane, guiding Maddy up the stairs, he held her for a moment, embraced her and spoke rapidly before pounding on the cockpit door, shouting instructions to the frightened flight attendant. He threw the pillowcase with the devices through the door. As he ran down the stairs and pulled them back from the aircraft, the flight attendant closed the door. Sebastian ran to Maddy and caught her before she fell. The air conditioning whirred and blasts of cool air washed over the cabin. The pilot advised everyone to fasten their seat belts as he was going to make an epic takeoff and get the hell out of here.

As the plane lifted off Sebastian held Maddy close as they sat on the floor of the aircraft. He removed the glass jars labelled '*water samples*' from her grip and was surprised to see a bruise on her shoulder - Skylar had fired a rubber bullet. He suddenly understood what had happened and although he was angry, he knew Maddy had been a part of the plan.

"That was crazy. What do you think we just witnessed?" The investment banker leaned over the seat to ask Sebastian.

"It was reckless in so many ways, but we were seeing a coup, a military takeover. Skylar had done so many things wrong they needed an excuse to remove him…we witnessed him shooting a civilian, the army shot him, rightly so, for harming a civilian." Sebastian found it difficult to comprehend, even as he explained it.

"What will happen now?" The banker's wife asked.

"Who knows. By the time they deal with the fresh water concerns, the damage done by the garbage and the recycling they may not have much of a life here. Perhaps they'll return to a simple life - fishing and diving."

Sebastian felt sad, imaging the disruption and destruction in their lives. Maddy had warned him - she questioned Skylar's motives from the beginning. He looked down at her, lying across his lap, sleeping as if nothing had happened. She was covered in dry clay, her feet blistering and yet even when sleeping she had a look of serenity - as if she knew she had succeeded.

"What a woman," he muttered to himself. "She's reckless and crazy and alive and definitely not like the other women." He smiled and closed his eyes. How could you not love someone like that?"

Indeed.

The Art of the Game

Lambert held up his hand and waved as Sebastian walked by his desk, to signal he had a message.

"You met a journalist last night at the reception and she wants you to meet her for a luncheon interview today. She was quite forceful, no excuses, she advised. You are to meet her at The Savoy Grill at 1 p.m." Lambert frowned. "She wasn't very pleasant, I must say."

Sebastian tried to recall who the journalist might be - he and Maddy had been introduced to so many media representatives last night. He would ask Maddy, she always seemed to keep it straight. He walked into his office, absently rubbing the back of his neck. Maddy always had a list of people and 'projects' she wanted to see or work with throughout the day, hopefully he could track her down before lunch. He felt so dependent on her, he shook his head. How had he managed before he met Maddy? He smiled as he thought about her morning sendoffs…she wrote him notes and left comic strips in his reports…he looked forward to finding her notes, especially in high level Council meetings, where the mood was sombre and often quite boring.

Sebastian walked into the Savoy, apprehensive about meeting Barbara Hartwood. Lambert had googled her and reported on her reputation as a nasty, unforgiving writer. Sebastian wondered why she would want to interview him at all.

Barbara waved as he stepped into the restaurant. She was seated at the premier table - with a clear view of those entering. She looked as though she was comfortable holding court in the room. Sebastian pushed her seat in as she sat down after greeting him with a familiarity he found unsettling.

Lifting one eyebrow, her trademark look, according to Lambert, she laughed at his discomfort.

"I ordered bubbly for us. Please don't tell me you prefer lager, my darling." She laughed, watching him squirm.

"Tell me about your CityScapes program. I heard your date gushing about the committee last night." Her approach was hard, her voice scoffing. She made him uneasy.

"Maddy, my wife, is quite enthusiastic about the program, about everything actually." Sebastian smiled and raised his glass.

"Well, I'm not interested in her. I'm interested in you, darling." Barbara ran her foot against his leg.

He moved his leg and looked around the room. She was enjoying making him uncomfortable.

Barbara asked a few questions about CityScapes as she sipped her champagne. She insisted in saying City, pausing before saying Scapes. Sebastian noted she did not take notes or refer to any information. He looked around the room, wondering again why he was here.

"So, my darling, shall we stop this pre-game shuffle and head upstairs?" Barbara asked coyly.

"What exactly is the game?" Sebastian asked, not looking up.

"Oh my darling man, surely you're not that naive. This is where we go upstairs, drink more champagne, you take me to bed. We meet every fortnight or so - you call me when you need a favour; I call you when I need a favour. No one gets hurt. We just have fun. It's simple." She smiled and reached over to touch his hand.

Sebastian recoiled and stood. "A few years ago, I might have been amused and flattered by what you offer, but now, my life is wonderfully full and I wouldn't consider jeopardizing my future. My apologies." he bowed. "By the way, I'm not your darling and I must go." He turned and walked towards the stairs and freedom.

At the table, Barbara motioned for the waiter and asked him to send the champagne to her room. She looked around the room and wondered if others had seen her guest walk out. She raised her eyebrow and smirked.

"Just wait and see what I do to you Sebastian Walker," she mumbled to herself. She stood and smoothed her tight skirt. She needed a moment to steady herself - she felt dizzy - not from the drink but from the dismissal.

"Ah, Hartwood, I see you only have a single column these days." She knew the voice but couldn't concentrate enough to see the man in front of her. She waved him away.

"It's too bad you haven't learned your lesson yet. People want feel good news not bitchy gossip. You're passé, my dear." He touched her arm, to steady her, not as a gesture of caring. Barbara shrugged his arm away and ran the back of her hand across her face, feeling the tears on her cheeks.

"Bugger off, you old fool." She hissed, too late realizing she was standing in front of Gideon Cleaves, the publisher of the paper.

She walked towards the door, hoping she would not fall. She recognized an old friend in the lobby and smiled, motioning towards the elevator. At least the afternoon would not be a complete waste of time.

Sebastian arrived at Bellmere House and slowly walked into the kitchen, where he could see Maddy preparing something at the range. The kitchen was warm and smelled of spices. The scene was one of a happy home; his wife, her cheeks rosy from the steam, was stirring and inhaling the aroma. She was laughing with someone on the speaker phone. It was a lovely scene - one any man would be happy to step into - he wanted to wrap his arms around her and kiss her neck. He held back, still uncomfortable with the encounter at lunch.

Maddy turned and greeted him with her usual delight at seeing him home. She tasted of cinnamon when she kissed him.

"Sweetheart, you're just in time. Drink?" She carried on with her stirring, pushing her hair behind her ear. A gesture he usually found so endearing.

"I think I need a shower first, can it wait?" He hoped the shower would take away the bad feeling he couldn't shake. He wanted to change, hoping to be rid of Barbara Hartwood.

"Certainly." Maddy smiled back. "Do you want company?" She asked mischievously, moving towards him.

"Just give me ten minutes." He loosened his tie and left the room, wondering why he was refusing her offer. Should he tell Maddy about his lunch? Would she understand why he felt so…unclean? He tried to think about something else. As he walked into the bedroom he sighed, the bed looked like a giant cloud - a cloud escape he enjoyed with Maddy. He quickly averted his eyes...the memory of what he had eluded on his mind.

He must have been in the shower for some time, eyes closed, letting the warm water run over his face, when he heard the concern in Maddy's voice.

"Sebastian, are you alright?" She was holding his towel, waiting to wrap him. "Are you feeling okay?"

He pushed the dial to stop the water and turned to her, stepping into the warmth of the waiting towel she offered. She reached up to kiss him and before he could think he told her what had happened at lunch and how it had affected him.

Maddy held him in her arms, listening without comment or changing her facial expression. When he had finished, exhausted in the telling, she touched his face and kissed him. A slow, soft kiss. He felt all the tension leave his body as he returned her kiss.

"Now I think I understand the reluctance of the women at The Club to speak up - it's difficult to imagine how they must have felt, keeping their disgust to themselves." He looked over her head.

"Maybe women have had more practice coping with shame." Maddy whispered.

Sebastian closed his eyes. "Maddy, you are stronger than I am. I watched you that night - you were angry, and you dared everyone to come forward and they did - for you - to add to your strength."

Maddy buried her face into his chest, enjoying the embrace and the warmth of his body. "We're strong in different ways. You always catch me when I fall - you hit that creep - no one else even showed any emotion." She smiled at the memory of Sebastian taking a swing and connecting with such force.

"Brute force doesn't make you a strong person." Sebastian seemed to be reflecting on past incidents.

"Well, you're my hero and right now I think my handsome hero needs to eat dinner, which I have lovingly prepared, just for you. Come on, grab your robe." Maddy moved towards the bathroom door, motioning with her finger.

Sebastian laughed at her and followed, stopping to don his robe. Was he really going to eat dinner in his robe? Another new experience, indeed.

The newspaper was sitting on the kitchen counter when Sebastian came downstairs for breakfast. He wondered if Maddy had seen the column. To his surprise Barbara Hartwood had not crucified him; instead, she had written an article on chivalry and how old world values were so endearing in a world of promiscuity and broken relationships. The article went on to warn romantics with a spoiler alert: beware…even the most confirmed bachelors prefer meals at home, with the little woman cooking at the Aga, over patronizing the trendiest restaurants in London in search of companionship.

Sebastian looked up as Maddy poured his coffee. She had an amused smile on her face.

He held his breath as he continued reading, fearful Maddy would be embarrassed if Barbara Hartwood wrote about his ineptness as a 'player'. He was not mentioned by name in the article.

"Maddy I did not say anything about cooking at the Aga…" he started to explain.

"Sebastian, it's better than you could have hoped for…every other man who has been defamed by Barbara has just thrown the paper across the room, upset and frustrated that they didn't say no to her charming offer - if they'd known there was a choice - if they'd known saying no would not have destroyed them, they certainly would have said no. Besides, we don't have an Aga." She kissed him on the forehead before sitting across from him.

Sebastian considered her words and reached for her hand. He could live with being labelled old-fashioned and chivalrous. The anonymity was comforting. So was having breakfast beside the woman you loved.

Weekend in Wales

Sebastian squinted and shaded his eyes as he walked out of the office, into the bright sunshine in Aberystwyth, a lovely seaside town in Wales The meeting had gone well: the design had been awarded the contract for the renovations to the courthouse. He had suggested Maddy plan a weekend in Wales and he was looking forward to being alone with her.

The sun was reflecting off the water, the warm ocean breeze caressed his face as he searched the waterfront. Across the road he saw Maddy, patiently waiting, sitting on the bench, her face turned up to catch the sun, her hands around her knees, her shoes under the bench. He walked across the road, dodging the traffic. He touched her shoulder and bent to kiss her neck.

"Ready to check in? I booked the Nanteos Mansion - you know they have the Nanteos Cup which is believed to be the the Holy Grail, the cup Christ and his disciples drank from at the Last Supper. It's a lovely story." Maddy looked up. "Meeting go well?"

They walked hand in hand towards the car, Maddy chatting about her walk through the town, down the beach. Sebastian sharing the good news.

Maddy had booked one of the luxurious suites at Nanteos Mansion. She had arranged for bicycles to tour the area. Sebastian noted the hills and wondered what he had agreed to.

They drove up the hillside to their accommodation - a stately manor overlooking fields of grazing sheep. The plan, Maddy explained, was to freshen up, have a drink in the bar before a lovely dinner in the manor and in the morning, after breakfast, they would ride their bicycles over to Devils Bridge Falls. Sebastian nodded, caught up in her excitement.

Sunshine and a light breeze made for a lovely day and the bicycle ride, albeit challenging, was interesting. After lunch in the Tea Room, they walked down the uneven stone steps to the Falls and sat in the shade, where Sebastian managed to close his eyes and fall asleep for a short kip. He reluctantly walked back to the bikes when Maddy tapped his shoulder.

The trails were well marked, and Sebastian led the way on his bike. He noticed a large rocky patch and made a mental note to take care...at that moment a rabbit ran across the path. He swerved and as his front tire hit the largest rock, he felt himself pitch forward. Maddy rushed over to tend to his scraped arm. She poured water over the wound and carefully removed the sand before applying ointment and wrapping the arm with gauze. She looked up at Sebastian, telling him she would kiss it better. He laughed and asked if she had anything in her bag for his bruised ego. They walked their bikes up the steepest part of the path and finally reached the road.

The ride back to the Mansion seemed long and Sebastian was pleased to step off the bike. They sat in the large bath, nursing their cocktails and tired muscles. Maddy had another great ride planned for the next morning. Sebastian begged off another bicycle ride and agreed to a hike instead.

"I'm sorry, I thought you enjoyed the cycling." Maddy shrugged.

"No need to be sorry. I'm happy to spend time with you, doing whatever you like, but after a day on that small seat I need a break. I'm happy to have you to myself." Sebastian raised his glass. "I may need more medical attention - now that I'm injured."

Maddy smiled and suggested a quick nap, or kip, as he called it, before dinner. She laughed as Sebastian bolted out of the tub, holding her towel for her. He kissed her as he wrapped the towel around her, suggesting they best hurry.

 # We Are Family

The guests at the dinner table were uncomfortable with the constant bickering between Larissa and Stan Jenkins. Every conversation seemed to revert to their issues with each other.

Maddy looked around the table, bored by the depressing mood the hosts had cast over the evening.

"Larissa, why don't you just leave Stan?" Maddy asked innocently.

Heads snapped, all eyes on Maddy as she dared to ask what they were all thinking. The guests were frozen, lips pursed, eyes down, waiting for the response.

"Why would I leave him? He's a good provider for the girls and myself, he's always been faithful, as far as I know." Larissa responded, hurt by the question.

"Why don't you leave, Stan?" Maddy continued. The guests still looking down, studying the silverware with great interest.

"I don't want to leave; I love my life." Stan raised his glass in a toast to his wife.

"If Stan was drowning would you save him Larissa?" Maddy was not giving up.

"Of course I would, he's my husband." Larissa seemed unsettled.

"Not a good enough reason. Why would you save him?" Maddy asked calmly.

Larissa stuttered, "that's what is expected. I wouldn't want to lose him." She looked helpless. "I love him." A tear fell down her cheek.

"Stan, would you save Larissa if she was drowning?" Maddy looked over at Stan, avoiding eye contact with Sebastian, who she knew would be wide-eyed and unsure of her next move.

"Yes, I would, no doubt in my mind. I love her." Stan responded, reaching for Larissa's hand.

"Great, let's have a toast to love and to kindness. Sometimes it's difficult to know if couples are in love." Maddy raised her glass.

"To love and kindness." The group raised their glasses and responded in unison, smiling at each other and hoping the mood at the table would now change.

Lively conversation followed as Larissa and Stan looked at each other and shrugged. Sebastian made eye contact with Maddy across the table and shook his head. He raised his glass to her, his head tilted, and gave her an amused smile. She had effectively saved the evening from disaster. He knew the couples at the party would be asking each other the same questions on the way home. He also knew he would save Maddy before himself…if that was love, he was in love. Indeed.

Larissa and Stan approached Maddy as she and Sebastian were preparing to leave the restaurant.

"Thank you for making us realize how petty our bickering must sound. We had an argument over the children's nanny on our way here tonight and we just couldn't leave it alone. We'll work on the good parts, not picking away at the bad parts of this relationship. Will you join us for Brunch on Sunday? We'd love for you to meet our children and see us at our best." Larissa clasped Maddy's hands in hers.

Maddy smiled and looked over at Sebastian, who nodded. "It's hard not to perform when you have an audience. We would enjoy meeting your family. Thank you."

"Sunday at 11 a.m. at the Hampstead house, Sebastian knows where we are. Thank you. It will be informal - just you two and our little family."

The couples waved to each other as they walked out into the night. Sebastian put his arm around Maddy, mentioning the chill in the air.

Maddy looked up at Sebastian and smiled. She hoped they never sniped at each other in public, that they were able to settle any disagreements in private, that they never lost sight of why they were together.

Sebastian looked down at Maddy and kissed her cheek. He hoped they would always feel this comfortable with each other. He stopped, pulled her close and kissed her, the kiss more powerful than any words. The kiss that promised what was to come.

Larissa and Stan were delightful hosts, and their children were exceptionally well-behaved. Maddy played lawn croquet with them as lunch was being set on the table. Sebastian and Stan surveyed an old greenhouse which was to be redesigned as a new playhouse for the girls. Maddy suggested a studio so the girls could paint and hang their work. The girls were excited and pleaded with their parents to start the rebuild immediately. Stan joined them for a quick game.

"Our girls have certainly taken to Maddy. Does she have children of her own?" Larissa asked Sebastian as she prepared his gin and tonic.

"I'm afraid not, although I do think she would have made a splendid mother." He thought of how attentive she was towards Henry.

Stan was heckling Maddy as she bent to measure her shot. Sebastian watched the girls high five Maddy after her turn. Stan always hit too hard and the girls laughed each time he drove the ball farther away.

"It's not golf, Father." They shouted and laughed.

"You know I was shocked when she called us out at the dinner table, but in retrospect her comments made us realize how petty we had become. I'm sure it took chutzpah to speak out."

"Maddy has a knack for speaking what others think…it could be that North American assertiveness - whatever it is, it seems to work in her favour. I do know she meant no harm."

"None taken. I rather like her. I see you do as well. After all these years, someone has finally captured your heart. Splendid."

Sebastian smiled and stood to greet the players. "Well done, ladies."

"May we show Maddy our new dollhouse Mother? Please. It won't take a moment." Larissa nodded and the girls grabbed Maddy by the hand and guided her towards their playroom.

Lunch was a noisy affair with much laughter and storytelling.

As their guests were leaving the family stood together to sincerely issue another invitation. "We've loved having you. Please say you'll come and see us when you want to get out of the city." Stan shook hands with Sebastian and air kissed Maddy on the cheek.

The girls ran to Maddy and thanked her for the craft gifts she had brought them. They promised to show her the finished product on her next visit.

The afternoon had been such fun - of course they would visit again.

On Top of the World

Henry's birthday celebration was attended by Grace, Davi and baby Chance; Christian and his latest girlfriend; Lambert; Sam/The Professor; Mrs B, the inspiration for so many of Henry's recipes; Audrey and the Buttons, who were growing so fast - soon enough they would outgrow their childhood names and become 'Jimmy and Jemma'.

Maddy and Sebastian had urged Henry to invite his best mates or classmates but he chose to spend the day with his family, the people he cared for...he said he wanted to celebrate with people who had been so kind to him when he was lost. Sebastian put his arm around Maddy, who had shed a tear at his decision.

The garden was set up *a la marché* with all of Henry's favourite foods - sushi bar; soufflé from Chez Henri; a taco station; pasta and of course, cake - Grace had produced a frothy, whipped icing cake in the shape of a lamb...totally *Instagrammable*.

Henry had taken an interest in photography, so the group gift was a beautiful Nikon camera with lenses and all the kit. Maddy had taken Henry on a shopping trip for new shoes and funky weekend shirts. He was becoming very aware of his sense of style and appreciated Maddy's suggestions. She forced him to make his own decisions when presented with a choice, and he was enjoying the challenge.

The Headmaster was pleased with the progress Henry was making at school and hinted that Henry might be ready for his 'A Levels'. Henry was hoping to attend Oxford and read Anthropology. He and Sebastian continued to work on architectural designs and he had attended several conferences with Sebastian and Christian, showing an interest in the climate talks - there were many young people at these gatherings. Henry and Maddy continued to visit art exhibitions and volunteer together at the Mission, serving meals and distributing warm clothing for the men.

Audrey sat back, watching Henry and Maddy touch each other's arm, hug each other and give each other knowing looks throughout the evening. She wondered how they had found Henry and how they managed to get him home. Maddy had not shared any details, just announced he was home. The boy was certainly settling in - even Sebastian seemed comfortable with him being here…she wondered why Maddy had not told her how this all came about. She would ask, again. As her best friend; she deserved to know.

After the guests had gone, delighted to be leaving with bags of *Henry's Own Cookies*, Maddy watched Sebastian and Henry clear the tables, laughing and working together, stopping to sample a bite or recall a funny comment. They were talking about an upcoming fishing trip Sebastian was taking with his CityScape Council - at the Conference in Barcelona the Count had invited a select group to his lodge north of Murmansk, in Russia.

It was a special invitation to be sure. Sebastian had been hesitant to accept but Maddy assured him it would be a wonderful opportunity for fishing and camaraderie. She had co-produced a television program there with Dag several years ago - he had been overwhelmed with the fishing and hunting experience - his enthusiasm at landing a salmon made the segment very popular. Maddy hoped Sebastian would take Henry fishing someday…

"Great party Maddy, thank you." Henry was beside her, holding a plate with cake and two forks. They sat at a table and shared the cake. Sebastian joined them, smiling at how comfortable they were together.

"We're all cleared out here…the kitchen is a mess but we can deal with that in the morning." He stood up and stretched.

"I'm off to bed. How about you two?"

"I'm knackered. The Buttons are too energetic for me. How does Audrey cope?" Henry laughed and shook his head. "I love my camera. I'm going to need some time to read what all it does. Good night and thank you again. It was really smashing." He leaned over to kiss Maddy and shook hands with Sebastian.

"Good night Henry. It's so lovely to have you here." Maddy sighed.

Henry turned to her, "it's lovely to be here, with you."

Sebastian started for the house, then stopped. He held out his hand. "Maddy, do you hear that? It's our song. Dance with me."

Maddy stood and took his hand. "You don't often ask me to dance anymore, how could I refuse?" She couldn't remember the song being their song, but no matter… they were dancing and it was heavenly.

"Indeed."

That evening, Lambert had arrived with a package for Maddy. It was a large envelope and although curious, she had not had time to open it. So unlike her to leave an envelope unopened. She noticed it on the sideboard as they walked, arm in arm, upstairs to bed. She looked back but kept walking, anxious to fall into bed. Tomorrow would be soon enough.

 Destiny, At Last

When Maddy opened the envelope the next morning she had a strange feeling - she shuddered and waited for a moment before taking the documents out.

"Something is wrong, dreadfully wrong...." she muttered to herself.

Another ticket to Paradise. It was too soon. Something must be wrong. It was not even a year since they had recovered Henry. Something was wrong.

Maddy sat at the table, staring at the instructions. The timing was good - Sebastian was leaving for his fishing trip, Henry was back at school...there was no question she would go. Now, how to let Sebastian know she was going; no need...she would be back before he returned. The matter seemed settled.

Henry and Maddy waved goodbye to Sebastian as he boarded the private jet. He turned back several times, hesitant to leave. He would be gone for two weeks and he was already sorry he had committed to the trip. Maddy had wished him a great time, she seemed preoccupied - she had mentioned a friend needed her for a few days. They had fallen asleep last night, in each other's arms, knowing they would miss each other.

Maddy, standing with her arm around Henry, blew a kiss across the tarmac and waved one last time. Perhaps next time Henry would be invited to go with the men.

"We better get you back to school, young man." She hugged Henry.

"Maddy, could we not go back to school today - I feel we should do something together - I don't want you to be alone."

Fighting back tears at his concern, she smiled, "What did you have in mind? Climbing wall or latest action movie?"

"Let's try the climbing wall and then see the movie. Pizza and popcorn for dinner?" He reached for her hand, smiling. This was code for *'let's hang out, no cutlery necessary'*.

According to the instructions - *no checked luggage; no devices or phone; watch for the Destiny signs; no names to be used* - Maddy boarded the plane, anxious to know what was happening. Sebastian knew she had something planned, no other details were known.

First Class was definitely the way to travel...when had she become so blasé about these things, she wondered. She must remember to thank Michael for the First Class tickets.

As she sat back and settled in for the long flight she realized she was anxious about what was waiting for her. She thought back to her first meeting with Michael Riley, a former classmate of Sebastian's. They had not been friends, but Sebastian remembered Mick O'Riley as a scoundrel of sorts - always in trouble, gambling and looking for a quick way out.

Michael, as he was now known, was a respected businessman in London, known for his ruthless behaviour, married to Francesca Bennett and her wealthy, powerful family - he seemed to have everything... fast cars, connections, mistresses and membership to the most exclusive places. Yet, he wasn't content...his restlessness and his love of sailing had appealed to Maddy. She saw a poor Irish boy with all the trappings, sad and looking for love. They became friends because Maddy didn't want anything from him - they met for regular lunches and sailing. Maddy introduced Michael to Henry, hoping they could sail together. Michael was thrilled with Henry's enthusiasm and ability as a sailor. Maddy, Michael and Henry were often seen together, preparing to go or returning from sailing. When Henry was called to Australia to see his dying grandfather Michael and Maddy were devastated. Shortly after Henry was gone Michael's boat exploded at the moor - no body was recovered and his wife was quick to pronounce him dead. It seemed the insurance company needed more time to investigate the accident before settling the claim.

Michael had found Henry in the outback and brought him back to Maddy...a gesture of love and friendship. Henry was back at school in London, settling into his studies and life with Maddy and Sebastian.

Maddy fell asleep with pleasant memories of dancing with Michael, sailing with Michael and Henry...

The heat was oppressive as the passengers walked across the tarmac to the small airport for passport control. The terminal provided shade but no reprieve from the heat. The line moved slowly and Maddy hoped there were cold drinks on the other side.

Once outside the security area Maddy looked across at the greeting signs for something familiar. She was out quickly as she had her bag with her. She walked toward the stocky, nervous man holding a blue sign with *Your Destiny Tours* written in black marker. When she reached him, he hastily took her bag and turned to go. He moved quickly for a short man, Maddy struggled to keep pace in the crowd.

The open-air jitney thankfully allowed the lovely breeze to cool her. Maddy smiled as she realized the dust from the sandy laneway was settling on everything, including her. She covered her nose and mouth and was glad to have her sunglasses.

Suddenly they were on a beautiful, deserted beach. The greeter/driver handed her a small cooler bag, a large towel and her carry-on bag. He pointed towards the water and left her in his dust. She coughed and looked around - taking in the scene - she was alone, very alone on the long, white sand beach. The sand was hot, there were no trees or shade - she walked into the water to cool off and found herself pulled out by the undertow. She tried not to panic as she gulped water, causing her to gag, the undertow tossing her about, scraping her knees on the rocks, finally pushing her towards the shore, she bobbed up to take a breath.

A second wave carried her back to the sandy shore, where she lay on the towel, exhausted. There were cold drinks and a sandwich in the cooler - she wondered how long they would have to sustain her. She reached in and opened a soft drink. A tube of sunscreen popped up and she laughed as she covered her salty arms and legs with the protective cream.

She fell asleep on the towel, using her bag as a pillow. She felt a presence and woke, shielding her eyes from the glare of the sun. The shadow standing over her was a man with long unruly hair, his face almost totally covered with hair, she might have screamed but she recognized his eyes. She sat up as he knelt beside her, touching her face and hair, not speaking, just swallowing her with his eyes. He stood abruptly and helped her up. He quickly grabbed the towel, the cooler and her hand and headed towards the small dingy down the beach. Maddy dragged her bag behind her and wondered where her shoes had gone. The sand was still hot under her bare feet.

The towel was set on the seat, the bags thrown in and the boat pushed out into the water before she realized she would have to wade out into the water again. She was careful to hold onto the side of the boat, but the water was calm and they both climbed in when the next wave went out.

They travelled in silence around the protected cove into the ocean. It was getting dark; she could barely make out the silhouette of the sailboat against the horizon. The waves lapped against the dingy and Maddy realized the motor was not purring. They were riding the waves, watching the pastel sunset, waiting for dark to approach and board the sailboat. Maddy looked around her - nothing but water, the shore miles away, no other boats, no danger. She wondered if The Captain was this careful when he was alone. So much for freedom on the high seas…was this the life you were forced to live if you ran away? It didn't seem right somehow.

The sound of the motor startled her, as they skimmed across the water towards the sailing vessel - she noticed the boat was now called *Destiny*. The Captain circled the sailboat, cautiously steering them away from the helm. He threw a line, pulling them towards the ladder. He deftly tied the dingy and helped Maddy up the ladder to the deck.

Maddy turned to see if The Captain was behind her, her eyes now accustomed to the darkness. He stepped forward and pulled her to him in a hurried embrace. He was holding her tight, as if she was a lifeline. She moved her arms around his back, burying her head into his chest.

"Thank you for coming. I have so much to talk to you about and so little time. I'm ever so thankful you came. Sorry about the cloak and dagger bit, but I think someone is watching me. Could be the insurance people, no body yet. I don't know. We must be careful - no names - sorry. So good to see you, I've missed you Blue Eyes." He whispered into her neck.

"You must be hungry. Let's get you settled and fed. Glass of wine?" He moved away and scurried into the cabin below.

Maddy followed him into the cabin and looked around in the dim light. The cabin was tidy; the table set for two. She sat and watched him prepare the meal, tossing herbs on the fish fillet in the frying pan, juggling the fruit bowl from the cold storage and pouring a glass of wine for her. He presented her plate with great flourish and sat beside her.

"Eat up. We have lots to catch up on." He was overly cheerful.

He watched her eat, he had enjoyed watching her eat when they had lunched in London, she was so aware of the flavours and the smell of her food - she made eating lunch an experience.

Maddy noticed he did not eat or drink and once again, that feeling of dread spread over her.

"Tell me what's going on? Can you talk about it? Are you alright?" She touched his hand, afraid he might back away and choose not to speak.

He stared at her for a moment, looked around the small cabin, leaned over to turn on a small speaker and when the music wafted through the cabin he began to speak, "No way to sugar coat this - I'm dying. I've known for some time it was coming, I mean, death is inevitable - I just hoped for more time. I've made arrangements to end the pain on my terms. Before I go, I need to tell you my story, all of it, so you can write it or destroy it or forget it." He touched her lips as she was about to protest. "You said you wanted to meet Mick O'Riley…well, here he is, just for you."

"Oh, I'm so…." Maddy was afraid to say the wrong thing.

"Shhh. Hear me out, please. I've got ten days with you, my last wish, so to speak." He chuckled. "You are the only person I trust."

He moved away quickly and retuned with a package.

"This is a laptop for you to record whatever you want to - it's clean and safe - no tracking device or signal."

Maddy struggled to understand his words, she heard him but didn't want to believe what he was saying. She could feel the tears on her already salty cheeks. She nodded, hoping he understood she was here for him.

"I can't kiss you or do any of the things I so want to do with you - we can't exchange body fluids…isn't that poetic justice?" He laughed, a maniacal laugh; a sad laugh. "Life is full of surprises. Who would ever believe that the woman I love is untouchable to me and that her ex, Dag, that big, goofy Amazon guy, would save me long enough to see you before I die." He laughed again. Taking her hand in his, he kissed her palm tenderly. When he looked up, his eyes were bright.

"I know you have so many questions but let me finish. I saw Dag, sorry, shouldn't be using his name, at a regatta, and asked him if he wanted to buy my boat. We smoked some weed and had a few drinks and he started talking about you - he thought you would love the boat because it was like an island, an island you could take with you wherever you wanted to go. It was a great idea, I could leave the boat for you and the lad…I just had to figure out how to do it."

Maddy was about to protest when he continued.

"In exchange for drugs that numb the pain, I sold him the boat - it was never registered after it was built so it was easy to complete the paperwork in your name. He said he owed you. He never even stepped on the boat - just signed it away to you. It's yours, Blue Eyes. You can go wherever you want…." He looked around the cabin and chuckled. "It's not much, but it's yours."

Maddy could not stop the tears. She felt a wave of sadness and suddenly her whole body was shaking. She cried out, not able to breathe, not able to stop the tears. The Captain reached for her, folding her in his arms, caressing her hair, rocking her back and forth, until she stopped heaving.

She stepped back, wiping her eyes with her napkin. She sniffed and collected herself.

"I feel so foolish, I'm sitting here crying and wasting the time you have left. I'm so sad it hurts, it hurts to know you are suffering. I'm crying because I'm sad to lose you, instead of being strong and being supportive for you. It's not fair. It's not right. You deserve to be happy. This is simply wrong."

He leaned over and touched her cheek, resisting the urge to kiss her, kiss her and kiss her and kiss her…

"Life is never fair, my love. You're here. That's all I wanted. I wanted to spend the time with you - I told you it was our destiny to be together and here we are. Perhaps not the best scenario, not the one I imagined, but we are together, and we have some time. A part of me will always be with you, in this boat. Karma is a bitch and it's time for me to purge all the bad things I've done and settle up. Can you help me with that? Will you do that for me? Will you be the writer of my wrongs? Will you be my confessor?" he pleaded.

Maddy nodded. She smiled at him and touched his face.

"Of course I will. I'm here for you. One favour?"

"Anything, my Princess." He smiled, bowing his head.

She pulled on his beard, "This has to go. I want to see my friend."

They laughed and embraced.

"Come and see your stars." He took her hand and led her up to the deck. They sat on a sheepskin rug, looking up at the starlit sky.

Maddy fell asleep, lying across his chest, his arm around her. The movement of the boat, the soft breeze and the mission ahead pulling her into a deep sleep.

The bright sun warmed her face as she stretched, aware that she was on the deck, lying on a rug with a thin sheet over her. She was fully dressed, and her skin was encrusted with a layer of salt. This is how a roast must feel when I rub the salt on it, she mused. There was a crashing sound from below deck and Maddy sat up suddenly, afraid The Captain may have fallen or hurt himself. She stood quickly, steadying herself against the railing. Rather than call out she took the stairs into the cabin and saw him, injecting himself with a long needle. His face contorted, his hands shaking as he watched the liquid leave the syringe. The cabin was in disarray, as if he had been in a hurry.

She watched her friend recover slowly. She felt useless, standing there, watching, shocked at the transformation.

"I'm sorry you had to see that. I fell asleep with you and didn't want to disturb you so I missed an injection. The pain was too much. Did I wake you?" He was himself again.

"Coffee or tea, Madame?" he asked in a cheerful voice as he discarded the needle.

"Tell me what to do. Let me help you." Maddy whispered.

He nodded. "Let's have breakfast on deck. I'll set up a tarp for shade and we'll get started." He set about making tea. "First, we need a swim. Come on." He darted up the stairs and waited for her on deck. He took her hand and led her towards the railing. They looked at each other and nodded before jumping into the ocean.

The water was lovely and refreshing. They swam, laughing and playing in the water like children. They sat on the landing, watching the water, alive with dolphins and fish, curious to see what the splashing was about. A quick shower and breakfast under the bluest sky imaginable - a wonderful start to the day.

Maddy was surprised when The Captain came up on deck with scissors and a shaving kit. He brought a bowl of warm water and handed the razor to Maddy. They laughed as the scissors changed the madman to a well-groomed, albeit longer haired, sailor. The scissors were needed to tame the beard, but the result was stunning - the white face of a handsome man suddenly appeared before her. She smiled and wished she could capture his face, smiling impishly, in a photograph.

There was no reason to speak - the friends enjoyed the morning in silence. After a short catnap in the heat of the day, The Captain appeared with a lunch basket, a fishing rod and two large sun hats. He motioned to the dingy and they set off to catch their dinner. Maddy realized they were not free to talk on the sailboat, so she waited for his cue.

Once they were away from the sailboat, the music softly playing, The Captain apologized for his clandestine behaviour. He asked Maddy about Henry; she told him about her meeting with the older man who held the key to her past; he asked about Francesca and the reports of his death; he wanted to hear about her various projects and finally, about her life. He wanted to know she was happy. He seemed pleased with her responses, especially knowing she was happy, well, as happy as anyone could be with Sebastian Walker. Maddy laughed and shook her head at his comments.

"You know, I could have had you kidnapped and brought here, against your will." He stared out to sea.

"No, you wouldn't have." She replied after a moment of reflection.

"You don't know what I'm capable of doing, the pain I'm capable of inflicting, even on those close to me. You have no idea…" His tone was menacing.

"I know." Maddy made eye contact and stared at him.

"Hah, you think you know. You're very naive. I went to Australia to find the lad, for you. I wanted you to come to the Maldives and sail away with us. You ruined my plan by showing up with my old schoolmate Sebastian Walker. Now here you are. No one knows where you are. They can't find you. What if I don't let you go? You don't know…"

"Maybe not, but I know you. You're my friend and you wouldn't hurt me. You are a good person and I believe in you." Maddy's voice was steady. "Don't ruin a perfectly wonderful day by trying to provoke me. Tell me what you need from me."

The Captain sat up and looked at her. "You really do believe in me, don't you?"

Maddy continued to stare at him.

"You really are something." He shook his head and touched her cheek. No wonder I love you."

Maddy put her hand over his and smiled at him. She felt her eyes tear and forced herself not to look away.

"Don't cry for me. No pity tears, please. No regrets."

"These are tears of happiness - I get to see you and spend time with you. I want to be here with you. If I had any regrets, they would be for the time wasted, for the time you didn't do what you loved to do, for the time you spent conforming and hating every minute." Now the tears were flowing down her cheeks.

He felt helpless as he watched her. He closed his eyes, willing himself not to reach out and kiss her.

"Okay, you win. I'm not despicable. I am your friend, and I would do anything for you, anything. Right now, we're going to have lunch, catch a fish for dinner and enjoy the day. Drink plenty of water, can't have you dehydrated before the story is done." The Captain, looking more like the Michael she once knew, poured a tumbler of water and spread out the lunch he had prepared.

Maddy gave a sigh of relief and waited for him to begin.

For two days they floated in the dingy after lunch - Michael talking, Maddy typing. She would stop to ask for clarification, he would stop to see if she was judging him. They laughed and cried over broken dreams, misunderstandings and cruel acts that changed his life. When he recalled childhood incidents his voice took on a thick Irish brogue, other times he sounded very English.

He was bitter when he spoke of his mother and his fiancée, Brigitte. His desire to fit in and be a part of London society had cost him the love of both women. His fiancé had been on her way to his flat in east London when the building exploded - she had screamed out, crying his name and sobbing in the rain. When a well-dressed man approached her and asked her name he produced an envelope of money, saying he was on his way to see Mick O'Riley with a payment. He was sure Mick, who was now surely dead, would want Brigitte to have it, to start a new life. She took the money and boarded a train for Birmingham where she met the dockhand she had slept with while Mick was in London, earning money for their wedding. Mick O'Riley, rough Irish gangster, became Michael Riley, respected financier, that night.

He had not been in the flat - he had been with Francesca Bennett and her father, making a deal with the Devil. He was to marry Francesca, grow the family business and become a successful businessman, endorsed by the Bennett family.

The deal was simple - *we take you in; you disavow your past and your family*…it was everything Mick O'Riley could have hoped for.

His mother, knowing Brigitte was pregnant, believed it was her grandchild. She never saw Brigitte again and she never forgave Mick for depriving her a grandchild, despite receiving a sizeable sum of money from his estate. He visited the village once, just to see if his mother was well - she had married the local grocer and was working long hours while he sat in the Pub…more of the same for his mam - he was heartbroken and sad to see her married to another drunk.

Money had bought him a place in society and a new name, an unhappy marriage and a few affairs, he felt his life spinning out of control - and then he danced with Maddy. He saw her as often as he could - she was easy to be with - she always made him feel like he belonged in the expensive suit or the khaki shorts or the oil-stained dungarees on the boat. She laughed at him and he didn't get angry; she teased him, and he laughed; she forced him to do things he enjoyed - she made him a better person.

Michael looked out at the horizon, the sun was setting and the breeze was picking up. Here he was with Maddy, at sea; alone at last with the only person he felt ever bothered to really know him. Now wasn't that just the luck of the Irish? He finally found the someone he had been searching for all his life and time was running out - all the money in the world could not buy him time.

He saw the questioning look on her face - he hadn't realized he had laughed out loud. He started the engine and headed for the sailboat.

They watched the sunset, their legs dangling over the side of the boat.

"You told me once lovers were fickle but friends were forever. I scoffed at you, remember?" Michael kept his gaze on the horizon.

Maddy smiled at the memory.

"Well, my darling Blue Eyes, there hasn't been a day since I escaped and started on this adventure that I didn't wish I had a friend to share the sunsets with…never thought about a lover, just wanted a friend."

Maddy reached for his hand and rested her head on his shoulder. They watched the sun melt into the water in silence - friends sharing the end of the day.

The time had passed quickly, too quickly - Michael was tiring; he was losing his strength and his focus. He showed Maddy the safe keeping compartments on the sailboat; the documents she needed, how to secure the boat and how to dock the boat. He made her study the information on the boat so she could recite:

> Valiant 42 with new Mack sails, 12-volt water maker,
> 60 lb Rocknell anchor, 55 gallon water tank, 90 gallon fuel tank,
> Bluewater Charts, latest Iridium GO, 6 man life raft, SSB radio,
> storm jib, storm drogue, solar panels, beautiful cherrywood interior.

He studied the charts with her until she was comfortable with reading them. They left the boat in the harbour in the prepaid slip.

The cab ride to the lodge was short. Maddy had packed the laptop in her carry-on, saving the notes on a USB stick. She told herself to be strong, for his sake.

"What do you want me to do with the story?" Maddy asked as they drove, holding hands.

"Whatever you think Blue Eyes. I know you'll do the right thing. It's really just for you - you once told me you wanted to meet Mick O'Riley - now you have. No one else cares." He looked out at the road for a moment, then he turned back to Maddy. "Let me have another look at you." He smiled and then turned away. "Do you think you could tell me you loved me? Just this once."

"I love the man Mick O'Riley became. I love the friendship I will always cherish and I love the man who brought Henry back into my life. I'm going to miss you but I won't stop loving you, my wonderful friend."

The Lodge was ready for Michael. Without the drugs he was delirious within the hour of their arrival. The attendant attached a drip to keep him hydrated - they would not discuss his care arrangements but suggested Maddy leave as per Michael's wishes. She held his hand until he fell into a fitful sleep. She kissed his forehead and took a cab to the airport. She smiled as she recalled the jitney ride on her arrival.

Had it only been ten days ago?

She heard her name as she stepped out of the cab. She turned and saw Dag running towards her. He seemed happy to see her.

"Everything go okay with your friend?" He asked, genuinely concerned.

Maddy nodded and then shook her head...she didn't know what to say. Her tears broke free like a flood gate opening. She sobbed into his chest.

"Hey, Mad, it was for the best. You know that, right?" His voice tender.

"Thank you for what you did. He was able to cope until today. Are you sure you can't make use of the sailboat?" She managed between sobs.

"Mad, you and the boy enjoy it. I'm not much of a sailor, get seasick too easily. You know me. It's too much work. Anyway, I'll keep an eye out for it and be sure it's ready when you want it. Just call me. Great excuse to see you, at least once or twice a year." He looked at the arrivals board. "I gotta pick up my guests. Are you heading home today?"

Maddy nodded and started towards the check-in counter. Dag stayed with her until she was ready to go through security. They hugged once more and waved goodbye.

The insurance adjustor, leaning against the pillar, noted the goodbyes and finalized his report. Madison Davis had indeed visited her friend Dag Andresen. The file was closed. No further investigation into the death of Michael Riley was required.

Maddy slept all the way to Frankfurt. The flight was delayed with weather - she realized she had no phone, and no one would know she was arriving. In the lounge she had started to send a message to Davi, with her expected arrival time, when she heard the flight to London was also delayed. She would wait to send a message home. It had been quite nice to be without a phone for a fortnight.

 # Welcome Home

Deirdre needed a drink. Her latest husband had taken up with the beverage cart girl at his Golf Club and although she wasn't surprised he wandered so soon after their wedding; she was surprised at how angry she was feeling. She walked into the Club and made for the bar. She noticed Sebastian sitting alone and could not resist approaching his table.

"Well, well, well. Trouble in paradise? How is it you are dining alone, again? Wherever can your garden mistress be?" She wondered why her voice sounded so catty.

"Deirdre, nice to see you. My wife, Maddy, you know her name is Maddy, is helping a friend. Why are you here alone?" Sebastian did not feel like sparring with Deirdre.

She sat across from him, resigned. "Same old story for me…lost another husband. Mother and Father are going to be so disappointed, yet again. Seems like your wife, Maddy, is always helping a friend somewhere in the world. How do you put up with it?" She was enjoying herself. She was not the only one alone at The Club tonight.

"I'm just back from a fishing trip and I expect Maddy home tomorrow. She's quite wonderful, you should get to know her."

"My Mother adores her. She goes on and on about Maddy this and Maddy that…it's really quite tiring, if you must know. My father can't wait to tell anyone the story of her landing that old airplane. Your Maddy seems to have taken all the good things in my life away from me." Deirdre signalled for a drink. "Including you. We used to be friends."

"Friends call each other even when they don't need anything. I've learned that. We were convenient but you only wanted to know me when you needed an escort, or you wanted to make someone jealous. Am I right?"

"That's harsh. Maybe somewhat true, but still harsh. You know, you were safe. There were rumours that you and your French friend were gay, especially after you both married those French girls…they were definitely into each other - don't look so shocked. You must have guessed. Ah, here's my drink. Another, right away."

Sebastian didn't respond.

"Here's Roger." Deirdre motioned to their old friend. "Come and join us, we're quite under the weather and in need of cheering." She moved closer to Roger, who sat next to her at the table.

"I was just telling Sebastian I think I need to have a child. My husband is far too busy so I may need your help. How would you two blokes feel about being sperm donors?"

Sebastian turned away in embarrassment for Deirdre. It was folly to get involved in this conversation. Deirdre was not at all maternal and by tomorrow she would be horrified by the very idea.

Sebastian stood, bidding good evening to his friends. He wished Maddy was here.

On the drive home Sebastian stared out the car window, not seeing anything but a blur of lights. He smiled as he thought about Maddy…how she would kick her shoes off the instant she got in the car, how he enjoyed falling asleep with her in his arms. The best times were when he woke first and waited for Maddy to stretch like a cat, across his body. She purred as she stretched and he ran his hand down her back, over her buttocks, letting her know he was ready. She smiled a sleepy smile and they made love, slowly and tenderly, her arms over her head, her body responding to his every touch. They moved together so naturally, and when they were spent, she opened her eyes, her expression pulling him in and letting him know she loved him. He moved on his side and she spooned him, filling in every space between them. They slept soundly until one of their alarms woke them with a soft melody.

He was pleased to have the memory because the house was dark and Maddy had still not returned home. He rubbed his eyes, in weariness. Wondering where Maddy was seemed to consume his life these days, and for that matter, his nights.

Crazy, So Crazy…. Why Not?

Late flights, connections missed…Maddy thought it best to take a cab into the city. She would make her way to the Club and surprise Sebastian.

The long delays and the time changes were wearing thin on Maddy as she entered the Club. She was excited and couldn't wait to have Sebastian wrap her in his arms. She needed to feel his strength and reasoning. She turned to leave her bag in the cloakroom and heard Sebastian speaking with his friend Roger. They were walking down the hallway towards the bar, watching the football scores on the big screen.

"Will you be telling Maddy about this baby situation?"

"I can't imagine why I would."

"Life is crazy, my friend."

"I just want my old life back; it was simple, no drama, no theatrics. No crazy women." Sebastian sighed.

"Isn't that what we all want? Women just seem to complicate things." His friend laughed and they greeted their colleagues at the bar.

Maddy leaned against the wall and found herself sliding down to the floor. She could hardly wait to see Sebastian but he was involved with someone and didn't want their life back. Michael had called her naive - now she felt naive and silly. She sat there for a moment, brushing the tears from her cheek, contemplating her next move. She stood up, gathered her things and walked out to the street, hailing a cab.

At the airport she walked slowly towards the departure board. She looked at the flight schedule twice before realizing she wasn't seeing the letters. Her heart was broken, her tears were unstoppable; she was too tired to think.

"Maddy, where are you off to?" Christian was staring at her, concern in his expression. "You look like you need a drink, come on."

Maddy followed her friend into the bar. She wiped her face and stared at her hands. When the bartender placed the drink in front of her she realized she had to snap out of her funk and make a plan.

"Prost." She toasted Christian. "Where are you going?"

Christian tossed back his drink and studied the wet rings on the bar before answering. "I don't know. I just need to get out of London for a few days. Just ending a messy affair, you know how it is."

"No, I don't. But I just left the Club where I overheard Sebastian tell his friend Roger he wished he had his old life back…oh, and he didn't think he would bother telling me about the baby…kinda ruined my surprise return. So here we are…running away and we don't even know where we're running off to. Aren't we a pair?" She laughed sadly.

"I usually go back to Hamburg and head for my sailboat. A few days sailing works wonders for your attitude. My wife is at a horse show, so I won't be disturbed - she never goes up to the summer house." He motioned for another drink.

"I can't believe Sebastian said anything that doesn't include you in his future, he is definitely crazy about you."

Maddy sat up. "Can you captain a thirty-six-foot sailing boat in ocean waters on your own?"

"Of course. I am a very accomplished sailor, you should know."

"I just happen to have a boat; would you like to run away with me and sail my boat home?"

"Where is your boat?" Christian was interested.

"Can you be away for a week or two?" Maddy was thinking fast.

"I have my laptop - I can do everything I need to do for a month or so from anywhere. You know I plan to retire next year. My wife will divorce me the day after I retire, can it wait until then?" He smiled a sad smile and shook his head.

"Look, we're both licking our wounds right now and if we leave tonight no one will miss us…who will care if we're gone for a while? Are you in?"

"What kind of sailboat?" He was warming to the idea.

"It's a Valiant 42 boat with new Mack sails, and…" Maddy took a breath, anxious to convince him. She stopped when she saw his expression.

"Why do I know this boat?" Christian was trying to remember how he had heard of the boat.

Christian looked around the bar and back at Maddy. "You are crazy but you make a good point…who will care and it does sound like you need my help…why not? I have vacation time and I can work remotely. The longer I'm away the better the situation here…messy affair." He was mumbling.

"Let's go. Finish up. It's quite a long flight." Maddy started for the door.

"You are definitely the craziest person I know, crazier than me. Where is it we are going?" He grabbed his bag and hurried to catch her.

Christian flirted with the ticket agent who eventually booked their flights with a stopover in Dubai. He was thrilled as his colleague would receive them for a night before they continued on to the boat. He had questions but he had not felt this excited for some time. It crossed his mind to call Sebastian and tell him he was taking care of Maddy but as they boarded the flight, he realized he didn't want to talk to someone who had ditched this woman, this woman he had seen change the world for his friend.

Christian smiled at Maddy as the flight attendant directed them to upgraded seats in First Class. "I still got it…" he chuckled as they settled in for the long flight.

After take-off they were offered drinks and a late-night meal. They declined the meal and opted for sleep instead. As Christian fell asleep, he wondered where the sailboat was moored; how Maddy came to have a sailboat; how she had planned to get the boat home if they hadn't met in the airport…so many questions, lots of time to get answers. Why did it matter? He was on a plane, going somewhere exotic, with his best friends' wife, to sail a boat, no idea when he would be back…what could possibly go wrong? He fell into a deep sleep, forgetting the young, scorned woman he had left earlier that evening.

In Dubai, Maddy and Christian were met by the local bank manager, an old schoolmate of Christian. They embraced like soccer mates and rapidly spoke German for several minutes before realizing Maddy was watching them.

"Why don't you two catch up. I'll meet you back here in the morning." Maddy offered.

"No. No. Nien, nien. We go to Ralf's for dinner and then a show, a big production. He takes us to the airport in the morning. Ya?" Christian seemed to forget his English suddenly.

Ralf was effusive in his agreement. "You will enjoy the show and my house is most comfortable. My family is in Germany, so we have the house to ourselves. Come, come. Any luggage?"

They all laughed as the travellers shrugged and pointed to their carryon bags. Ralf assured them they would find everything they needed at his home; his wife was an avid shopper.

The next morning Maddy and Christian boarded the flight with headaches from a whopping hangover. The evening had been fun, but neither could remember getting to bed. They slept until the plane touched down at the Velana Airport, near Malé, in The Maldives.

The heat was oppressive and their wardrobes unsuitable, so the first order of business was shopping for shorts, cotton shirts, a dress and sandals for Maddy. Arriving at the marina, they looked like vacationers.

Christian was busy familiarizing himself with the boat when Maddy left to get supplies. When she returned, he was in the cabin, whistling as he poured over the charts and documents. Maddy removed the price tag from the captain's hat she had purchased for him and placed it on his head.

"Now you look the part, Captain." She laughed as he posed for her.

"Maddy, whoever designed this boat, built this boat and set everything up especially for you…this boat was made for you! Even the registration… how did you get this beauty? She's very seaworthy…when shall we set sail? I can't wait to take her out…"

Christian stopped as he realized while he was so excited, Maddy looked sad. She smiled at his enthusiasm but all she could see was the ghost of Michael showing her the boat, loving the boat, waiting to die.

Destiny set sail the next morning, the Captain looking proud and sure of himself. His mate wistfully focused on the horizon. She would not be back here again. Michael was resting here, finally at peace.

The days flew by; the sunshine gracing each morning, the soft ocean breezes cooling them at night. Christian embraced the wind each day, making good time. He was living his dream and Maddy was the perfect mate - she caught fish, made lunch, sat on deck with her laptop writing each day. At night they searched for constellations and discussed the next day. They were easy with each other - they danced on deck to the soft music she played, they ate in silence, enjoying the wide-open spaces and their own thoughts.

Christian was able to answer his email messages and take care of business each afternoon - he was becoming a younger version of himself; a free spirit of the world with a job that allowed him the freedom of sailing.

When his phone rang, disturbing the soft breezes, he answered impatiently. Maddy seemed oblivious to his conversations, at times he wondered if she allowed herself to be distracted from her writing.

The call from Sebastian was a wakeup call; Christian was missing the presentation they had worked on - did he intend to participate? Christian hesitated before responding - his friend was concerned about his absence - what if he mentioned Maddy? Would he tell Sebastian she was here with him? Should he express his anger at Sebastian for letting her go? He looked over at Maddy, her limbs tanned, her hair golden, bleached by the sun, her expression so like a child - no worries, no complications. He turned his back and did what he had to do; what he knew he should do; what he hoped was the best for all involved.

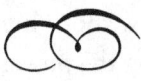 And Yet Another  Second Chance

Sleep would not come so Christian crept up on deck and once again, was astonished at the brightness of the stars. The night sky had given them ample light to play chess or backgammon. Christian sighed as he recalled their games…Maddy sitting cross-legged across from him; the board on the stack of life jackets; their half-eaten dinner off to one side. It was a ritual - he would rub his hands and ask for odds, then he would want to know what his prize would be for winning. Maddy would consider his question and he would quickly suggest one more day of sailing when they arrived home.

Maddy would frown and consider this and then she would touch her chin and smile that mischievous smile that made him grasp his hands to stop him from reaching out and touching her face, pulling her towards him and kissing her.

After what seemed like ages, she would answer, with a grin, that if she won there would be two days of sailing when they got home.

He would consider this and eventually agree. They would both start laughing, unable to stop, falling over.

The game began serious enough; they were both good strategists, but as the final moves became apparent, he would let her win, much to her delight. He had racked up several weeks of sailing - Maddy called it a win-win situation.

Tomorrow they would arrive in port and the magic would be over. They would have to decide on their next move - keep sailing or moor.

Christian realized he was sad - the trip across the Indian Ocean had been the best sailing he had ever hoped to experience. How could the weather have been so perfect? How could his travelling companion be so ideal? How could he go back to the office and the drama of each day? He had enjoyed his remote office, the fresh salt air, the sunshine, the catch of the day for meals, no outside distractions and, he had to admit, he had enjoyed being alone with Maddy. They had developed a quiet routine and he found himself wondering how strange life would be without her laughter, her positive approach to everything, her relinquishing the power of the wind to him - the Captain. He would miss her enthusiasm at seeing dolphins playing, her excitement at spotting a turtle, her early morning fish feeding, her afternoon swim and her delight at catching their evening meal.

He heard her behind him and closed his eyes. He felt like a teenager, unsure of the next move. So unlike him to feel out of control, to fight with himself over right and wrong.

"Are you worried about mooring in the morning?" Maddy asked in a small voice.

"No. No, I'm just taking a last look at the stars." He sighed.

"I'll leave you alone to enjoy the view. Good night Christian. Thank you." She touched his arm softly and he felt the shock go through him. Maddy went back down into the cabin, leaving him alone on deck with the stars mocking him.

Christian woke on deck, the sun beating down on him. The wind was right and the sails snapped as he set their course for Goa, India. The charts indicated an easy arrival at the sailing club, where they would be welcome, despite their worn and sun-faded clothing.

Maddy appeared on deck with coffee and a breakfast sandwich. She looked tanned and healthy. She was wearing his shirt over her bathing suit; his expensive, custom-made, monogrammed business shirt - the only item of light clothing on board with sleeves. They sailed in silence, disappointed yet excited, to see land ahead. Smaller boats came out to them, offering food and souvenirs, a tow into the harbour, haircuts and chai. They laughed and shouted *'no, thank you'* or *'borem korum'* at the enterprising and persistent salespeople.

It was a production worthy of the stage, manoeuvring around the vendors, but they finally arrived at their designated moor. Lines were secured and for the first time in weeks Maddy and Christian set foot on land. They laughed as they walked towards the Sailing Club Office, arm in arm, aware of their sea legs on the wooden docks.

A young man was running towards them, waving and shouting.

Maddy stopped and looked over at Christian, tears rolling down her cheeks. "It's Henry. What is Henry doing here?"

Christian smiled and motioned towards the clubhouse. Maddy looked over and saw Sebastian walking towards them, an anxious look on his face. Maddy stumbled against Christian; she needed time for her heart to stop beating so fast.

"We need their help to get home. Come on, let's see what happens. Please, Maddy. I believe there is a great deal to clear up." Christian stopped and waited for Henry.

Henry was like a puppy, jumping up and down, waving his arms, hugging Maddy, shaking hands with Christian, asking questions through the whole welcome.

"Were you scared being out there alone? Was it awesome? Can I go with you? I can be helpful, I'm a good sailor. Maddy, we missed you. Why didn't you call? I'm so glad to see you, both of you. Come on, Sebastian is waiting. He thinks you'll want a steak tonight; you must be tired of fish." Henry prattled on, his excitement spiralling into a frenzy.

After their peaceful existence on the boat Henry's enthusiasm was jarring.

Christian and Sebastian shook hands and then, awkwardly, they embraced. They spoke in hushed terms while Maddy tried to answer all of Henry's questions.

Sebastian looked unsure of how to greet Maddy. He touched her face with one hand and then the other, looking into her eyes, willing himself to go slow. He wasn't sure either of them were ready to fall into the others arms…there were too many unanswered questions.

Maddy looked up into his eyes and blinked to stop the tears she knew were waiting to fall. Sebastian saw the confusion and sadness in her eyes and wanted more than anything to make her smile and come back to him. He reminded himself he was angry.

"Maddy, you look wonderful. I'm pleased to see you are alright. Your friends will be delighted to know you are alive and well." Sebastian struggled for the words he wanted to say…he had rehearsed this on the plane. Why did he sound mechanical?

"I wondered how long I would be punished." He looked away.

"Punished?" Maddy was confused. "I don't understand. This is what you wanted." She was upset that her tears would not wait until she was ready for them.

"What don't you understand about a man returning home early from a fishing trip because he wanted nothing more than time with the love of his life, only to find she is gone; her phone and belongings in the house; no note - no indication of when she might return, if at all. Why wouldn't you consider being alone without word a harsh punishment?" Sebastian tried to keep his voice calm.

"What would you call a month of no contact with the only person you want to come home to every evening? Isn't punishment depriving someone of something they love and require to breathe? Why Maddy? I just need to know why? What did I do to make you run away?" He wasn't sure he was ready for the response; his heart was beating so fast, so loud in his ears, he could hardly hear her words.

"It wasn't punishment Sebastian; it was what you said you wanted more than anything. It broke my heart to hear you say it, but I love you so much I thought I had to go so you could be happy again." The tears would not stop, she wiped her hand across her face with an angry gesture.

"I don't understand. What are you talking about? You are the only good thing in my life. The house is unbearable without you - every room reminds me of you - every night too long. What did I say?"

"Sebastian, I went directly to the Club when I got back. I hurried there because I needed you to hold me and tell me everything would be alright. I was so tired. I heard you and Roger talking about the baby and whether you would mention it to me…and then you said what you wanted more than anything in the world was to have your old life back." Maddy was sobbing now.

Sebastian reached for her shoulders and shook her lightly. "Maddy, you had been gone for over a week and all I wanted was to have you home…home with me. I was at the Club for meals - I couldn't bear to eat alone at the house. I went by every day to see if you were back but there was no word from you, and I felt my heart breaking into pieces after every visit." Oh how he wanted to fold her into his arms, stop her tears and never let go.

Maddy was confused. She wanted to believe him; she had thought about him every day for the past month.

"I'm sorry, it's a long story but I thought I was doing the right thing - freeing you. It wasn't easy…and seeing you now, I can't believe I didn't fight for you. I should have fought for you…I should have reminded you that we had a great life together…why didn't I?" Maddy searched his face for the answer.

"Why didn't you? Indeed."

Maddy smiled, despite herself.

"You find that amusing?" Sebastian was hurt.

"No, I'm sorry. I missed hearing you say *indeed*." She smiled at him.

Sebastian tried not to look into Maddy's eyes, her beautiful misty blue eyes, now even brighter with the tears, the sunshine and her tanned face. He wondered how long he would stay angry with her - he wasn't sure he could explain how much he loved her.

"Sebastian, I know you're angry with me and we have lots of stories to catch up on so we can understand what happened. Right now, just kiss me." Maddy touched his face.

He hesitated for a moment, closing his eyes, wondering if this kiss would betray him, or her.

Maddy leaned forward and touched his lips with hers. She teased his lips with soft kisses and before he could think, he was responding, his lips hungry for hers, his body craving hers…he willingly gave into the kiss - he felt Maddy's arms around his neck, her body close. He felt dizzy from the smell of her hair and her touch. He may not have reconciled how he felt but his body and his heart were still in love with this woman, this woman who could cause him great joy and excruciating pain.

On the boat Henry pointed at the embracing couple and smiled. He looked up at Christian. "Does that mean Maddy will be coming home with us?"

Christian looked over at the boy, managing a smile, even though his heart was breaking. He just realized he had strong feelings for Maddy. "Yes, it appears we will all be going home, together." Henry extended his hand for a *high five* and they both laughed.

Maddy heard the laughter and nuzzled into Sebastian's neck. "Come and see my *Destiny*." She pointed to the boat.

Sebastian was confused until he saw the name of the boat, shining brightly in gold script.

"Captain, permission to come aboard." Sebastian called up to Christian, collecting himself.

"Aye, aye First Mate, if you plan on traveling with us. Permission granted." Christian was pleased to see his friend, even if he was to lose the girl. They would all be friends, just as they had been before, he hoped.

After a tour of the boat the group walked over to the hotel for lunch and cocktails. Henry fell asleep in a hammock near the water; Christian wanted to take a long shower with hot water…he joked it was easier to be celibate for a month than be without a good shower. Maddy and Sebastian went for supplies, leaving a note in Henry's pocket, in case he should wake up before they returned.

As they walked, hand in hand, Sebastian felt years younger, just being with Maddy. She was alive and standing beside him; she was still the woman he had fallen in love with…surely that was worth celebrating.

After dinner, at the steak house, Christian suggested he and Henry sleep on the boat; they had charts to review. He thought Maddy would like to take a long bath at the hotel. Sebastian was delighted with the arrangement. They agreed to meet on the boat the next morning at 8 a.m. with coffee, ready to sail.

Maddy and Sebastian sat in the bathtub until the water gave them a chill. They laughed and talked and shared their fishing stories. Maddy made her way into the bedroom and Sebastian heard a deep sigh. When he walked into the room she was lying across the bed, stretched out like a starfish, fast asleep. He smiled, recalling her narrow berth on the boat. Sebastian carefully slipped under the mosquito netting and laid beside Maddy. He could hear the air conditioner purring softly; the white moonlight flooded the room and Maddy, her body toned, her hair draped over the pillow, was snoring lightly beside him. This was not how he had imagined the night unfolding, but he felt a sense of joy, lying beside her, once again.

Maddy sat up and felt disoriented - the bed was larger than her berth on the boat. She looked over at the window and saw the outline of the man she had been dreaming about. She slipped under the netting and joined him at the large window, placing her arms around him and pressing her body against him. He felt cold and her body warmed him.

"Come back to bed, I've missed you." She whispered, not wanting to disturb the darkness of the night. "I must have fallen asleep, I'm sorry."

"Maddy, I am committed to you in every way, but I can't go on like this. Weeks not knowing where you are; not knowing if you're coming back. My heart and my head are confused - we're good together; my life is complete with you and yet…"

"I'm here now. Come back to bed." She moved her hands down his chest.

He caught her hands and stopped her. "Sex isn't the answer Maddy. I can't stop thinking about you and Mick O'Riley or Michael or whatever he calls himself. I know that's where you were. You were with him. Did you two have a laugh about leaving me or did you not have time to think about me?"

Maddy stepped back and a wounded animal sound escaped her lips. "Well, if you were going for hateful and hurtful, you just hit the jackpot. Congratulations."

Maddy searched for her clothes in the dark, she wouldn't dare turn the light on and show herself exposed, naked, to this stranger standing before her.

"Maddy, the men in your life have loved you without asking anything in return - they have, I have, been content to love you for the sheer privilege. Is there any future for us?" He asked, trying not to sound desperate. He heard Maddy moving around the room and suddenly he saw the light from the hall.

"Maddy, where are you going?" His heart was pounding.

"I'm going to lick my wounds." Her response was cold. She tried to slip out of the door but the chain lock stopped the door.

Sebastian leapt across the room and slammed his full weight onto the door, with such force Maddy was frightened. She stepped back and wrapped her arms around her waist, closing her eyes to keep the tears back. Maybe she really didn't know him at all.

"Damn. I'm trying to convince you to make a commitment and instead I frighten you into running away, again. I'm making a mess of this, aren't I?" He sounded contrite.

Suddenly Maddy was giggling and sobbing, tears flowing down her cheeks. She leaned over, trying to stop the giggles but it seemed all the feelings she had been holding inside for a month were surfacing and she was powerless to stop the emotion flowing out of her body. She was crying and laughing, trying to catch her breath. She loved Sebastian; his words stung; she thought she had done the right thing leaving him - freeing him...

Sebastian watched her reaction and felt helpless - he moved forward and held her in his arms. He kissed her eyes, her neck and her tear streaked cheeks. He whispered how sorry he was over and over again, waiting for Maddy to stop shaking in his arms. He carried her to the bed, struggling to get through the mosquito netting. He lay beside her, wishing he had said nothing, wishing she would fall asleep in his arms.

Sebastian woke an hour later, careful not to wake Maddy. He watched her sleep, listened to her breathing, inhaled the smell of her. She turned and stretched, the gesture so familiar. His body responded hungrily to her leg moving up his thigh.

Sebastian held her and whispered in her ear, comforting her, assuring her she was safe. She responded by kissing his neck and his chest and as her hands moved down his body he knew that he had never loved anyone the way he loved Maddy. They moved together, taking turns pleasing each other, touching and kissing until they fell asleep, not wanting to be apart. Sebastian was sure he heard Maddy whisper *I missed you* before she fell asleep.

Soft music filled the room and Maddy stretched, smiling as she recalled the workout her body had experienced. The alarm meant they had to go, Christian and Henry would be anxious to sail. Sebastian wrapped his arms around her and rolled over to look down at her. The sun made her hair gold and her eyes sparkle.

"Good morning my darling." He kissed her neck.

"Good morning." She drawled in a soft, low voice. "Hey, none of that, not right now. We have to get going. Shower?" Maddy was kissing him between her words.

Sebastian looked over at the clock and groaned. He pushed back the sheet and picked Maddy up as he stood. "Shower it is, but I'm not done with you, not for a very long time."

As they stood at the door of their room Maddy stopped Sebastian before he opened the door - the door that would let the world in.

"Sebastian, there's so much more we have to talk about; so much I have to explain - I can't do it now. We don't have time. Michael is gone, he left me the boat, Dag was involved…it's too much. I adore Henry, but you are the love of my life. I need you…I've spent hours wondering if you were angry at my being late all the time; you're so punctual - I wondered if I wasn't thin enough, like Deirdre; I wondered if you were upset by my speaking out when you have such a controlled filter…I wondered why…" Maddy didn't get to finish her thought. Sebastian had wrapped her in his arms and his lips stopped her words.

Sailing with a crew was a challenge for Christian as he had come to know everything about the *Destiny* - it was agreed that Henry would crew and the others would prepare meals and handle entertainment.

Maddy continued to write, fish and enjoy the freedom the boat allowed them to experience. The boat seemed smaller now with two more people on board.

Sebastian woke and heard only the lapping of the water against the boat. He stepped up to the deck and saw the outlines of Maddy and Christian as they did what seemed like a familiar yoga routine. They didn't speak, they were concentrating on their moves, as the sun rose above the horizon. It was a magical scene…one he dared not disturb. He quickly dismissed the jealous twinge at seeing the couple sharing a morning ritual. Of course, they had been at sea for most of a month, together, with little or no distraction. He quietly returned to the cabin, waiting for an invitation to join them for breakfast.

"Thank you for arranging this Christian, I'm forever in your debt. I was frantic, not knowing where Maddy was, if she was alright." He cleared his throat. "Henry is definitely a sailor, under your tutelage." The men were alone on deck.

"Sebastian, if you hadn't called and shown up when you did I might have done something inexcusable. Don't screw this up...don't let her go. I think the boy will be a fine sailor and with the boat closer to home we should have many opportunities to sail together. Everybody is happy." Christian raised his coffee mug.

"Everyone except you - I'm sorry to hear about your wife. It's not easy to live apart." Sebastian was sincerely sorry his friend could not find the happiness he and Maddy had shared.

"Ach, it's inevitable that we should divorce. I will give her the house and keep the northern cottage. It won't be any different. Our relationship was always about acquiring social standing with horses, not with each other, not my work, not London. You know, I've had so many affairs, looking for something to fill the void but the time I spent with Maddy made me realize I've been working too hard at making a relationship happen...don't punch me, but she is a great companion - she was just so easy to be with. You are a lucky man."

Sebastian nodded, understanding his friend, knowing he was a lucky man. He tried not to think what might have happened if Maddy had walked out of the hotel room. Lucky. Indeed.

"Michael Riley left her the boat, did you know? I think Maddy was with him when he died. He paid for the boat but I brokered the deal, a year ago. Poor guy, all he wanted was to be free."

"He's free now. I'm sure having Maddy here was a comfort." Sebastian looked out at the vastness before him; clear blue sky, deep cyan coloured sea and only the slight sound of the wind in the sails to disrupt his thoughts. "It must be lonely out here, alone." He wasn't sure if he had spoken out loud.

Christian turned his face towards the sun, squared his shoulders and sighed. "You are never alone out here. I'm not looking forward to returning to my desk and the closeness of my office walls." He smiled wistfully. "It's been a helluva journey."

 # Home Stretch

"It's all settled, my old schoolmate, Gamal Habib, you met him at the Barcelona Accord, Christian, he seems to have an influential position with the Egyptian government and has arranged for us to be ferried with the convoy through the Suez Canal in two days. It's a big favour and we must take him to dinner the night before. He'll meet us in Port Tewfik at Suez. He has clothing for Maddy - she'll need to be covered, just for the ride." Sebastian announced as the group convened for lunch on deck.

"How exciting for Henry. We better study some history today so we can speak intelligently about what we'll see." Maddy looked over at Henry.

"It should take us a day to get north and then we'll be in the Mediterranean - just like that. Well done Sebastian." Christian raised his glass.

Everyone took a moment to digest the news. For Maddy it meant the end of an adventure; for Henry it meant sailing into the Mediterranean; for Sebastian it was time to be back at home, back to life with Maddy; for Christian it was time to get back into his office - he had to admit he wasn't looking forward to life off the sailboat, not yet.

"Tomorrow we moor in Port Tewfik, pick up more supplies, meet this friend and start up the waterway tethered to a ship; why haven't we ever gone swimming at night?" Christian asked Maddy as they sat on deck, taking one last look at their night sky.

"Here's why..." Maddy grabbed the head lamps and headed to the prow, laying down on the deck, looking down at the water. Christian joined her, taking the headlight she offered. They watched the fish under the light, a silent ballet in the water, the water changing colour, almost neon. They giggled and pointed like children, watching the spectacle below. Michael had shown Maddy when they were at sea and she had not been ready to share the experience with anyone until now.

Sebastian, sitting below in the cabin, reviewing a report, heard the giggling and felt a twinge of envy that his friend and his lover had spent time together alone - he had not had the luxury as Maddy was always surrounded by her friends. He listened to the chatter and then Maddy padded down the steps into the cabin, a sad smile on her face. She sat on the bunk and looked over at Sebastian.

"Sometimes it's just too much."

Sebastian knew she was talking about Michael and her time with him. He wasn't sure how to console her. He put his papers aside, removed his glasses and sat next to her, his arm around her. They fell over, lying together on the narrow bunk. He held her, reaching over to close the light. He ran his fingers through her hair, respecting her silence and letting her know he was there for her. She fell asleep in his arms.

Sebastian, Christian and Gamal sat at the Tiki Bar, enjoying a beer, discussing the position paper for the upcoming meeting - now called a Climate Summit. Maddy and Henry burst into the bar, barely able to contain themselves.

"Ah, here's Maddy." Sebastian stood to greet her.

"We found the best crew shirts and we got a starfish, a beautiful starfish on the beach." Henry was wired.

Gamal couldn't take his eyes off Maddy - she was bronzed by the sun, her hair wild and blond, her eyes dancing…he hadn't seen anyone this fresh and alive since his young niece got her own phone, years ago…now she never showed any enthusiasm. He wanted to know this woman before him, unsure of her role in the group.

"So pleased to meet you Gamal. How can we thank you for arranging this passage for us? We're so excited." Maddy felt she was gushing as she shook his hand.

"Let me see the shirts." Christian laughed, uncomfortable with the look on Gamal's face.

Henry held up the wildest, bluest shirts imaginable. He looked so proud of his find.

"The best part is that we found a dress for Maddy in the same colour. Isn't that totally brilliant?" Henry wasn't afraid to sound uncool - when had that happened?

Dinner was a festive affair, although the four sailors had issues with the rolling, even on land. They laughed as they passed dishes, pretending to be rolling at sea. Christian and Sebastian sat on either side of Gamal, eager to hear how his work was progressing. Maddy and Henry were able to catch up on his schoolwork and his volunteer projects. When Maddy looked up she was rewarded with smiles from Sebastian and winks from Christian. She sighed as she realized how fortunate she was to be surrounded by these men who were so important in her life.

The next morning, they said goodbye to Gamal, inviting him to London, so appreciative of his assistance. The *Destiny* was tethered to a container ship, large fenders to keep them away from the barnacled side of the ship - it was necessary to be adjacent to the boat as the size of the convoy would not allow for the sailboat to follow the ship.

The ride through the Suez Canal was slow, the sand banks repetitive, the sun blaring down on them - Henry retired to the cabin with his sunburned nose - suddenly too cool for the zinc oxide provided.

As the container ship slipped into the port, pulling up the lines and waving goodbye, the sailboat motored out into the Mediterranean.

They stood together, silent, as Christian steered the *Destiny* towards Montenegro.

The meeting was in Kotor and the Bay of Kotor was a perfect safe harbour for the sailboat. As the crew walked away from the mooring heads turned, the blue shirts were hard to miss. The group walked arm in arm, towards the lights of the town, laughing and swaying as they went in search of dinner and a last night at sea.

The men realized, reluctantly, they would need business clothes for the meeting. They were pleased to follow Maddy on a shopping expedition. Maddy and Henry climbed the Ladder of Kotor, their labours rewarded with an amazing view of the bay area, while the men attended their meeting.

The last night on the boat was bittersweet. Flights were booked for the next day; arrangements made to leave the boat until Christian and Henry could return. Christian was to fly back to London with Henry, who had missed too many school lessons; Maddy and Sebastian were heading to the Villa Mirage in Italy before returning to London. Sebastian left Maddy and Christian alone on the deck - he knew they needed time to process their adventure and how they were going forward. Christian had changed - it would be interesting to see how he coped with London and his previous routine.

As the group emerged on deck the next morning, they laughed as they realized they had all donned their gaudy blue uniforms, as a gesture of team solidarity. Sad goodbyes at the airport and suddenly Maddy and Sebastian were alone.

Villa Mirage was operating as a retreat, with several rooms already occupied. The grounds were impeccable; the facade of the building sandblasted and welcoming; the interior fresh and minimalist; the staff serene and professional. Father Dom was delighted to see his friends and review the progress since their last visit. Maddy's friend Giselle was the perfect manager for the Villa - she brought her calm resolve to the operation and the guest comments confirmed it was a delightful and enlightening destination.

Maddy and Father Dom walked along the vineyards, Maddy anxious to confess her part in the death of her friend Michael. Sebastian felt they needed time together - he and Father Dom would have time to discuss the vineyards and planting after dinner.

"Your design was perfect Sebastian. Are you pleased with the result? It's just as I imagined it." Maddy twirled in front of him, her delight visible.

"Your vision was so specific - how could it not be perfect?" He laughed.

After dinner, when their friends had departed, they walked through the public areas, the available rooms and then into their suite. So much had happened since they first arrived at the Villa, then known as the Villa Contessa - so much had changed in their lives...Sebastian opened the balcony door and took Maddy's hand.

The garden was alive with colour, even at this late hour. He looked over at Maddy, her eyes bright in the setting sun, her diamond earrings sparkling, her face radiant; he knelt in front of her and in the most serious voice he asked her to marry him, to spend the rest of her life with him.

Maddy knelt beside him and asked him to marry her, to spend the rest of his life with her.

They kissed and neither heard the other say *yes*.

You've Got A Friend

Audrey burst into the kitchen. "I've got five hours before football practice, enough time for you to tell me what's going on."

"Good morning Audrey. Coffee?" Maddy laughed at her friend. They had not seen each other for some time.

"Maddy, where did the boat come from? How could you just disappear and not tell us where you were? Do you know Sebastian came over to the house, frantic, looking for you - I don't think he believed me when I told him I didn't know where you had gone. You know everything about me and yet, your life is a big secret…it's not right."

Audrey took a sip of her coffee and looked around to see if there was anything to eat. Getting the children off to school in the morning was a daunting task for someone who had enjoyed quiet mornings in bed for so many years.

"Audrey, I'm sorry. I left in a hurry, there was no time to contact you - I left my phone here and barely made the flight. It was important. So many things went wrong and suddenly it was time to come home…here I am." She sighed and pushed a platter of muffins toward Audrey.

"It was delightful to see Henry and Sebastian and we're all home now. Isn't that what matters?" Maddy looked over into the garden, recalling the events that led her to leave, return and leave again, hurt and disoriented. It seemed too big a story to share, now that everything was settled.

Audrey was trying to understand how it all transpired. "But where did you go?"

"It doesn't matter, I had to help a friend - a dying friend who needed me. It wasn't pleasant but it provided closure, I suppose."

"Where did the boat come from? You never said you had a boat - I didn't know you sailed, except with that creep Michael Riley."

"Audrey, it was crazy...so many things happened and I'm just trying to make sense of everything myself." Maddy shook her head. How could you explain what happened without revealing the wrongful disappearance of Michael and the drugs and the eventual exchange of the boat? It was too complicated.

"Maddy, people don't just find boats and sail away...come on."

"It doesn't matter now. The boat was a gift. I'm trying to bring it back here. Enough about me. How are things going with you and Jeffrey? How are the Buttons?" Maddy keenly wanted to change the subject.

"It's been awful. Jeremy spends more and more time at the office. He doesn't miss a football practice but he's never home anymore. I think he's going to leave me. I've been miserable......I really needed you - I missed you and your shoulder to cry on, I'm okay now but I am ready to make a break and start a life with the children, away from London. The children take all my time these days." Audrey sighed.

"I felt abandoned by you Maddy." Audrey stared defiantly at Maddy.

"I'm sorry Audrey. I'm sorry I wasn't here for you."

"Oh, don't be sorry, it's not your fault you can just run away to far off lands, without notice or making arrangements or telling your best friend. You have no responsibilities or cares, you just take-off whenever...you go to Argentina, you take off for the Villa and spend time with your Italian friends, you go to places where there's lovely sunshine...without a care, without consideration for the people you leave behind." Audrey wiped away a tear and slammed her coffee mug onto the counter.

Maddy wanted to laugh at the theatrics but the tears on Audrey's cheeks made her draw back in shock.

"What are you saying? You love being a mother and taking care of the Buttons - you're very dependable and responsible. Look at you - you're perfect. Your hair and makeup are always amazing, even at the soccer, I mean football practices; you dress like a movie star; you have lovely children and you wear heels all the time. You are a beautiful person and I'm so fortunate to be your friend."

"Maybe it looks that way, but don't you remember that I wouldn't leave the house when you first met me? It's not enough to be perfect - everyone wants to be like you, including me. I just hate it when you aren't here, and we can't talk about things. Can't you just tell me what you're doing so I don't worry? Is that too much to ask?" Audrey carefully dabbed at her eyes with the back of her hand.

Maddy could not help thinking that Sebastian would produce a handkerchief right now, if he was here. She put her arm around her friend, not sure what to say.

"Come on, let's see how the renovations are going next door and then we'll head out to lunch - liquid lunch, if you like." Maddy smiled at her friend.

"I'm still miffed at you. Don't you ever disappear without telling me where you are…understand? There's only so much a person can take." Audrey looked over with a critical eye. "You really should invest in lipstick, it would make a world of difference and your hair, why does it always look like you just jumped out of bed?" Audrey sniffed and composed herself. "Promise me - no more running away. Unless I'm with you!"

Maddy chuckled. "I'll work on the running away thing. Okay?"

Audrey linked arms with Maddy and the two friends walked into the garden.

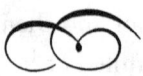 # Easy to Forget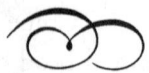

Lambert invited Sebastian and Maddy to attend the opening of his playhouse pantomime - he had a lead role and was anxious to have them enjoy the production this evening.

Sebastian walked into the house, calling for Maddy, loosening his tie and pouring himself a scotch. He had hoped they would have a quiet night at home after all the mayhem of the last few weeks. The flickering flames from the fireplace in the sitting area looked inviting. He sat on the sofa enjoying the warmth of the fire.

Maddy padded down the stairs and leaned over the sofa to embrace him.

"Sebastian, I can't imagine we will want to eat after the show, so I made us a charcuterie platter to snack on before we go. Is that alright with you?"

Sebastian smiled, enjoying the scent of her. "Good idea. After Italy I'm not sure I can sit down to another meal. Come and join me."

Maddy kissed his ear and whispered, "I'll be right back."

Sebastian closed his eyes, content to be home, content to know Maddy was here, waiting for him, content to know their lives were back on track.

Maddy placed the board with deli meats and a lovely display of cheese on the side table. In her other hand she had a bottle of wine and two glasses. She was wearing a simple black dress and her hair was pulled up in a messy do. She had thrown her colourful pashmina on the back of the sofa. Would he ever tire of looking at her?

When Davi knocked at the door to announce it was time to go the pair reluctantly stood up and walked towards the garden. As they neared the car Sebastian took Maddy's hand. "Are you forgetting something?"

Maddy looked up at him and smiled. "No, I have our theatre treats in my handbag." She held up the black cloche. She waved her shawl.

"I wondered if you thought shoes might be appropriate." He smiled as he gazed at her bare feet.

Maddy followed his gaze, brought her hand to her face and started giggling. "Oh my, imagine that…won't be a minute. Completely forgot. Sorry."

She ran into the house to retrieve her shoes as Sebastian stood by the open car door, smiling at her bohemian moment. When she returned she was carrying a pair of black slippers in her hand. She was still giggling. Sebastian found himself smiling all the way into the theatre, Maddy leaning against him, her feet tucked up under her on the seat. It was a delightful habit he enjoyed; it belonged to them.

He closed his eyes and recalled the day Maddy had changed her outfit in the car - he had been shocked when she pulled her sweater over her head and slipped into a silk top. She had laughed at his discomfort, assuring him people changed in the car all the time. She offered him a fresh shirt to change into. He had refused. All evening, as he sat in the sticky heat of the outdoor theatre, he wished he had changed. Maddy had somehow produced an ice cube and rubbed his wrist - how had she known, he wondered.

He pulled her closer, contentment washing over him.

The production was entertaining, the costumes delightful - Lambert could not have played his role any better. Maddy slipped Sebastian lemon bonbons and whispered in his ear, giving him goosebumps…everything was alright in his world.

Indeed.

I'm Dreaming of a White Christmas

"Another stellar office party. Thank you Maddy." Lambert hugged his friend, feeling the effects of one too many holiday cocktails.

"You are most welcome. It's such fun to see the families enjoying themselves." Maddy smiled and popped a chocolate covered cherry in her mouth.

"Any plans for Christmas?"

"I think we'll take Henry skiing in France. Philippe has invited us to spend the holidays at his chalet. Sebastian has one more appointment with the heart specialist next week - if that's okay, we're off. What will you do Lambert?"

"I'm in rehearsals for another pantomime, don't you know. If there's room I'll tag along with you - I never learned to ski but I can whip up fine evening feasts for you all." He laughed, more to cover his embarrassment at inviting himself than at the thought of preparing gourmet meals.

"If you don't have plans you are most welcome to come with us. I don't think Christmas is a good time to be alone." Maddy was sincere.

"You will never have to spend Christmas alone, my dear." Sebastian responded, placing his arms around Maddy. He overheard the end of the conversation as he walked into the room.

"Lambert is alone for the holidays. Wouldn't it be great if he and Henry could be roomies? He's also volunteered to produce fabulous meals. Are you okay with that?" Maddy leaned into him.

Sebastian realized it would be mean-spirited to express any concerns as Maddy was always including others, ensuring they were cared for. "The more the merrier...but let's talk about the meals...Lambert, you realize you may be challenged by Henry and Maddy in the kitchen."

Henry was a quick study on the ski slopes - he was no longer a gawky adolescent. He took lessons in the morning and joined Maddy after lunch, following her down the long groomed trails - meeting with Sebastian and Philippe for an apres-ski aperitif. True to his word, Lambert prepared elaborate meals - from raclette to Beef Wellington. He tried skiing but enjoyed shopping more - leaving the others to tire themselves out on the mountain.

Christmas morning was delightful - Maddy had surprised Philippe by inviting Giselle to join them. After a big breakfast the group sat around the small Christmas tree and opened their gifts. There was much laughter, many hugs and thank you's...Maddy sat back into Sebastian's arms, smiling up at him. It was chaos and she was loving it.

They played games and watched *It's a Wonderful Life* before sitting down to a magnificent turkey dinner. Everyone claiming it was the best Christmas ever.

Sebastian held Maddy in his arms when they finally went to bed, alone at last. Maddy reached under the pillow and handed him a small, neatly wrapped package.

"This is for you."

"I thought we had opened all our gifts earlier. What's this?" He slowly opened the box to find a gold-plated compass. On the back it was engraved with the words:

Sebastian
love will always bring you home
Maddy

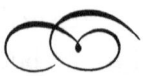 Moral Dilemma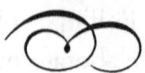

Maddy looked around the expansive foyer, everyone dressed in their best - it was a prestigious affair - long dresses with sparkling necklaces and white gloves, the men in black tuxes. Sebastian had just been beckoned to add his thoughts to the draft for the congress address in the morning, leaving her to her own devices for at least the next twenty minutes.

She was enjoying a moment alone; not forced to make idle conversation or smile at silly, weak jokes. She walked up the red carpeted stairs, running her hand lightly over the railing, admiring the detail in the polished wood. She was lost in her thoughts, humming to the orchestra playing an unlikely rock tune when she felt a hand on her back.

"Trying to escape?" Dermot, the American Ambassador asked, his eyebrow cocked.

Maddy smiled back at him. "Just enjoying a moment…"

"Let's enjoy it together. I know a place at the top of the stairs where you can hear the music, dance unseen and really go to town before my security team find me."

Maddy laughed at his American gusto. The two friends continued walking and laughing, his hand still on her back.

Sebastian looked up from his conversation, watching Maddy ascend the staircase, hating himself for leaving Maddy alone, especially with Dermot. Sebastian likened him to a puppy dog every time he was around Maddy. Christian coughed, jostling his attention back to the group. *Yes, of course, let's continue and get back to the reception.*

"Where have you been? It seems like ages since I've seen you. First you're away on a mission and then it's the holidays…too long." Dermot asked as they made their way to the landing.

"I was helping a friend. What's new with you? Did you have a nice Christmas in Washington?" Maddy asked.

"Have lunch with me tomorrow, please. This friend needs your help." Dermot was serious for a moment. "Lunch, tomorrow, noon at your little bistro *Chez Henri*? It's important. I'll fill you in on everything."

Dermot saw Sebastian heading toward them and nodded his greeting.

The two men spoke for a few moments, then Dermot moved on, brushing his lips across Maddy's hand. He winked and walked away just as his security team appeared.

"Sorry, it couldn't be helped. I hate to leave you alone, but you always seem to be cared for when I do." Sebastian smiled and took her hand.

"Come on my handsome Prince, we better dance before the clock strikes midnight and I turn into a pumpkin." Maddy laughed.

Sebastian led her to the dance floor, unsure about the midnight curfew and how anyone would turn into a pumpkin. He would ask Lambert, who always knew about these things. Right now, he was dancing with an enchanting woman and she was smiling at him, she had called him a Prince and he felt like one.

Indeed.

The next day Maddy hurried through her morning appointments, visiting Mr Simpson at the bookstore - he wasn't looking too well these days. She stopped to see Mrs Bing to arrange the flowers for the hospital gala; she checked in with her neighbour Esme to ensure the staging for the house was coming along - it was to go on the market in the next week or so - Esme and Gordon were moving to Cornwall to be closer to their daughter and grandchildren; then she checked in with Grace and little Chance, who was, without question, the most beautiful toddler ever.

She arrived at the bistro right on time and was greeted by Henri, the Chef, with much gusto. She promised to bring young Henry by for dinner and then joined Dermot at his table. He stood, kissed both cheeks - he never really learned the air kissing part of the exercise, preferring to plant a kiss on each cheek. Just as they sat and had their napkins whisked across their laps, a flushed Audrey appeared and sat down at the table.

"Sorry, am I late?" She was breathless.

Maddy was delighted and surprised to see her friend, they had not had time for a visit since the holidays. She looked over at Dermot, wondering if he had invited Audrey. He seemed confused, especially when Audrey reached for his hand across the table. Maddy took a sip of her water and wondered what was about to happen.

"Maddy, we both love you, adore you actually, and we wanted to talk to you first. Don't stop me, I've practised this for hours...Dermot and I want to see each other...it started out being a job, working together and then we realized we were attracted to each other..." Audrey rolled her eyes. "Can you imagine?" She took a sip of water, looking around for the waiter, wishing she were gulping white wine instead of water.

"Anyway, before you say anything, I mean, after all, you lead such a charmed life, you may not understand. Just let me just say this - we are not falling in love or leaving our families or anything, we're just enjoying being two consenting adults who are lonely and need a sexual release. There I said it." Wine was desperately needed now.

Dermot moved his chair back in shock, wondering if the women were playing a joke on him. He looked at Maddy, waiting for her to laugh. Her reaction was unsettling. She had actually winced at the charmed life comment.

Maddy stared at the two of them and wondered what they expected from her. Was she to condone their behaviour? Should she be upset or happy for them? What about the children? What about Jeffrey? Dermot was married...was there a happy ending here?

"Well, I must say this is unexpected. You don't need me here...I'll let you two enjoy your lunch together. It looks like you have things to discuss." Maddy stood and pushed her chair in. She backed away from the table, still processing the news and wondering why they felt they needed to include her in the affair. Why had Dermot invited her?

"Maddy, wait. I need to talk to you...not about this...this is news to me, believe me. I wanted to ask you about something else...please don't go." Dermot followed her out of the restaurant. "Maddy, why would I get involved with Audrey, of all people?"

"Dermot, you can call me later but right now, you need to talk to Audrey. Should I be happy for you?"

"No, I don't need to talk to Audrey - she's delusional. I don't know what she's talking about. I just wanted to talk to you..." The sound of an incoming call seemed to puncture the air. Dermot looked helpless; a ringing phone in one hand - his friend walking away - a strange person sitting at the table waiting for him. He felt the urge to swear out loud, at the injustice of it all.

 *Reflections on the Beach*

The nurse greeted Sebastian at the door, speaking anxiously about his mother as they walked towards the room.

"Good morning Mr Walker, I'm sure Belle will be pleased to see you. I do think your dear mother needs some encouragement from you or perhaps some motivation to eat her meals. I don't want you to be shocked at her memory loss. She has moments of clarity, recognizing music and voices but more often than not she seems to loose herself in her own thoughts. The doctor says he has done all he can, for the moment."

"I appreciate your concern - we saw her before Christmas, and she seemed fine. I'm just returning from a trip abroad and anxious to see my mother. Is she still interested in the life board on the wall?"

"She walks me through it everyday…it is a wonderful tool. I wish other families would provide the same map of a life for their loved ones. Mrs Walker was very clever with the photos and timelines. We haven't seen Mrs Walker for some time. Is she alright?"

"She's fine. She left me at the door, apparently she had a delivery." Sebastian glanced out of the hall window and saw Maddy standing in a circle with several of the male residents.

"She appears to be making friends." He smiled as he watched her laughing with the older men.

"Oh, she's very popular with the gents. She brings them copies of old Playboy Magazines…she has a friend who found boxes of old issues. I was aghast at first, but your wife is very convincing and she made a strong case for allowing the residents to have access to their favourite boyhood memories so how could I refuse…the gents enjoy talking about their wartime memories and I guess the pinup girls gave them solace - look at them - they will sneak a look and hide them and forget where they hid them." The nurse sighed, sad to state the reality.

"Here we are." They had stopped at the room door. "Hello Belle, you have a visitor. Look, Sebastian has come to have tea with you." The nurse used a practiced cheery voice that somehow seemed insincere as they walked into the room.

Sebastian was indeed shocked at the blue-skinned woman sitting in the chair. Belle had refused to eat for the last week and she was fading away. He knelt before her and touched her fragile hand.

He was rewarded with a smile, but the spark had gone from Belle's eyes. She leaned forward and whispered "Let me go to George. I miss him. He's waiting for me and heaven knows he's waited long enough." She closed her eyes and brought his hand to her cheek.

Sebastian was touched by her wish and her tender gesture. He was afraid to hold her; she looked paper-thin and he thought he might break her if he wasn't careful. He understood her wanting to be with George; of course, she was missing him. He felt useless, sitting beside the woman who had spent a lifetime sacrificing her own happiness for him.

He sensed Maddy was beside him before she spoke.

"Hello Belle, isn't it a wonderful day - Sebastian is here and the sun is shining. Shall we have tea?" Her voice was soothing, and Belle responded with a smile, her eyes open and her arms out for Maddy.

"Yes, tea would be lovely. I haven't seen Sebastian yet but I do hope he comes by. Maddy, you take George's cup - he knows you like the pattern." Belle was lucid as she reached for the teacup Maddy placed in her hand.

"Ah, here's your handsome son now. Sebastian gets more handsome every day, don't you agree?" Maddy motioned to Sebastian who leaned over and kissed Belle on the forehead.

"Belle, you look lovely today." He tried to keep his voice light.

Belle looked up and studied Sebastian for a moment. She turned to Maddy and nodded. "He's always been a handsome boy, takes after his father."

Maddy laughed and the two women continued talking, chatting really, about nothing in particular. Sebastian watched as Maddy continuously reminded Belle he was there. Belle ate a cucumber sandwich and lemon mousse with Maddy - insisting they share the small, prepared lunch. When Belle announced she was getting tired it was Maddy who helped her into the bed, covered her and held her hand until she fell asleep.

As they walked out to the car, Sebastian took Maddy's hand in his, turned and rested his forehead on hers. "Thank you for being so patient with her. She doesn't know me anymore."

"Sebastian, she won't be here long. She's ready to join George and we should just enjoy being with her while we can. You are in her heart, you know, maybe not in her vision, but you are always in her heart. Let's not go back to London, let's stay here and just be with her."

They drove to the cottage in silence, Sebastian wondering if Maddy would take care of him in his final days; Maddy wondering what she could do to make Belle comfortable in her final days. A walk on the beach would do them a world of good.

Sebastian and Maddy visited with Belle every day, returning to the cottage, more discouraged after each visit. Belle would take a few bites of food if Maddy was there, but she was fading away before their eyes. A week later Belle took her last breath, Sebastian and Maddy by her side.

Although sad, they were relieved their beloved Belle had not suffered.

The Celebration of Life was held at the home where Sebastian had grown up, happy memories of times with Belle and then with Belle and George. Maddy had arranged for Grace to cater; The Professor had arranged the music; Audrey had staged the house with ample seating; Rod had taken a series of photographs from photo albums, chronicling the life of Belle and framed them so the walls showcased her colourful life. Maddy was thrilled to see happy moments with Sebastian and George; friends and special occasions featured throughout the lower level of the house.

Friends and acquaintances poured through the house all afternoon, paying their respects for a woman well-loved. Sebastian and his childhood friends greeted all the well-wishers, patiently listening to recollections and long, involved stories that reinforced what a lovely soul she had been.

Rod, Helen and Josh had grown up with Sebastian and spent many hours in this house - Belle was affectionately known by all as their *'after school auntie'*.

Maddy kept a close eye on the food, the drinks and Sebastian - he had yet to shed a tear for the woman who brought him into the world and protected him from the truth for so long. She knew he cared; he was just not equipped to deal with the emotion, yet.

"How are you holding out?" Maddy waited for a break in the arrivals. She touched his shoulder and offered a drink.

"I'm fine. It was good of you to invite my old group of friends to be here with me...they loved her too. Everything else seems to be under control - thank you." He smiled at her, aware of how much she had arranged. Maddy had taken care of the arrangements after discussing everything with Belle - Sebastian had been busy with the solicitors discussing the estate, not sure what was expected of him.

When the last neighbour left the house the group of friends convened in the kitchen, where Maddy had set a light supper for them. They drank many bottles of wine reminiscing and laughing over past conversations and episodes with Belle and George. It was a fitting tribute to Belle. Philippe was staying at the cottage, Henry and Christian were invited to stay over with Rod, while Helen and Josh were pleased to have Audrey and the Buttons at their home. Maddy and Sebastian were alone in the house.

Maddy helped Sebastian up the stairs to bed; hoping the wine would bring him sleep. She closed the door and left him in his boyhood room, still adorned with posters and sports equipment from his youth.

She hurried through the clean-up, pleased to see there wasn't much left on the trays. Dishwasher loaded, kitchen cleared, trash taken out - she sat on the sofa and admired the photos on the wall. She fell asleep on the sofa, soft music playing, the lights low.

Sebastian woke with a heavy heart and a throbbing head. He looked around for Maddy and with effort, threw his feet on the thick carpet and waited for his body to respond. He padded down the stairs to find Maddy asleep on the sofa. She was all he had left...she was his family. He touched her cheek, hoping not to wake her. She stretched and opened her eyes, smiling when she saw him.

"Good morning Sweetheart, how are you feeling this morning?" She sat up; sorry she hadn't thought to have coffee ready - he was sure to have a headache.

"You've already cleaned up. You're amazing. Yesterday was perfect. I'm sorry I was so little help to you. It was quite overwhelming…thank you." He sat beside her and waited for the room to stop spinning.

"Hang on. I have just what you need…" Maddy jumped up to make coffee and get him a headache tablet. "Maybe you need a Bloody Mary…"

Sebastian was lying on the sofa when she returned with her tray. She set it down on the table and covered him with the blue pashmina Belle always wore across her shoulders. Maddy watched him sleep and wondered when she should tell him Audrey had expressed an interest in the house; to move here with the Buttons; leaving London behind. They had never spoken of the affair - Dermot was adamant that they were not involved and Maddy didn't want to upset Audrey, who seemed fragile these days. Maddy guessed she was going through a rough time if she wanted to leave Jeffrey and start anew in a different community.

Audrey had been upset with Maddy for not sharing the purpose of her mystery trip and the month-long disappearance. In the last week Audrey had cancelled site visits, saying she was meeting Christian for advice on swimming lessons for the children; she had dinners slated with Christian - he was loving the Buttons and her cooking; she had called Maddy to say she didn't know what to do with all the flowers Dermot was sending her; she had sent Maddy text messages about how the children were enjoying sailing and how patient Christian had been with them. Maddy had smiled at the vision; Christian was patient, and he was an excellent sailor, of course.

At the funeral Maddy noticed Christian and Henry together, clearly avoiding Audrey. The Buttons had not run to Christian and Maddy wondered why they wouldn't embrace their sailing master as they did Henry and Sebastian. She shook her head, wondering if she were overthinking the situation - she would wait and speak with Audrey before mentioning the house to Sebastian.

Sebastian stirred and Maddy had no idea her musings had eaten up over an hour. She knelt beside him, ready with water and a headache tablet. He smiled gratefully.

"What time is it?" He whispered, his head still throbbing.

"It doesn't matter, go back to sleep." Maddy ran her fingers through his hair. "I'm right here watching over you. I haven't had much time to sit and think…it's very cathartic. You can't imagine what issues I am solving sitting here."

Sebastian smiled, even in his hungover state he could imagine all the plans Maddy would be hatching or how many couples she would be matching or how many pies her capable fingers would be in at any given time. He closed his eyes thinking of her. She had been so kind and loving with Belle, George had loved her and now she was taking care of him.

It was Maddy who had opened the secret door to his life - he had grown up believing Belle was his loving aunt, the aunt who took him in when his parents died. Maddy had been relentless in pursuing the details… Belle and George had been young and in love, Belle was sent to the Villa Contessa in Italy to have her son, denied the right to see George or include George in her life by her parents, who controlled her inheritance. The baby boy was left in her care when his parents had reportedly died at sea. Sebastian felt loved and George, always identified as a close friend of Aunt Belle, was the masculine influence in his life. Maddy forced the truth from Belle as George lay on his deathbed…it had been difficult to digest but Maddy had given them the gift of time, to be together as a family before George passed away. Maddy and Sebastian had been married by the pastor in the hospital so his parents, Belle and George, could witness the happy moment. There was still legal paperwork to complete, but both felt they were spiritually married to each other.

Maddy pursued the connection with the Italian holiday villa, suggesting they visit on their honeymoon and once again, she triumphed. The Contessa was so besotted with Maddy's passion to have Sebastian know his past she made an unbelievable gesture in selling the villa to Maddy for Sebastian. The Contessa had been in mourning for most of her life as Sebastian, the baby boy born to the English guest, was to be left in her care - she considered Sebastian to be her long-lost son. The Contessa passed away having spent her last days with her reclaimed son. Maddy had transformed the villa and the village, with the help of Father Dominic, into a growing concern.

Sebastian couldn't recall if he had ever thanked Maddy for pursuing her instincts and putting all the pieces of his life together. Initially he had felt she was meddling; eventually he came to realize she needed order, to fix things, to make sense of things - none of that mattered now - she was his life.

Fog blanketed the coast, rolling over the beach as the man and his dog approached the path. The German Shepherd sat patiently as his master leaned over and fumbled with the leash. The man stood, rubbing his back, and heard the waves crashing, it was difficult to see very far down the beach. He spied a couple walking hand in hand, stopping to embrace or pick up a treasure. They seemed to be choreographed in a sad, slow dance.

"Way you go, lad." He was surprised the dog was still sitting, patiently, watching the couple on the beach. Usually the dog would bound down the path and chase waves, digging at air bubbles on the sand.

The couple started to climb up the cliff towards the caves - only locals knew where the caves were - it was folly to go up there today, but they seemed to know the way. The woman, her hair buffeting around her head in the wind, sat on the rocks holding her knees, resting her head. She handed the man a small container. He seemed reluctant but he carefully held the vessel and disappeared into the cave.

The man and the dog watched, motionless. They seemed mesmerized by the couple on the beach.

Wiping his face with both hands, the man emerged from the cave and helped the woman stand. They embraced and started down the rocks, looking as though they were floating across the jagged, wet surfaces.

They walked along the shore to the stairs leading up to the cottage on the bluff. As they started up the stairs the woman turned, stopped and waved, just as the fog allowed a ray of light to shine through. She must have seen the man and his dog on the path. It was a wave that said thank you for allowing us to grieve alone on the beach.

The dog perked up and barked, bounding down the path to chase the next wave. The man waved back, drawn in by the mystery. The dog had sensed they needed time. He wondered what he would tell his wife when he got home…best to savour some moments on your own, he decided.

At the top of the stairs Sebastian looked back at the dew-kissed rocks - Maddy had suggested they scatter Belle's ashes in the cave along with George's ashes. Belle had been happy there with George. Sebastian had been conceived there. Now Belle and George were together. Sebastian knew he would always think of them when he stood here with Maddy, at the cottage, overlooking the beach, listening to the waves. He wiped away a tear and smiled as he walked into the cottage.

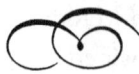 # Lavender

"What have we here?" Sebastian asked as he walked into the kitchen, dropping his attaché case on the chair, leaning over to kiss Maddy. It was comforting to be back in London, at Bellmere House. The air was quite fragrant…he couldn't place the scent.

"We're making sugar scrubs for Henry's school fair and I'm just about to add the lavender." Maddy had jars lined up on the counter, beside a sugar bag and bottles of oil. She was mixing something in a large bowl and spooning the mixture into the jars.

"Would you mind tightening the lids on the jars? Henry had to be back at school. I won't be a minute and dinner is ready whenever you are." Maddy flashed him a smile.

Sebastian was rewarded for his lid closing with a warm embrace and an offer to have a treatment. He wasn't sure what that entailed but Maddy had already taken his hands and rubbed them with the coarse, lavender scented mush. Now he was instructed to rinse his hands. He raised his eyebrows at the process and proceeded to pour the wine. He did notice the mild scent on his hands but felt it would be *unmanly* to mention anything.

His morning shower with Maddy included a sugar scrub of his back and arms…it was pleasant enough and having her gently dry his back and arms was a nice way to start the morning. He wished her well with her scrub sales and left for the office, smiling, as he always did when Maddy was excited about one of her many projects.

"Did you just smell your hands?" Lambert, his trusty but nosy assistant asked, amused.

"Who smelled your hands?" Christian asked as he walked into the office, dropping his papers on the side table.

Sebastian, clearly uncomfortable, cleared his throat and pulled at his sleeve. Christian was quick, he reached out and bent to sniff the hand.

"Lavender. My masseuse uses the oil on me. Very nice. Did you have time for a massage?"

Sebastian was now flushed, much to the delight of Lambert, who had not left the room.

"Maddy is making sugar scrubs for Henry's school fair and I'm the guinea pig. I thought it might dissipate through the day but here I am with you two, talking about my lavender-scented hands. Unbelievable."

"Tell her I'll get some for the ladies in my office - they love that sort of thing. It makes your hands soft." Christian rubbed the top of his hand to show Sebastian what he meant.

"Enough about the hands. You received the first draft of the council proposal?" Sebastian hoped that was the end of the discussion on his hands.

'Maria said she would join us later, at your house." Christian made himself comfortable on the sofa, his papers on his chest.

"Maddy didn't say anything this morning. Perhaps we should head to the house. I'll call her and…"

"I have Maddy on Line 1. I thought you'd want to confirm." Lambert, as usual, had beaten him to the punch.

"Hello my darling. Are you expecting Maria this evening?" Sebastian enjoyed calling Maddy - he never knew where she was, but it was exciting hearing her voice over the sounds of wherever she happened to be.

"Oh Sebastian, I left you a message earlier. PC is in town, visiting from Texas. He dropped off a rather large roast of beef this morning along with a case of wine and we're having everyone to dinner. Why don't you and Christian come home and work on your draft until Maria gets here with PC? Christian prefers the sofa here to the one in your office."

Christian sat up and nodded his agreement.

Maddy continued, "Henry is baking a scrumptious chocolate cake, it's Thursday after all. Get here when you can, bring Lambert with you, we have so much food. Everyone else should be here by 7 p.m."

Sebastian wondered who everyone else included but he knew with Maddy more was better than less. "We'll make our way home now, is there anything you need us to collect on the way?"

"No thanks. Just you." She laughed and blew him a kiss before clicking off.

"Let's go." Christian jumped up. "My driver is outside." He rubbed his hands together; dinner was always an event with Maddy.

Dinner was indeed an event - PC was excited about sharing his latest acquisitions, which would allow him to travel across the pond more often. He had winked at Maddy and then looked over at Maria.

The dining room table was filled with friends - Grace and Davi, baby Chance, Henry, Lambert, The Professor, Christian, Esme and Gordon from next door, PC and Maria, who was looking much more relaxed these days. Sebastian sat on his courtly chair at the head of the table, raising a glass to the group. He never tired of looking across the table at Maddy, her blue eyes dancing, her cheeks flushed - when he caught her eye, she flashed him that lovely smile, the smile that warmed his heart. He looked around the table at the friendly faces, laughter and conversation…the scene before him was exactly what Maddy had envisioned when she had suggested a redesign for Bellmere House - Sebastian's family home. It was a happy place these days.

Christian carried an empty platter into the kitchen and stopped to talk with Maddy. He wanted to know how she was and if she thought it would be acceptable to take Henry sailing with him in Hamburg.

Maddy commented on how nice it was for the Buttons to learn to sail and Christian looked confused. He was not aware they were sailing - they were too young. Maddy shook her head, shrugged and said she had heard he was spending time with Audrey and the children. Christian laughed and then realized Maddy was not kidding. He hugged her shoulders and assured her he was not interested in having anything to do with Audrey. He thought she was a little unbalanced but she was a friend of Maddy's, so he tolerated her foolish behaviour. He walked out of the kitchen shaking his head and wondering why Maddy would think he had time for Audrey.

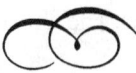 Have You Ever Seen the Rain

Davi was surprised the meeting was over so early - he had not expected to collect Sebastian until later in the day. Sebastian was pleased he would have more time with Maddy - she usually had something interesting planned on Saturday.

"You'll have enough time to go to the Rain Dance." Davi exclaimed in an excited voice.

"What is a rain dance?" Sebastian wondered why he would want to go.

"Maddy organized a street fair to celebrate the last five days of rain… it's a wonderful event. Grace is at the bookstore with Mr Simpson. I will go there now. They are offering tea and scones. The flower shop is selling roses - you know, like raindrops on roses." He chuckled and continued. "There are colourful rain boots and ponchos for sale and food trucks, oh and a contest for the best artistic umbrella…it's a lovely way to defy the rain."

"You say Maddy has something to do with this?"

"Yes sir, Maddy arranged to have the radio station broadcast from the street and she has been on the radio all morning, inviting people to come out and enjoy the rain. Mr Patel is selling samosas and very delicious roti wraps. The gelato cart is out on the street….there is a band and it's very festive." Davi was waving his hands.

"Maddy sent your Wellington boots and a poncho for you, just in case you were home early."

Sebastian shook his head in amazement. Maddy hadn't said a word this morning at breakfast. Of course, he had expected to be in the meeting for most of the day. Now his curiosity was piqued - he hoped there were some hardy souls at the fair so Maddy wouldn't be disappointed.

As they neared the neighbourhood the traffic slowed. Davi was excited, pointing out the parked cars and the groups of people walking along the street. Sebastian laughed out loud - he was amazed at the crowds. The music, the umbrellas, the families, the smell of the food trucks, the sheer madness of people enjoying the rain…it was festive, indeed.

Sebastian donned his rain poncho and boots, hoping he wouldn't meet anyone he knew - he must look a sight - and walked into the madness. Before he could find Maddy he was accosted by the flower shop owner, Mrs Bing.

"Don't just stand here gawking, help me get more roses…so many roses, so many people buy roses in the rain…crazy idea but good for business. Careful, don't drop."

Sebastian had to agree as he carried the long boxes outside to the table. Mrs Bing loved Maddy and her crazy ideas but he found her manner unsettling. He moved on quickly, working his way through the crowd. He stopped and smiled as he watched children jumping into a large puddle pool - their squeals of joy were infectious.

He waved at Mr Simpson, who was standing in the doorway, smiling and greeting his customers. Mr Patel waved him over for a naan wrap, the Pub next door offered a beer tasting; everyone was certainly in the spirit. Still no Maddy. The band was playing a mix of songs about rain and the crowd was loving it.

Maddy was leaving the radio booth when she spotted Sebastian. She waved enthusiastically, looked up at the rain and shrugged as he laughed at her. They met and embraced. Several people followed Maddy, needing her attention for some critical detail.

"Well, this is a fine way to spend a rainy day." He yelled above the noise.

Maddy beamed and looked around at the mayhem. "Isn't it great?" She mouthed. "I could use your help…I need a reliable and trustworthy scrutineer to count the votes for the best umbrella art. Mr Jamieson from the Umbrella Company is going to announce the winner and use the design for a limited run…isn't that amazing? I love your poncho, by the way, very sexy."

Sebastian nodded and wiped the rain from Maddy's face. "I'm ready to do whatever you require, my Rain Goddess." He smiled at her, feeling immensely proud of what she had pulled together. Five days of rain was indeed depressing and yet, here people were, laughing and enjoying themselves in the very rain that might have kept them indoors for another day.

At four o'clock the rain stopped - the crowds cheered, and the band began playing 'Here Comes the Sun'. The crowd joined in, singing along, providing a fitting conclusion to a perfect day. The Rain Dance had worked…the rain was defeated and everyone was leaving the neighbourhood in good spirits.

As the crowd dissipated the street was strangely quiet; the vendors packing up; volunteers sweeping away any litter; the band enjoying a drink at the pub. Maddy joined Mr Simpson and Grace for tea, marvelling at how busy they had been all day. Sebastian found them, sitting at a small table, laughing and exhausted from their impromptu event. He took a photo of the group, surprising himself that he thought about taking a photo - Maddy usually handled that department. He knew they would be pleased with the satisfied looks on their faces when they saw the photo.

The day, however unconventional, had been a success.

Mr Simpson invited the group to a light meal and soon enough the conversation turned to Maddy's suggestion for the bookstore. She had approached Mr Simpson with a plan to purchase the store - adding a coffee shop for Grace and Davi, reading room for children and a best seller area - leaving the upper level for his treasured and classic books, which Mr Simpson would continue to operate. Maddy had not yet convinced every one of their role but with a buyer for the west end coffee shop, Grace was uncertain about the future. Esme and Gordon were hoping to sell their home and Mr Patel had hinted that his wife's health was making it difficult to operate the take-away. It seemed logical to Maddy that Grace would sell, move nearby, live in the house and have Auntie and Uncle take over the building from Mr Patel. Who could argue with her logic?

"I love Maddy like a daughter, her ideas have made me think about the future and I'm excited about the changes." Mr Simpson was addressing the group. "I can see Grace and Davi are hard workers and they would do well here. Maddy brings the children in and reads to them - it's wonderful to see." He wiped a tear away. "I'm just not ready to sell."

There was a moment of silence as everyone at the table considered what that meant…they looked over at Maddy, more concerned that she would be disappointed.

"What I would like to propose," Mr Simpson continued, "is that you go ahead with the coffee shop idea, set up your children's reading room and the best seller area. I will be here to help in any way I am able…I want you to succeed. You make the changes and run the business. You keep your profits and someday we'll talk about you buying the building. Is that fair?"

There was a collective gasp as he finished speaking. It was too good to be true…this man was offering them a wonderful opportunity without any financial restraints.

Maddy hugged Mr Simpson and smiled over at Grace. "You're going to have work hard at getting new customers but today was a good start. By the way, the Bagel King rep handed me a card and suggested you add bagels to the menu." She turned to Sebastian, who was astounded at the proposal, and squeezed his hand. He smiled at her enthusiasm.

"I hope Sebastian will help us with the drawings and the construction." Maddy looked so hopeful it would have been mean-spirited to refuse.

"I trust Maddy and I thank you for including me in your plan. I'm looking forward to working with all of you." Mr Simpson winked at Maddy. "When will you start?"

Grace and Davi spoke in unison, "Right away. We have an offer and if our partners, Maddy and Sebastian agree, we will sell and move over here." Grace looked over at Maddy and Sebastian with tears of joy tracking down her cheeks.

Mr Simpson smiled. "Excellent. More tea?"

What a day. What a day, indeed.

Rescue Me, Please

The ladies were gathered for lunch at the Club, hearing the detailed account of a recent wedding at a Spanish Resort. Everything that could go wrong, had gone wrong.

Maddy felt a hand on her shoulder and turned to look up. Deirdre was standing beside her. Maddy smiled a tight smile, not sure what to expect.

"Can we talk?" Deirdre asked, looking unusually uncomfortable.

Maddy stood beside Deirdre, nodded and waited.

"I haven't been very nice to you, mainly because I couldn't figure you out, but Sebastian seems happy with you and my mother cannot stop praising your many talents. You seem like a nice person and if I was the type to seek out new friends I might consider getting to know you better." Deirdre shifted from one foot to another. She had obviously prepared for this.

Maddy nodded encouragement, amused by the monologue.

"The thing is, I need your help. I've been asked to Chair a fundraiser for a cause very dear to my heart, however, I am hopeless at this sort of thing. I can write a cheque, no problem, but organizing and pulling off something worthwhile - not my bailiwick. Everyone, and I do mean everyone, tells me you are genius at this sort of thing." Deirdre seemed to lose steam. She crossed her arms and looked at Maddy.

"Will you help me? Please?"

Maddy took a deep breath and looked around the room, she needed time to digest what was happening.

"How can I help you?" Maddy asked, already planning a blockbuster event in her head.

"I need a theme…I need an idea…something different, something that will raise enough money to make me look good in the eyes of my parents, who, by the way, don't believe I can handle this…" Deirdre looked pained. She was wringing her hands, nervously, as she spoke. "Understand I am not an organizer - I'm not good at this, at all."

Maddy smiled, "You know we will have to work closely together. Are you prepared to do that?"

Deirdre looked as though she might cry. "Oh yes, of course. Does that mean you will help me?"

"Let's meet at the Club tomorrow for lunch. You have your ideas ready and we'll get started."

"Thank you Maddy. You can't know how much I appreciate this."

"Let's give London something to talk about." Maddy put her hand out.

Deirdre hesitated and then reached out to shake Maddy's hand.

"This is going to be brilliant." Deirdre walked away, imagining a grand event. That hadn't been so hard. Maddy seemed willing to help her…she'd show them she could be a better person, with Maddy's help, of course.

Later that evening, in bed, Maddy mentioned the encounter with Deirdre and asked what Sebastian thought. He was quiet for a moment, then he leaned over and kissed her. "I think it would be wonderful for you two to become friends and I know Deirdre would appreciate your help."

Maddy arrived at the meeting with several ideas for an event and was not surprised to hear Deirdre had no thoughts or ideas. Deirdre confessed she was a blank page when it came to these things. All she had with her was a photo of Deirdre and Creighton as children - the little girl proudly wearing a princess dress and tiara; beside her, his arm protectively around her, was a jaunty cowboy, with red boots and wide brimmed straw hat.

Maddy suggested a cowboy theme, using the photo on the invitation and Deirdre agreed it would be a fitting tribute as Creighton wanted to be a cowboy all his life.

Maddy proposed Decades as the venue and laid a plan for a fun evening - Deirdre was delighted to have Maddy take over with the planning and details. She clapped her hands and thanked Maddy and ordered a drink. She could hardly wait to tell her parents the event was really going to happen.

The two women worked well together - Deirdre taking her assignments from Maddy seriously and diligently.

Sebastian heard his colleagues discussing the event with enthusiasm, feeling proud of Maddy, who had not shared the plan with him. He knew there was to be a Boots & BBQ Night for Cowboys & Cowgirls at Decades Night Club. He could only imagine all those who Maddy had corralled to help out for the event but he believed it would be a fun, if not a disparate, evening. Lambert had already purchased his white Stetson and western boots.

Sam, resigned to being called The Professor, was pleased to work with Maddy and convert his night club into a western club - he had found a great country band; gregarious PC from Texas had provided the mechanical bull and straw cowboy hats; Grace was planning the barbecue complete with corn on the cob, baked beans and corn bread, with the help of Henry; Audrey had asked to be on the decorating crew but her schedule with the children did not allow her to participate in any of the meetings.

The greatest challenge was teaching Deirdre how to line dance - she was eager but had no rhythm. Sam patiently worked with her and Maddy was pleased to see the two of them laughing together and teasing each other.

Over the months they worked together, Deirdre confided in Maddy - sharing stories about her life she had not dared discuss with anyone else before. Her older brother had been a model son, an outgoing athletic boy with many friends. Creighton had been her idol. He was on the transplant waiting list as a result of a freak accident - he passed away before a donor was found. Her parents had been inconsolable - not only had the heir to the family business been taken from them but now they were left with a spoiled daughter who had no head for business.

Deirdre felt lost without Creighton in her life - she married the first man who seemed interested in her family business, hoping to gift her parents a suitable heir. After several attempts at marriage, she realized she had no appetite for it…her parents certainly had tired of the steady line of suitors and her continuous return to their home. She had enjoyed Sebastian as a friend and escort; he was not interested in her fortune or in making demands - it was an easy friendship. Deirdre also confided that Sebastian had been friends with Creighton and she believed he felt obligated to assume the role of big brother.

The Creighton Foundation was established by the family to assist with organ donations as a result. In order to create awareness with the public the family decided to hold an event to raise the ante and get the message out. Deirdre felt it was her responsibility to make the event a success - cathartic for her family and timely for the medical community at large. She was thankful to Maddy and said so repeatedly.

Deirdre was quick to cajole friends and acquaintances into purchasing not only a ticket but a table and soon the "Big Event" was sold out.

"Audrey called today and asked if she could sit with us at the fundraiser - she was too late to get a ticket - we talked about it and I guessed you would be too busy to sit down anyway so, of course, I agreed." Sebastian casually remarked as he poured a drink. "I wondered why Audrey wasn't on your committee, but I knew you would want her to attend." He walked up the stairs with his drink in hand. "I have an early morning."

Maddy looked up as he left the room. She was spending so much time on the details and wondered why Audrey would call Sebastian for a seat when she was on the committee and had not shown up for the past two meetings. Her absence was adding to the workload Maddy had already taken on. She shrugged and smiled, thinking of how nice it would be when she was alone with Sebastian for a few days. Surely, he must feel neglected. She had planned a lovely getaway as soon as the event was over.

The next evening Sebastian called Maddy to say Audrey had asked him to take the children to their football practice as she was tied up in a meeting. Maddy suggested he bring the Buttons home with him for grilled cheese sandwiches - their favourite. It was agreed he would be home for dinner with the children. Maddy stopped working on the seating charts to set the table and prepare for dinner.

It was dark out when she looked up, realizing it was long past dinner. She heard Sebastian walk into the kitchen and ran to meet him. "What happened, I was expecting you. I was looking forward to seeing the children. I hardly see them anymore. It's so strange that Jeffrey wasn't at their game - he plans his day around their games and practices."

Sebastian loosened his tie and kept walking towards the stairs.

"Audrey came to the practice. Her meeting ended early. She had promised the children they could eat at their favourite restaurant." He leaned against the door frame. "The meal took so long to arrive Jemma fell asleep on my lap." He smiled, remembering how she had crawled onto his lap and tucked her head in his jacket. "Anyway, we just got them home. You might have called to see where we were. Audrey said she saw you at Decades just before she joined us, so I assumed you were busy with the event."

He turned and walked upstairs, noticing the table had been set with colourful plates and napkins. If he hadn't consumed so much wine he might have apologized to Maddy.

"I did call. Audrey's phone was off, and you didn't pick up. I haven't been anywhere this evening." Maddy realized Sebastian had left the room. She sat at the table, resting her head on her folded hands and wondered why Audrey would say she had seen Maddy. Why was her phone off?

Maddy was too tired to prepare anything to eat at this point…she was too tired to move. She stood up, stretched and switched the lights off. She saw her shoes near the sofa and dragged herself over to pick them up. As she bent down, she fell back on the sofa - it felt so soft and welcoming.

Maddy woke with a start and realized her neck ached and she was still wearing her clothes from the previous day. She sat up and looked around the room. It was morning and the birds were loudly singing in harmony. She stood and stretched as she walked towards her laptop. She did a double take as she noticed the time…it was mid-morning. She ran up the stairs to see if Sebastian was still in bed but he was gone and the house felt cold and empty. Maddy stood in the shower, letting the water wake her up, struggling to get on with the day.

"Oh Sebastian, I waited dinner for you. I didn't realize you'd be late. Have you eaten?" Maddy was following Sebastian as he walked towards the stairs, loosening his tie.

"I stopped at my Club. I'm going to bed."

"Sebastian, what's wrong? Have I done something to upset you? We've hardly spoken in a week. I know I've been focused on the fundraiser…"

"I'm tired Maddy. Not tonight…" Sebastian didn't turn around to look at her, he just walked up the stairs to the bedroom, leaving her to wonder what was going on.

Sebastian seemed preoccupied when Maddy called and asked him to join her for lunch.

"I haven't seen you much this past month and I want to try the new restaurant Aqua in the Shard building. Do you have time to join me?"

"If it's quick. I'll meet you there. Today is filled with client appointments."

Maddy's spirits would not be dampened. "Great. I've made the reservation. See you there...how will I know you?" He usually laughed at the question but today he just disconnected the call without a response.

Sebastian was aware Lambert was watching his reaction. He tried to smile but he was feeling sorry for himself - in fairness, he had agreed Maddy should help Deirdre with her event; but he had not expected her to be so involved. He felt left out. Audrey reminded him he was being abandoned for Maddy's old friend, Sam and of course, the American, Dermot. Audrey was crushed that Maddy was also cutting her out of the planning. Audrey thought Maddy wanted all the accolades...that didn't seem like Maddy, but people changed...

Maddy arrived at the office early, to surprise Sebastian and walk with him to the restaurant. She looked radiant in a knee length, light blue coat dress with a colourful scarf loosely thrown around her neck.

Lambert stood as he saw her push the door open. "Mad, Sebastian has been trying to call you. He can't make your luncheon, Mad, so sorry."

At that moment Jemma ran out of the boardroom, calling for Maddy.

Maddy crouched down to catch the little dynamo, happy to see her. Jimmy followed his sister into the reception area.

"Maddy, yippee, you came to lunch as well."

Sebastian walked out of his office and stopped when he saw the children and Maddy in a happy embrace. He looked over at the boardroom where Audrey was casually unpacking a takeout order on the table. She had a demure smile on her face.

"Sorry, not today darlings. Sebastian and I have a luncheon date but it is so good to see you both."

"No, Maddy, Mommy brought our lunches here for a picnic with Sebastian. Join us, please. Please. Mommy, can Maddy have a picnic with us?" Jimmy was begging, his hands in front of him, prayer-like.

"I'm sure Maddy is too busy for us. Let's sit down, shall we? Sebastian, you sit here. Come along children. We don't have long." Audrey smiled sweetly and sat down at the table.

Sebastian had not spoken. He looked at Maddy, at the children and at Audrey, who was not acknowledging Maddy. The children each took a hand and led him into the boardroom, waving sadly at Maddy. He turned back to see Maddy, looking dejected but oh so becoming. When he looked back a second time she was gone.

Lambert and Maddy enjoyed an expensive, but delicious lunch at Aqua. Lambert insisted on treating...he was incensed with Sebastian and his behaviour towards Maddy.

"Maddy, that woman is evil. She knew you had lunch planned - I told her myself. She drops in for coffee, needing advice; bringing him gifts...it's really inappropriate. She is very, very unhappy with you. Why is she trying to undermine your efforts for the fundraising event?" Lambert touched Maddy's hand, as a concerned friend would do.

"I don't know what's going on Lambert. I have been so focused on the event maybe I'm not making enough time for either of them. Audrey is on my committee, but she hasn't been able to attend a meeting, actually, she has made several contrary calls and I'm having to explain or grovel a lot. Sebastian is just distant. I'm taking him away right after the event on Saturday. I'm looking forward to spending some time with him...he's working so hard."

"He's not. I can tell you he's so behind in his sign-offs; I'm worried he can't seem to focus on his own business these days. I hope the time away with you works...it usually does. Do you think we can share this dessert, it sounds divine, as the Americans say."

Lambert returned to the office and found Sebastian staring out the window, his feet propped up on the window ledge. He had an unopened file on his lap.

"Sebastian, I've worked with you for such a long time and I know something isn't right. What's going on?"

Sebastian stared at Lambert, wanting to hear about lunch, wanting to tell his trusted employee how he felt...yet how do you describe a jealous, self-pitying feeling to another man? Audrey was constantly asking for his help or advice; Maddy didn't need his advice - Audrey needed him to help with the children; Maddy didn't need help - Audrey was hurt by Maddy cutting her out of the planning; Sebastian was also hurt...Audrey had hinted that Maddy was planning to run off with Dermot right after the event. They had been planning something for ages.

Lambert picked up the snow globe Maddy had sent Sebastian when they were going through a difficult time, it seemed so long ago. He tossed it from hand to hand, watching the snow swirl in the globe, over the figure of a woman reaching out for the man below. He hoped Sebastian remembered the significance of the snow globe as he dropped it loudly on the desk and walked out of the office.

"Where is Maddy now?" Sebastian called after Lambert.

"She always thinks better when she's walking the beach." Lambert wanted Sebastian to go to the beach house and find Maddy - find Maddy and settle this silliness.

Sebastian left the house early, hoping to reach the beach house before Maddy went for her morning walk. He walked around the building to the outdoor deck to see if anyone was on the beach and there she was, not far from the bottom steps. He saw her wave at a man leaning against the rocks. Sebastian sat on the first step watching Maddy greet his schoolmate Rod. He felt a pang of jealousy as Rod picked Maddy up in a bear hug. They walked down the beach, his arm around her shoulders, stopping to pick up shells or jump away from the surging water. At one point Rod took Maddy's hand and they followed something towards the rocks, crouching down to observe.

Sebastian weighed his options - he could leave and drive back to London; he could wait right here for them to notice him and they would have breakfast together or he could climb into the bed and wait for Maddy to return - she would be cold and taste of salt, and he would warm her.

He shook his head and wondered if Rod would come back to the beach house with her. He opted for the safest path and went to the local coffee shop for breakfast, alone.

As he was leaving the shop, coffee in hand, he saw Rod drive by. Maddy would be alone at the beach house. He would have a shower with her...or sit in the large bathtub with her.

His phone rang, breaking his resolve. Davi was calling to remind him of his appointment, wondering where he might be. If he left now, he could just make it on time. He started the car and headed for London.

"Hi. Do you have time for lunch today?" Maddy held her breath. "I really have to talk to you and we don't seem to be in the same place much these days."

"Maddy, today isn't good for me, I'm sure Lambert told you I will be out for most of the day. I'll be late, don't wait up." Sebastian didn't want to know where the conversation would lead - if Maddy wanted to tell him she was leaving, he wasn't going to make it easy for her.

Maddy sighed as she looked at her phone. Sebastian had ended the call without a goodbye. Something was definitely wrong - hopefully the time away, just the two of them, would fix this.

There were so many last minute details to attend to - Maddy added several shopping items to her list - she wanted to have all of his favourite things on the menu. She was looking forward to getting away after the event…but right now, she needed to confirm the lighting and sound arrangements.

My Heroes Have Always Been Cowboys

"Breathe Deirdre. It's going to be a great evening...you managed to sell all the tickets; the band is awesome; the films on each floor are showing westerns; one screen has only photos of Creighton; the literature is by the door in the takeaway bags - there are sweets in the shape of boots and hats in the bags as well; the digital camera is set up for the mechanical bull; the photo booth is popular; you look amazing and the red carpet will make everyone feel special...I'll let you know when we're ready for the line dance. Enjoy the evening." Maddy assured her nervous Co-Chair, squeezing her hand.

Deirdre hugged Maddy. "Thank you. Everything is perfect. Thank you."

"You done good." Maddy smiled at her, thinking about all the work that led to this moment, the change in Deirdre and the joy she felt seeing her friends rise to the challenge for this evening.

Guests were arriving and there was a buzz in the night club. Maddy walked over to Sam and Dermot, who were also looking very western and pleased with themselves.

"Maddy, we've taken toy guns away from most of the cowboys...just in case." Sam shook his head and laughed. Dermot lifted the canvas bag as proof.

"You both look like authentic lawmen, I must say." Maddy leaned in between the men and kissed both on the cheek.

"Thank you." she whispered as she moved away to greet Deirdre's parents.

"How does she manage to make blue jeans and a white cotton shirt look so good?" Dermot asked Sam, as they watched Maddy make her way through the crowd.

"It's the red bandana…and the boots. Ah, come on, she would make a bed sheet look good." Both men laughed and nodded and raised their glasses in a toast.

"Sam, the place looks great and the guests are loving it. That booth with the custom 'Wanted' poster is genius. Everyone will have one on their wall come Monday."

"It's all Maddy…every detail, everything you see, she planned."

"You should leave it this way - it really rocks as a country and western dance hall." Dermot was impressed with the decor and the vibe.

"The next owner can make that decision. It's time for me to sell and enjoy my well-earned golden years." Sam smiled, his eyes following the crowd. "Come on. We better see how things are going upstairs."

The event was in full swing; the crowd embracing the music, the food and the mechanical bull. Maddy looked around and watched Sebastian approach, a worried look on his face. She wondered if she should tell him she was kidnapping him tonight. He looked so handsome in his jeans, denim shirt and boots, except for the solemn look on his face, he was a hot commodity.

"Are you having a good time, Cowboy?" She smiled up at him as he stood beside her. She had not seen much of him for the past few weeks leading up to the event and she could hardly wait to whisk him away for a few days of romantic seclusion. She was ready to go as soon as the function was over.

"It seems to be a great success. Congratulations." Sebastian looked around the room. "Maddy, I don't think there will be a good time to have this conversation so I'm going to say this now…"

Maddy blinked, not sure what to expect. One of the lighting men approached Maddy with a question.

"Just give me a moment." She smiled and focused on Sebastian.

"I know you plan to leave later this evening and I hope you will be happy, you deserve to be happy. I love you and because I love you, I have to let you go. I'll stay at the house for now, but you have several options. The beach cottage is yours; of course and Villa Mirage is yours. You won't be destitute, I'll make sure you are taken care of - you won't have to worry about anything." He could not look at her, could not chance being drawn in by her blue eyes. He convinced himself this was best for both of them. Why did all these people need to speak to Maddy at this moment, he wondered.

Maddy felt her chest tighten; her face was on fire; she could not breathe; could not cry with all these people around her; could not scream at him; could not digest what was happening. She was paralyzed. Sebastian, on the other hand, was cool and rational, leaving her in the middle of the biggest event she had ever choreographed.

She was trying to think, trying to shrug off the many hands touching her arm or shoulder, congratulating her or asking for assistance with a particular detail.

"Can we talk about this later? I'm not sure what you want from me right now. I'm in the middle of an event…can this wait?" She asked, although she really didn't want to discuss this later. She just wanted him to go. She just wanted to play this back in slow motion so she could laugh at the joke.

"I think it's best if I go now. You carry on. You'll be fine. You don't need me." He almost said he wished they would remain friends, he almost said he was sorry, but thought the best of it.

Yet another hand on her elbow. She knew Sebastian was agitated by the constant interruption.

"What about Henry? What happens to Henry?" She had to know.

"He needs stability. I will continue to look at adoption. Surely you would agree that would be best for him?" Still no eye contact.

Maddy felt as though a knife had been pushed through her abdomen. She concentrated on not giving him the pleasure of seeing her cry. She wanted to scream at the people needing her constant attention.

"Please Sebastian, just let me finish the program and we can talk." Another hand on her arm, congratulating her on a lovely affair. Maddy wanted to scream. She looked over and saw Audrey walking towards them. Audrey placed her hand on Sebastian's arm and asked if he was ready to go.

Maddy's throat was thick, her chest heaving, her legs were like jelly - she wasn't sure she could walk away. Maddy had so many questions - her head was spinning. She turned away; afraid Sebastian would touch her.

She closed her eyes and turned suddenly, "Sebastian. Kiss me goodbye."

"Maddy we both know that kiss would betray us." He turned away.

Sebastian moved Audrey's hand from his arm and they walked out through the crowd to the foyer. Audrey didn't look back but as they walked out, she was hoping he would place his hand on her back as he always did with Maddy. Sebastian did not.

Maddy somehow made it to the Maintenance Closet, locking herself in the small room. She leaned against the wall, hoping her chest would not explode. Tears were raining down her cheeks. She felt betrayed by her best friend and the love of her life…would she ever see the Buttons again? What about the projects she and Audrey had been working on? What about Henry? Could she see Henry? What would happen if they saw each other on the beach at the cottage? What if…why…how…

Audrey had been calling Sebastian and they had been with the children…it had seemed so innocent…had Maddy been so completely unaware of how neglected Sebastian was feeling?

Taking a deep breath, Maddy shook her head and wiped her face. Of course, she had to realize she had disappeared to help a friend, leaving those closest to her wondering where she was, when she would be back. Why was this happening tonight? Of all nights…why tonight?

She heard laughter and realized she didn't have the luxury of feeling sad or hurt right now…there was an agenda to follow, an event to shepherd. She walked out into the crowd, pleased to hear the music, the laughter, the sounds of people enjoying the evening.

"Hey, where have you been? I've been waiting to dance with you all evening." Dermot was at her side. "This is a Five Star night…great party. I'm going to hire this band for my next affair at the Embassy. As a matter of fact, I intend to hire the party planner as well. I made a personal donation to the cause. Did I do good?" He stepped in front of her, shocked at the tears and her sad face.

"What happened Maddy? What's going on?" He seemed genuinely concerned.

"Let's dance. I can't really talk right now." Maddy looked towards the dance floor.

Dermot took her hand and gently led her onto the crowded dance floor. He held her tightly and looked around the room as they two-stepped to a popular country tune. His mind was reeling - the woman he couldn't have was hurting and he wanted to be her hero. Who took her smile away? Who dampened her spirit? He was ready to fight.

"Thank you." Maddy whispered. She dropped her hand from his shoulder and moved away.

He couldn't let her go, not when she looked so broken. "Talk to me Maddy. I can't let you walk away. Do you want to go somewhere quiet to talk?" He would not let go of her shoulders. He hated to see her so distressed.

Maddy closed her eyes and bit her lip, not sure she wanted to speak to anyone right now. She looked up and saw the concern on his face.

"Sebastian and Audrey left together so here I am, free, free at last." She tried to smile but her face betrayed her - it was a night of betrayals. She wanted to run away…somewhere far, where no one knew or cared who she was…somewhere far, where there were no people she could hurt or people who could leave her.

"Maddy, I'm so sorry. I can't believe they would do this to you, of all people. Come on, let me take you home. Deirdre and Sam have this, they don't need to see you like this. Come on." Dermot had his arm around her and was leading her towards the back door, away from the crowd.

Outside in the back alley, near the trash bins and stacks of empty bottles, they stood in the harsh streetlight, unaware of the soft drizzle.

"Scream! Scream at the top of your lungs. Scream until you get all the anger you feel out of your system. Go ahead." Dermot encouraged her.

Maddy smiled, despite herself. "What are you talking about?"

"They say it helps. I hate to see you hurting…please scream. I'll feel like I'm helping you if you scream. Loud, real loud, like a banshee."

Maddy put her head down and cradled her face, wiping the rain away. Then she screamed; she screamed for the sadness, the loss, the hurt, the pain of the unknown. She screamed until she was hoarse.

Dermot wrapped his arms around her and whispered, "That's my girl. It's okay, I'm going to take care of you. We'll all take care of you, all of us.

You're gonna be alright. I promise you, it's gonna be alright. You're gonna be fine, just fine."

Maddy collected herself, moved away from him and looked out at the alleyway - she could run and make the street easily, disappearing into the busy traffic and leaving all of this behind.

"It won't do any good to run, Maddy. Let's talk about what you do now. I know it's still stinging but you need a plan. You have to get through this night - so many people are counting on you. I must be in Washington next week - come with me. I'll be a perfect gentleman. You can have your own suite in the capital. I'd love to show you my town. Please Maddy, come with me. Get away from here - until you're ready to face things. You've been a wonderful friend to me - let me be a friend to you." Dermot was so serious Maddy smiled back at him and touched his cheek.

"Let's see what tomorrow brings. Right now I need a drink."

"Of course, I'll get us a drink, you sit here for a minute. I'll let Sam know you had to leave. Please just wait here for me."

Maddy looked up at his concerned face. She touched his cheek and whispered, "thank you Dermot. You're my favourite Ambassador."

Moments later, Dermot returned to the alley, drinks in hand, having given Sam the abbreviated message and excused himself. He looked up and down the alley, but she was gone.

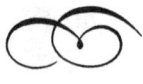 (When Did You Fall) Out of Love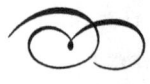

"I found her. I found her. It wasn't easy but I found her." Lambert burst into Sebastian's office waving a piece of paper. "I knew I would."

Sebastian stood up, his heart pounding. "Where is she?"

"She booked a fortnight at Applecross, it's in Scotland, in the northwest, about 60 miles from Inverness." Lambert was clearly excited.

"I know Applecross. Would Maddy still be there?"

"She purchased petrol a few days ago in Fort William - no charges since then. I looked into flights to Inverness, stopping at Edinburgh…you can leave first thing in the morning, rent a car and be there before the sun goes down. Shall I…"

"No, I can get there faster by driving. I can be there in the morning." Sebastian walked out of the office, turning to thank Lambert.

The overland pass to Applecross offers a magnificent ride, rising over 600 metres in five miles - in good weather the pass is a dream for motorcyclists. The narrow single lane has several lay-bys for oncoming traffic - the tight ascending turns and the views are spectacular. Riders are rewarded with a pint at the Applecross Inn at the end of the road.

A tired, but exhilarated Sebastian arrived at the Inn, removing his motorcycle helmet and gloves, barely able to step off the bike. He breathed in the fresh air and surveyed the area. It truly was a special place and he was so pleased Maddy had chosen this for a getaway.

He walked into the Inn, stretching his back and shoulders - it was a long ride, and he wasn't as young as he thought he was. He ordered a pint and asked at the reception if Ms Davis was at the Inn. The barman leaned forward and asked why he wanted to know.

"I'm her husband." Sebastian responded without thinking.

The older men at the bar looked at each other, eyebrows raised. "So you're the fella who couldn't make it." They laughed. "She might be out walking - she'll be back soon enough."

Sebastian nodded and took his drink outdoors to the wooden table, to wait. The sun was warm on his face and the reflection on the water made him squint as he looked up and down the coast. He hoped he wouldn't fall asleep before he saw her. Rubbing the gold compass in his hand, he could feel sleep overcome him.

"What are you doing here?" He felt a hand on his shoulder. He shook his head and looked up to see her, shrouded in sunlight.

He had rehearsed what he wanted to say all the way north but as he saw Maddy he was overwhelmed with shame and guilt. "I came to bring you home. I have so much to tell you. What I did was inexcusable and I need to explain…I came to ask you to forgive me."

Maddy sat beside him. "We can talk later. You look awful. You need to get some sleep. Did you really drive up on the bike?" She was pleased to see him driving the motorcycle - the vintage Triumph had sat in the garage for years, gathering dust, before Maddy had her friends restore it and ensure it was in working order. It had been a touchy gesture as Sebastian said he wanted to work on the bike but never had the time…he had been delighted when Maddy presented the shiny, working motorcycle to him. They had planned to take a trip…

"It's good to see you Maddy. I think a few hours of shuteye would be the ticket." He suddenly felt the weight of his twelve-hour drive, the anticipation of seeing Maddy and how she would react, overwhelm him.

"Come on. People will talk if I leave you here. Can you walk over to the apartment? It's just over here." She pointed to the glass front building.

Maddy gathered his helmet and gloves and started walking, holding him up.

"Maddy, let me sleep for a few hours. Please don't go anywhere, we have to talk. Please tell me you'll be here when I wake up."

Maddy nodded and opened the door for him. "You can take this room. There's a shower…did you bring a change of clothes? Never mind, I'll check your bike. Let me take your jacket and boots off and get you into bed."

Sebastian fell asleep before Maddy removed his boots. He dreamed of walking the beach with Maddy, having a candlelight dinner with her smiling face across from him, dancing with her under the stars…

He woke to the smell of coffee, birdsong and sun streaming through the window. He sat up in the bed, shook his head and realized his body was stiff from the long ride. He showered and dressed, thankful that Maddy had brought his things in from the bike.

"Good morning. Did you sleep well?" Maddy was on a yoga mat, stretching her torso, bent over her knees. He stopped to watch her - breathing to calm the desire to run across the room and hold her face in his hands before kissing her.

"Like a log, dead to the world, I dare say. Thank you."

He stood before the full-length window, looking out at the view. "This was an excellent choice for a getaway." He was unsure what to say next. "Would you like to walk with me?"

"Lunch first. We can walk after you've eaten. How about an omelet, toast and coffee?" She stood and walked into the small kitchen.

They walked against the wind in silence, both lost in their own thoughts.

"I knew I made a mistake as soon as we got in the car. Audrey couldn't wait to tell me how her plan had worked to perfection and how she knew you were done with me. I couldn't get back to Decades fast enough. They said you had disappeared. I wasn't able to beg you for forgiveness that night. Is it too late now?"

Maddy did not speak for some time, she seemed to be concentrating on a gull, gliding back and forth across the water. "I need time. You broke my heart, and I can't forget how horrible that felt. I'm not ready...not yet." She brushed a tear from her cheek. She had watched him sleeping and wanted so badly to lie beside him and hold him, but the hurt was too raw.

Sebastian felt as though he was falling into a well. Beside him was the woman he loved. He had hurt her and now he had to let her heal. He would have to do whatever it took to get her back into his life. He sighed. "I never meant to hurt you. I believed you were leaving me."

"Why didn't you ask me? Why didn't you wait until we were alone? Why did you walk away in front of five hundred guests? Why didn't you tell me how you felt when we were at home - why were you so cruel to me when everything I was doing was for your friend? I worked so hard on that event because Creighton was your friend and I wanted you to be proud of me. Why didn't you use your compass?" Maddy couldn't stop the tears. It felt good to be angry with him.

He reached for her face, but she flinched and turned away. He felt as though his hand had been scorched. They stood in silence for what seemed like an eternity.

"I have to respect your wishes and give you time, but I want you to know I will be waiting for you. When you're ready, please come home. My feelings for you have not changed - I will always love you. I'll stay the night if you'll have dinner with me, and I promise I will go tomorrow at first light. It's a long drive and the way home won't be as motivating as the drive here."

Maddy nodded. As they walked back to the apartment Sebastian reached for her hand, and to his delight Maddy did not pull her hand away. He turned to her and wrapped his arms around her, feeling her cold cheek against his neck. Time - the killer of hope, the trap that robbed you of happiness, the only thing she asked for...time. He would give her time and never let her go.

The next morning, true to his word, Sebastian embraced Maddy before donning his helmet and driving away. Maddy watched the bike turn the corner to the pass, took a deep breath and started walking along the water. Sleep had been slow to come last night - she tossed and turned - her mind in conflict. She loved him, of course she did, but she was angry and rather than react to every nuance and word she wanted time to get over him - or not.

As she walked, she felt the rain on her face, biting into her cheeks and forcing her to squint. She should turn back. She realized she was crying - sobbing and trying to catch her breath. She wanted to be angry at Sebastian; she wanted him to hold her; she never wanted to see him again; she wanted to hear his voice…she stopped and leaned forward, hands on her knees, trying to breathe. She was muttering to herself, telling herself that love was not worth the pain, she was better off alone, she would never again love someone and let them hurt her…

Someone was calling her name. She felt she was losing her mind. The sound of her name was closer, louder. She turned and fell into the arms of the man she knew she loved.

"I can't leave you. I can't imagine life without you. Maddy, I love you. I need you." Sebastian was shouting against the wind, holding her, protecting her. She looked up and felt his hands on her face, he looked into her eyes and then he kissed her…his lips hungry for her. She threw her arms around him and pulled him closer.

The older couples walking towards them agreed the scene was out of a movie…the motorcycle on the road, the helmet dangling from the side mirror, the rider in his leather jacket running to his fair maid on the sand, holding her in an amorous embrace - their imaginations believing he would now carry her to his bed. It was indeed romantic.

Sebastian and Maddy barely made it into the apartment before shedding layers of clothing. Sebastian carried Maddy to the outer door, knowing she never locked doors. He struggled with the latch, pushing the door open, careful not to drop her. In the small porch area he stood Maddy up against the inside door, flung his jacket on the floor, unzipped Maddy's coat and pushed it off her shoulders. She opened the second door, kicking her boots off, throwing her gloves and scarf on the floor. By the time they reached the bedroom door they were embracing, hungry for each other, hungry to hold each other and be one. Maddy laughed at Sebastian as he hurriedly tried to shake his riding pants off, forgetting he had his riding boots on.

When they finally fell on the bed, naked, they were laughing between kissing and touching and rolling across the quilt. Sebastian rolled over pinning Maddy's arms on the bed, looking down at her, his breathing heavy, the laughter over. As he studied her a small gasp escaped his lips; he was overwhelmed with the vision in front of him.

Maddy blinked as tears fell. She looked up at him, panting from the laughter, the production of undressing, the delight at having him so close, beside her. They both wanted to say so much, to tell each other how they felt, how they missed each other, how they wanted to move forward…Sebastian leaned down and tenderly kissed Maddy, a kiss that confirmed everything he wanted to say and more. Maddy responded, knowing everything was going to be alright.

Waking up with the last rays of the day bathing the room in soft pastels the couple held each other and talked, not wanting to move or break the spell. Maddy, cradled safely in his arms, touched his chest.

"Why did you do it?" She asked in a whisper.

Sebastian cleared his throat, collecting his thoughts, wondering where to start…how to explain the unfortunate circumstances that resulted in hurting the woman he loved. He placed his hand on hers and began to relate the series of events, the misread signals, the feelings of inadequacy, Audrey's mission to have Maddy to herself…when he explained how he had returned directly to the Club, realizing his error in judgment, Maddy sat up, confused.

"I can't believe you came back to Decades…what about Audrey?"

"I ran back. Dermot and The Professor assured me you had gone. They wouldn't let me in, and I know they would have enjoyed punching me out. Audrey is in a facility, well looked after by professionals. Jeremy tells me she will be there for some time. She had a breakdown. It seems the children were too much."

"I'm sorry to hear Audrey is not well." Maddy turned away. "I did leave Decades right after you left. I drove here. I was angry and confused and so hurt."

"Oh Maddy, I've made such a mess of things. Davi stopped the car and I ran back to the Club. Lambert is upset with me…he was relentless in his search for you - prevailing as he always does. Christian was worried about you, of course, and Deirdre became your biggest fan. I don't want to be without you in my life. Please forgive me. Please come home." Sebastian pulled Maddy into his arms.

"I'm trying to move forward, and I am pleased you are here but I do need time - I just can't go back to London right now. Luckily, I have commitments with the Coastal Council so I need a week or so at the beach house and then I have to be at the Villa for the financial team review. I wouldn't feel comfortable presenting an idea, a major change, and then walking away, without encouraging the makeover and the details I felt so passionate about. I also want to see the harvest in - I can't wait to taste our first wine."

"I'll wait for you - as long as it takes. Will you let me stay here with you until it's time to go? It's important."

"I think we need some time to get to know each other again. To trust each other again. This was supposed to be our time. Let's enjoy it and not think about next week. Right now, I'm starving. You better feed me. Dinner." She threw off the covers and offered her hand. "Shower or bath?"

Sebastian smiled and took her hand, pulling her close. He kissed her neck and held her in a firm embrace, thankful for the time they would have together. He had grown up believing that British men do not show their feelings, they are to be reserved and proper. Meeting Maddy had changed all that…he wanted to shout out his feelings, throw caution to the wind and be the man she would love forever.

They walked, they talked about taking a motorbike vacation, they prepared meals together, trying new recipes - on rainy days they sat across from each other on the sofa or lay across each other, holding hands, reading. They worked on a jigsaw puzzle, played cards and backgammon, staying up late and sleeping late the next morning. They researched more water purification plans and waste options for Maddy's island project. They made love and they danced, holding each other with loving arms. The days and nights passed too quickly as they sadly waved goodbye to their refuge at Applecross.

Sebastian believed it had been worth the drive. Indeed.

When We Were Young

Arriving early in the morning, Colonel Oliver Wainwright III requested his driver standby as he walked into the Villa Mirage. He asked for Madison Davis and was directed to the breakfast room. The señora was at the yoga session and would be down soon.

Entering the room, admiring the decor and noticing the soft music, he felt nervous, his usual calm demeanour on edge.

"Hello, welcome to Villa Mirage. I am Giselle, the manager here. Is Maddy expecting you? She didn't say."

Oliver turned to the woman, taking in her dark eyes and compact figure - he sensed she might appear feminine and petite but there was a fire behind those eyes.

"I'm an old friend. I'm taking her to lunch." He offered his most charming smile and bowed slightly. "Would you prefer I wait for her down in the courtyard?"

"No, please have a seat. Maddy usually goes to the early yoga class - she should be along for breakfast anytime now. Coffee?"

He nodded and sat at a small table by the window, where he could watch for Maddy. He felt like Gulliver in Lilliput…the room was calming enough but his tall frame seemed to dominate the space.

He caught his breath as Maddy appeared in the courtyard, intent on the conversation between two other women. She stopped to explain something and waved goodbye. She seemed to explode into the breakfast room…the energy around her almost palpable.

"Good morning Oliver. You found us." Maddy leaned over and brushed his cheek with her lips. "Coffee? You're early for lunch."

Oliver reached for her wrist, stopping her forward motion.

"Are you trying to drive me crazy?"

"I'm sorry?" Maddy asked, confused by the question. "Would you prefer tea?"

He laughed and a rich and joyous sound filled the room as he shook his head. "Here I am, a Marine, with a rather good track record for staying calm in dangerous situations; I've seen combat and been recognized for keeping a cool head. You bounce in here with that 'dare you to join me on an adventure' smile and I'm nineteen again, watching the sweet sixteen-year-old blonde with a bouncy ponytail take over a room of bored students, challenging all of us to put down the rule book and have some fun. And we did have fun…despite the trouble you got us into. I can't believe you're here beside me, making me feel like a teenager on a first date."

Maddy looked away for a moment, remembering that first day of class, so long ago, meeting the other students, older and more mature, more serious and focused on learning Spanish. All the students were children of diplomats, except Maddy. She was told she was enrolled by her host family - they had limited English; it made sense that she should learn to communicate with them. Her parents were travelling for work and hoped she would enjoy living with a family and learning a new language.

"Bogota seems like a lifetime away…it's changed since we were there." Maddy smiled at him. He was still handsome, there was no doubt about that. "Are we on a date?"

"You bet. I know I asked you for lunch, but it seems I have a quick JAG consultation in Sicily. If I check in at the base I get another day of leave… join me?" Oliver hoped she would see this as an adventure.

"The Maddy I knew would never turn down an opportunity to take an impromptu leap of faith." He smiled at her, eyebrows raised, in a challenge.

"The chopper is available, and we can be done by late afternoon if we leave this morning." He held his breath until he saw the mischievous smile on her face. He was willing her to accept his invitation.

"Dinner in Taormina? You can see the sea and Mount Etna from the town."

"If Madame wishes, certainly. We'll get a car from Catania and drive there. I've heard it's beautiful." He wondered why he could not stop smiling. "Anywhere else you'd like to go or see?"

"Agrigento, on the southwest shore is also lovely. Great restaurant on the waterfront...I think the ancient ruins on the hillside in the Valley of the Temples are more interesting...sorry, you have a day and I'm planning a vacation."

"We have time. Pack an overnight bag and we'll do both." Oliver stood and held Maddy's face in his hands. "Thank you. Thank you for reminding me there are lovely places to see and enjoy." He sighed, hoping he had not scared her away by being so intense. "We should go. We have a big day ahead of us."

Maddy laughed and waved at him as she breezed out of the room. "Give me fifteen minutes."

Oliver sat down, ran his hand back and forth across his forehead as he looked out at the courtyard, seeing only the face of a young girl he had locked in his memory for so long.

Giselle knocked lightly on the bedroom door. "Maddy, are you going with him?"

Maddy turned and sat on the bed. "Gigi, he's an old friend. We were teenagers in Bogota - we had a lovely summer. He's leaving for Cyprus and I'm sure he just wants a few hours of reminiscing about our youth."

"He's dangerous Maddy. He's too darn handsome and confident for his own good. He looks like he's used to getting what he wants..."

"Oh Gigi, I'm broken, damaged goods...what would he want with me?" Maddy looked away.

"I don't like how he looks at you...does Dermot know you two are taking a little jaunt? Better still, does Sebastian know?"

"I'm just going to dinner in Taormina...Dermot is at a Summit in France. He and Oliver were college roommates. I will tell Sebastian I'm going on an adventure trip. All perfectly above board. Believe me...I'll be very good."

"Heavens, I know you will...I can't say that about your marvellous marine. May I help you pack?"

Maddy hugged her friend. "I thought I'd take something blue."

They both laughed as Maddy opened the closet door to a rack of blue creations by Sorento.

The chopper was ready for their passage from Florence to NAS Sigonella Navy Base in Sicily when they arrived at the airport. Oliver was pleased to see Maddy was a seasoned flyer, at ease with the headset and very aware of the routing, pointing out landmarks.

In his uniform, Oliver appeared taller and even more commanding, saluting the welcoming officers ready to guide him through the NATO site. Maddy and the pilot, Jazz, were left to wait in the Officer's Lounge. They played backgammon, shuffleboard and enjoyed a light lunch as they waited.

"I'm thinking there will be quite a negotiation going on right now." Jazz smiled at Maddy.

"The Colonel will be vying for one of the Commanding Officer's private cars. He has a sizeable collection on base."

When Oliver appeared in a shiny blue Lamborghini, Maddy and Jazz winked and fist-punched each other…they had guessed correctly.

Maddy touched the driver's door and smiled up at Oliver. "Can I drive?"

Oliver laughed and instinctively reached to hug Maddy. He laughed and whispered in her ear, "only when we leave the base."

"Fine." Maddy smiled up at him and walked over to the passenger door, running her hand across the car.

Oliver shook his head, realizing he had just agreed to let the young girl with the dimples convince him to let her drive this very expensive car on Italian roads. He wondered if he would ever be able to say no to the woman beside him, especially when she smiled and lifted her chin, as if issuing a challenge. He had forgotten the spell she cast with her dimples and blue eyes. Thankfully, she had her sunglasses on now and he could concentrate on the road ahead.

They arranged to meet Jazz in two days, tossed the bags in the small space and drove off the base to explore Sicily.

Maddy and Oliver travelled well together, stopping for gelato or a cold drink on the drive south. They sang along with Carole King, James Taylor and Neil Diamond - laughing at the memories each song evoked from their summer together, so long ago.

"You know we've gone viral on social media." Oliver laughed as they sat on the stone wall enjoying their gelato.

Seeing the confused look on Maddy's face, he scrolled through the messages on his phone and played the video of their dance at the Embassy.

"I can't imagine why someone filmed it, but here it is, another great memory." He handed her the phone.

The memory of that evening came flooding back to Maddy. She smiled and shook her head. When she looked over at Oliver he was watching her reaction. He wanted to touch her cheek and tell her how much he enjoyed watching her smile; how that simple smile lit up the room - how he wanted to kiss those dimples and tenderly brush his lips against her eyelashes… how the memory of that smile had kept him on point in many a tough situation. Before he acted like a fool he tossed her the keys and let her drive instead.

Delicious seafood, quiet music and a perfect sunset over the water was their reward for choosing to stay in Agrigento. They strolled through the street market holding hands. The moon was bright, the breeze light as they sat by the hotel pool and talked, sipping on a lovely wine.

"Tell me about your life after Bogota, not just the highlights…I really want to know how you got here." Maddy touched his arm, encouraging him to begin.

"It's not that exciting, really. My future was to be in banking or foreign service, my father's dream - not mine. Sometime during my teens he realized I wasn't going to make a living racing yachts or playing tennis, so he painted a life for me as an international financier. Just to be sure he started buying property along the east coast. Martha's Vineyard, Long Island, beachfront properties…it's taken me years to sell them off. It was his way of saying if you can't make a living, I can at least leave you a legacy." He shrugged. "Maddy, I have the means to make you a happy woman."

"You can't buy happiness; you must know that."

"I suppose I do, but everyone wants to do something that will make a difference. What do you want?"

Maddy looked over at him and leaned forward. "I want to figure out a way to turn garbage into something productive like water and building materials. There has to be an affordable way to reuse the waste. It's for a small island off the coast of northern Africa. A developer changed the island way of life to accommodate a project that will never operate - the islanders are living with the devastation and although we were able to find water, by digging a well, they won't survive long on that limited water supply. Lofty, I guess, but it will require passion and money. I have the passion…" she smiled wistfully and shrugged.

"Maddy, I've never met anyone like you. That is a lofty project but there are organizations, NGO's, looking for challenges exactly like that. Let me think on it. I may be able to help you with your happy wish."

Maddy closed her eyes and visualized the village as she knew it and how she wished it could be. Her thoughts were interrupted by Oliver touching her hand.

"Here you go again…changing my plans. After a summer in Bogota and time with you, I changed my major to law."

Maddy sat back and shook her head. "No way."

"You questioned everything. Every rule, every suggestion, every authoritative comment - you made me realize my world was boring. First year college I accepted the lectures and studied. Suddenly, it's my sophomore year and I'm questioning why certain laws have been instituted. I tried to imagine how you would interpret a certain clause and bingo…I was the nerd with the *'what if'* attitude. I was recruited by the Marines and offered a full ticket; combat, officer and legal training, if I signed on. That's when I met Dermot. He was a rule follower, a perfect student - he saved me many times. I owe him." He looked away and took her hand.

"Let's call it a day and start off early tomorrow, shall we. It's been a lovely evening." He stood and gently pulled Maddy up, looking into her eyes with a strange expression.

"What's the matter Oliver?" She asked as his gaze rested over her head, at some far-off point.

"Do you recall the bird incident?" He dropped his hand and looked into her eyes.

"You mean the tree climbing incident?" She laughed. "I dared you to climb that tree…I felt so bad."

"You saved my bacon with my host family. They were ready to send me back to the states. They were beside themselves with worry and before I even climbed down from the damn tree you were taking over, managing the situation." He smiled as he relived the event in his mind. "You had tears in your eyes, and you were holding a birds nest, explaining how I had saved the nest from the cat who had climbed up the tree."

"They were so lovely and understanding. I remember hurting so bad after I jumped but I could see your host family was angry. I couldn't let you take the blame. I found a nest in the bushes and let me tell you, the tears were real. I thought I had a broken leg." Maddy chuckled.

"That simple gesture, of you saving me, making me a hero instead of a delinquent, was a turning point for me. My host family thought the world of you and suggested we invite you to their *Club de Tenis* every weekend… they never asked where the cat came from or realized you already had the nest in your hand when you pretended to take it from me. They had no idea you were the first one up the tree. I didn't have siblings so I had no experience on how to salvage a bad moment…that one incident had a great impact on my life. It made me realize things aren't always what they seem." He cleared his throat. "And that, my fair maid, has made the difference in so many trials through my lifetime."

Maddy reached over and squeezed his hand, wondering how such a confident, imposing figure of a man could be so tender. "Your father would be proud of the man you've become."

Sebastian raised his eyebrows and smiled. "Thank you. Goodnight."

Alone in her room, Maddy fell onto the bed and giggled, thinking how gallant Oliver had behaved all evening; acting as if he were her personal security guard. For the first time in a long while she wondered what she would do if there was a knock on her door.

When the sun peaked through her window she stretched and headed to the swimming pool for a morning swim, only to find Oliver in the centre lane, swimming laps as if he were training for time trials. She had forgotten he was a water baby.

They met at the deep end of the pool, treading water. Oliver took in the colour of the water, the clear sky and Maddy's eyes - he needed to focus before he did something foolish. He continued with his story, looking up at the sun.

"So, you asked…I got married to the rich girl next door, parents ecstatic; bride and groom not so happy. I stopped paying for the tennis lessons when I realized the tennis pro was the father of the expected son. It's hard to be a good husband when you are on a mission for months. I tried getting married again and failed miserably…it seems the uniform is only enticing when it's on. Joining JAG was a no-brainer; trading combat for courtroom warfare. Somedays I long for the sanity of combat rather than the obscurity of justice. Here I am, still a Marine, working with the United Nations and the Department of Homeland Security - following up on persons of interest." He stopped and wrapped his arms around Maddy. "You're getting a chill, let's have breakfast, shall we."

Over platters of fresh fruit and yogurt, they recalled the summer in Bogota…laughing at the memories, the silly things teenagers do, the fun they had, away from home.

"You were the best pen pal. I waited for your letters and read them over and over again. True story." Oliver held up his right hand.

"My last letter from you said you were leaving Paris and heading to South America. No word after that."

"South America was supposed to be healing but Dag found me and we spent months travelling remote areas - by the time we returned to Canada my life had taken a totally different direction."

Neither spoke as they watched the sunlight dance on the water.

"You're a woman, maybe you can help me solve a mystery." Oliver was suddenly serious.

"Glad you noticed…" She paused for effect, "that I'm a woman." She looked out over the pool.

"Oh my dearest Maddy, I know very well you are a woman. It took great control to be with you as a teenager and it's not any easier right now. I was a teenage boy with raging hormones, afraid to make a move and scare you away…I wanted your friendship, however crazy, more than I wanted sex. I don't know why I'm telling you this now."

Maddy turned to look at him, her voice tender, "that's lovely." She reached out and took his hand. After a moment she asked, "what's the mystery?"

He cleared his throat. "Why is it that when you're courting, an old fashioned way of saying dating, women never want children - they want a career and a life of travel and freedom. Once you get serious, they want a baby; they need children in their life. They leave you when you remind them of their goals. Why is that?"

Maddy weighed her response, "I'm not sure I'm qualified to speak for all women. Perhaps they have big goals until they fall in love with you.

They know you'll be gone for a while, and they want a part of you with them, to nurture and love while you are away, saving the world. I don't know…could have something to do with the biological clock ticking…"

"Did you want children, Maddy?"

"It was never an easy option. My Paris lover, Paul, was too old. Dag had grown children who worked with us and he said he was too old to go through that again. When I met Sebastian it was just too late."

"Disappointed?"

"No, I had such a busy life - I was always travelling and experiencing adventures, there wasn't time to dwell on it. Hey, come on, we can't change the past or dwell on what might have been. But now I have Henry and he is a gift. I told you about him yesterday."

"Hmmm. He's a lucky boy. Hey, one more swim before we head over to Taormina?" He was standing, his hand out. Discussion over.

Maddy smiled and took his hand. When she was standing she turned quickly, and fell into the pool, pulling Oliver in with her. When they came up out of the water, Maddy was laughing, shaking the water from her hair. Oliver wiped his face and pointed at her, "you are still a brat." He splashed her with a wave of his arm.

Maddy laughed, coughing up the water she had swallowed.

"You know what this means, don't you?" Oliver moved towards her; a menacing look on his face. Maddy stared back, her eyes wide in disbelief. Surely, he wouldn't. When they were teens, he would stride towards her and pick her up out of the water, on his shoulders, throwing her into the air over his head. It was a game they played in the pool. She realized he was serious, and she felt an uncontrollable urge to scream, just as she had so many years ago. She started backing up, flipping water at him, hoping the other guests who were arriving at the pool side would realize they were just having fun, being silly. Oliver overpowered her and came up under her. She struggled to keep her balance on his shoulders, giggling like a schoolgirl. He grabbed her ankles and tossed her into the air. As Maddy sank to the bottom of the pool she felt as though they were teens again, no baggage, no complicated feelings - just teens, having fun.

"Let's go, shall we." Oliver held out his hand as he climbed the ladder out of the pool. "Sicily is waiting for us."

The drive north towards Taormina was splendid in the sunshine and they spent the rest of the day exploring the towering town. They found a quaint villa and booked dinner, overlooking Mount Etna. The guitarist encouraged the patrons to dance - Maddy and Oliver were the only dancers on the small platform, but they didn't seem to mind.

"How many cotillions have you had the pleasure of attending? I'm sure you were in demand as you make quite a handsome figure in your uniform." Maddy teased.

"Thankfully none. I was sent out to dangerous missions with real enemies, not debutantes."

As they danced they continued exchanging stories of their lives.

"Dermot tells me he met you in a reverse Cinderella story."

Maddy smiled as she recalled their first meeting. "That's a good way to describe how we met. I was late for a banquet and he was the guest speaker - he and his security team were behind the door when I rushed into the foyer, I almost knocked him down and I did drop my shoes." She saw the look of confusion on Oliver's face and continued.

"I was running through the lobby barefoot because you just can't run in slingback shoes, can you? Anyway, we chatted, and security were getting fidgety about the shoes…it was weird. I walked away and he was still holding my shoes…it was funny to be called back to retrieve your shoes. Later in the evening his henchmen came to escort me to the Mezzanine where we danced - Dermot said there was a protocol for dancing, and he refused to dance with the Mayor's stout wife. After that we became friends. He really didn't know anyone who wasn't in the Embassy. Anyway, we just got along, and he fit right in with my friends." She stopped for a moment, realizing she would miss him.

"It was lovely to see him in Florence, but I know it's just a quick stop for him before he goes back to Washington."

"He cares about you, very much." Oliver whispered.

"I care about him and wish him all the best in Washington. He's a good friend." Maddy smiled.

Oliver nodded. They danced in silence, lost in their own thoughts.

"Have I told you how much I'm enjoying your company?" Oliver whispered into Maddy's hair.

"I've enjoyed our time together as well. I'd forgotten how much I missed you after that summer." Maddy looked up into his eyes.

"I could fall in love with you, all over again, you must know that."

"Oliver, please, you're leaving tomorrow, and you'll be gone for six months. I can't fall in love with you. My heart is still navigating through the healing process. I seem to be destined to have the men in my life leave me, sometimes for years, sometimes for days. Come to think of it, I leave them too. You don't want to get involved with me." Maddy closed her eyes.

"Well, that is encouraging. Maybe someday you will realize you care for me. I can wait. I've waited for almost 30 years." He kissed her forehead. "Will you write to me?"

"Sure, what's your email address?"

"No, I mean letters, like you used to…I would wait for your letters and postcards. I would run to the postbox to check for your news. Then I would try to construct grand sentences to let you know how great my life was; just in case you wanted to come and visit." His voice cracked.

"Am I really a *person of interest*? Is that why you came to Florence?"

"Oh Maddy, short answer…I've known Dermot most of my adult life and he's always been a prime candidate for office. He was doing so well and then he took the posting in Florence and the *Machine,* the powers that get men elected, were concerned that he had lost focus. There had to be a reason he stepped off the escalator to the top. It seems you were his Achille's Heel. We had to know if you were going to bring him down. As it turns out, you were good for him. Your friendship has kept him out of trouble, so to speak. No indiscretions, no political gaffes, no scandals to uncover. I requested the assignment when I saw your name. I hope you understand." Oliver was searching her face for a sign - a smile, a frown, acknowledgement, anything.

"You could have asked me." Maddy sighed. "I do understand the situation and I would never do anything to hurt his career. On the other hand, I'm pleased you remembered me and that we had this time together. I will write and I hope I see you again." She reached up to kiss his cheek. "One more dance or are you ready to call it a night?"

"A few more dances, if you please. I need six months of moments with you in my memory bank. It's going to be lonely in Cyprus."

Gazing at the moon as they walked back up to the Inn, holding hands, they took turns recalling the highs and lows of their lives as adults and the music they attached to the experiences. There was no shortage of interesting conversation.

Oliver stopped under a streetlamp, placed his hands on her shoulders and held his breath as she looked up, a quizzical look on her face.

"Maddy, you've told me you can't get involved with me right now and I respect that, however, I need you to understand that I am not giving up - it took me years to find you and I'm not prepared to walk away. I'm a Marine - *Semper Fidelis*. Understood?"

Maddy saw the intense look in his eyes and bit her lip, touched by his sentiments. "I don't know what to say…"

"Don't say anything. We will be together at some point, I know it. You can call me for anything, anytime. I intend to be in your life again."

"Good night Oliver, and thank you for another splendid day." Maddy reached up and kissed his cheek.

Giselle placed the cups of tea and a platter of buttery croissants on the table and sat next to Maddy.

"So, how was your visit to Sicily? You know I'm dying to hear all about it. Did he try anything? Did he ask you to go to Cyprus with him?"

"Oh Gigi, slow down. It was wonderful. Oliver was a perfect gentleman and we had fun just hanging out. It felt good to laugh. He had so many stories about that summer in Bogota…I'd forgotten how much trouble we got into. He let me drive the Lamborghini." Maddy shook her head, as if clearing her thoughts. "You know Oliver told me about some of his defence cases - many of them are harassment or exploitation charges. He was so easy to be with." She sighed. "Enough, everything okay here?"

"Everything is fine but I'm glad you're back. I have a few things to run by you, although I'm worried about you. You're working too hard and I hope you don't make any rash decisions right now."

"Don't worry about me Gigi. I just have a lot of balls in the air at the moment…I'm fine." Maddy sighed.

"Dermot told me about what happened in London - it was unconscionable and incomprehensible. I can't believe you didn't tell me. I can only imagine how hurt you were…but then Philippe said Sebastian went north to Scotland to explain what happened and you asked him to be patient…to give you time. He'll be here in a few days to complete the work on the cottage. We've enjoyed working with him, he's very professional. Philippe tells me he has changed since he met you - he used to be perfunctory but now he seems more empathetic and open to sharing ideas."

"That's good news. I hope the cottage will be ready for you when you get back from your honeymoon." Maddy smiled and looked away.

"Gigi, I'm sorry your children won't be here for the wedding. It's your big day and I want you to be happy." Maddy touched her friend's arm.

"I'm fine. I hardly know them anymore. They wouldn't approve of the wine or the winemaker - their beliefs are no longer compatible with the Western world, I'm afraid. They seem to enjoy the Arab way of life."

"Well, that's too bad." There was a silent moment between the friends.

Giselle shook her head and squinted at Maddy. "You're concerned you won't feel the same when Sebastian gets here, aren't you?"

Maddy shrugged. "I don't know. I just don't know. I'm too old to be making these choices. Oliver's visit was such a wonderful surprise but my heart belongs to Sebastian. Why would I take the leap and start over again when I just have to make every effort to forgive and move on with what was supposedly my perfect life?"

"Not many people will ever have to make such a sublime choice - seriously, Sebastian or Oliver? I don't envy you." Giselle clicked her tongue and shook her head.

"Okay, just stop. No choice. I love Sebastian and I can't wait for him to get here. Tell me what's happening here at the Villa." Maddy stood, indicating the conversation was over.

"Fine, I know you want to change the subject. First a word of caution… Maddy, beware - charming, handsome men are heartbreakers - you do what makes you feel happy. Whatever you decide, I'm here for you, my friend. You keep telling me I deserve to be happy…now it's my turn to tell you."

"Thanks Gigi. If indeed I have a choice, one option is in Cyprus, the other is in London…we have work to do here and the harvest is coming on soon. Most importantly, we have your wedding to plan. What's on your list?"

 # Don't Give Up On Me

"Have you seen this video Sebastian?" Deirdre asked as she sat down opposite him at his regular table in the Club.

"Most likely not." He responded, not sure he wanted to have dinner with Deirdre again. His nights in London were lonely but he and Maddy spoke each day and he planned to travel to the Villa on the weekend.

"It's marvellous. It's Maddy, I'm sure. Look at this." Deirdre was not giving up. She shoved her phone into his face. "It's at the Embassy in Rome and your friend Dermot is there and all of a sudden this Adonis in a uniform shows up and she's leaving but she turns around, so obviously they know each other, and they dance, and it takes your breath away and then she walks away…watch it. It's breathtaking, it's *très romantique* and it's oh, so Maddy."

Sebastian watched the small screen and smiled when Maddy turned around, an amused expression on her face. She seemed to be familiar with the officer and the music. He held his hand out and she slowly walked towards him, looking radiant. Everyone else had moved to the edge of the dance floor. They danced, as if they were floating, staring into each other's eyes. They spoke and suddenly Maddy placed her hands on his chest and walked away, before the music ended, leaving him on the dance floor. He bowed and the video ended.

He handed the phone back to Deirdre, who was watching his expression. "That is an old friend of Maddy's - they went to language school together when they were teens. He's a JAG officer; he does legal work and he just left for a peace-keeping mission in Cyprus."

"It was very romantic, the dance. I wish I could dance like that. You only dance with Maddy, don't you?" Deirdre looked wistful. She waved at the bartender; a drink was needed. Sebastian was very calm and that meant she would have to carry the conversation. It was hard work being a woman who couldn't dance. "They look like more than friends…don't you think?" She was hoping for a rise out of Sebastian.

Uncomfortable with the silence, Deirdre continued, "Why are you sitting here with me when you could be living your best life with Maddy?" She raised her glass again; catching the eye of the bartender. It was going to be a long night. No response from Sebastian.

'Sebastian, has Maddy forgiven you? She seems like a forgiver. She helped me and I was never very pleasant to her."

"She's magnanimous, she's simply a lovely person who wants to help people - forgiving is part of the package."

Deirdre sighed. "Maybe she could introduce me to her Marine friend - who doesn't love a man in uniform? He's very dreamy."

Sebastian looked up at his long time friend and companion. He wondered if anyone was pining for Deirdre in the same way he was missing Maddy.

In their daily calls Sebastian had little to report but Maddy always seemed to have entertaining stories about her days and nights at the Villa in Italy. She had explained that Dermot was in Florence as the Acting U.S. Consul General until a replacement could be assigned. Maddy was hosting receptions with him. She related amusing stories of the receptions and how excited Dermot was to be returning to Washington with a new title and responsibilities.

Dermot's roommate from college was flying in before his tour of duty and would attend the reception in Rome with the U.S. delegation. Maddy was floored when the roommate turned out to be someone she had known at a summer language course in Bogota. The students at the school were from diplomatic families and somehow Maddy's father had arranged for her to attend while her parents travelled. She had been the youngest in the group and had lost touch over the years with the elite group.

Oliver Wainwright III was now with JAG, handling court martial cases and interpreting international laws abroad. He was enroute to Cyprus for a six-month tour of duty, handling any conflicts as they arose. Maddy laughed as she described being so tired at the reception in Rome - anxious to get in the Embassy car and return to the Villa, when she heard a song they had listened to repeatedly that summer, so long ago. She turned and recognized Oliver immediately. They danced to the song and she left before it ended so she could make it home before falling…she wasn't sure if she was tired or lonely. Working in the vineyards was more taxing than she had imagined.

Sebastian found it difficult to concentrate on his work after talking to Maddy - he missed her and wanted to be with her. Her life was filled with people and events, unlike his. He laughed out loud when he recalled her saying they only had two weekends and then three more sleeps before seeing each other. Two weekends and three lonely, restless sleeps. Indeed.

Sebastian did not feel it was necessary to tell Deirdre that Maddy had gone to Sicily with Oliver, enjoying a few days away as he toured the U.S. base. Maddy had insisted Oliver was a perfect gentleman and a good friend. He hoped she was right. All he knew, for certain, was that he missed her.

Anne Marshall

August 25

Dear Oliver,

    Thank you for being such an outstanding gentleman on our mini vacation to Sicily. It was wonderful - exactly what I needed.

    I hope you are settled into your digs in Cyprus. I also hope you have a peaceful tour of duty - no mishaps. Promise me you'll be careful and stay out of trouble. Tell me about your living quarters and your daily routine - or can you divulge this secret information? I wanted to ask you about your legal duties and if you are hearing court cases while in Cyprus...we just ran out of time.

    It occurred to me you never took me sailing....I just happen to have a 36 foot boat moored in Kotor, Montenegro....maybe someday you'll be in the neighbourhood. She sails like a dream.... the challenge is on!

    The harvest will begin soon. Our random grape testing has been positive. The readings have shown 24 Brix which is about right. When you return to the Villa Mirage, I promise there will be a bottle of our best chianti for you! Fingers crossed.

    Dermot is hoping to hear from the State Department on possible replacements (you probably already know this). He will receive the delegation prior to the upcoming G7 meeting. He is acting cool, but I know he sees this as his last hurrah before returning to Washington. Thinking positive thoughts.

    Take care. Watch for falling stars.....what good are they if no one sees them?

My best

Maddy

 Broadway for the Soul

"Are you really flying into New York City for the weekend?" Father Dom asked as he passed the platter of pasta and meatballs.

"If you can handle things here, I will go - it's been ages since I've seen a live production and I love New York." Maddy smiled and waved her hands in the air.

"You've been working so hard it would be cruel of us to deny you a weekend of mindless pleasure in the *city that never sleeps*. Just a weekend, mind you, or you will need retraining when you return."

The group of friends at the table joined in the laughter and ribbing, confident Maddy would return rejuvenated and ready to tackle even more.

"How did this come about?" Philippe asked as he raised a glass of wine in a toast to Maddy.

"Dermot's nephew is a pilot and he's getting married, so he sent passes for his European friends and relatives to attend. There was a free seat, so Dermot arranged for me to fly over and take in both an off-Broadway and a current hit while they celebrate the bachelor party and attend the wedding. I'll see some friends while I'm there and we'll fly back to Milan on Monday. I have to admit I'm excited, but I will miss you all terribly." She pouted, as they laughed and applauded her attempt at remorse.

Sebastian had not been as positive when she told him of her last-minute plan. Maddy had invited him to meet her in New York as she hoped to see Ephrom and Harvey Gold - he regretted he couldn't get away on such short notice; he also regretted that he didn't make the effort. Indeed.

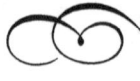 Getting By With a 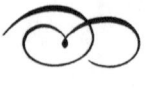 Little Help From My Friends

The midday sun was beating down on the vineyard, a light breeze whispering over the rocky soil. The plump Sangiovese grapes promised a fine chianti and it was a perfect autumn day for harvesting. Father Dom and Maddy walked slowly through the rows, carefully filling their baskets with random bunches of grapes for testing.

"It's time for lunch and some shade, I think." Father Dom suggested, looking over at Maddy, fanning himself with his straw hat. "Did you enjoy your time in New York City?"

"Oh Father, it was exceptional. I saw my friends for lunch and dinner, soaked up the theatre - the tickets were amazing. Just being in New York again was…" Maddy considered how best to describe the exhilaration of being anonymous in the noisy crowds, moving with traffic, catching glimpses of store windows and street vendors as she walked in the city. "It was crazy enough to make me not want to miss the flight back here on Monday morning."

Father Dom chuckled, realizing Maddy was telling him what he wanted to hear. They had missed her, even for the few days she was gone.

"Whew, a cold *limonada* would be most welcome." She sighed, wiping her forehead with the bandana she removed from her neck. "You think they'll test well? They look so ready. What do you think?" She leaned over and plopped a fat grape into his mouth, laughing. She hoped their first harvest produced a great wine.

As they approached the courtyard at Villa Mirage, they noticed others sitting at the table, enjoying a glass of wine. Maddy's heart skipped a beat. She looked over at Father Dom who had also noticed the guests. He reached for the basket in Maddy's arms and motioned for her to go on ahead. She gave him a grateful look and with a cry she ran towards the group.

Sam, The Professor, was bouncing baby Chance on his knee while Grace and Davi laughed at something Philippe and Giselle were saying. It was a beautiful sight. Maddy felt a wave of homesickness as her friends looked up and waved.

There were hugs and tears before the group settled into their seats for lunch, a grand affair with pasta, salad and platters of antipasto.

"Please tell me you don't eat like this every day?" Grace exclaimed.

Father Dom gave the blessing and the friends all started talking at once, anxious to catch up and hear about the wedding plans for Giselle and Philippe. Grace excited to share her wedding cake design. The Professor offering music choices for the ceremony and reception.

Maddy sat back and smiled, enjoying the warmth of friendship. She looked at the happy faces and wished Henry and Sebastian were here as well….

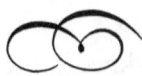 # Audrey

Reflecting thoughts

I just know, I can feel it...Maddy will sneak into this place and motion me towards the door. She'll say, "forget what the doctor says, we have to get you out of here" and she'll have a black cape for me to wear. We'll tiptoe down the stairwell and out the back door to her waiting car...I'm keeping my shoes by the bed, just to be ready.

She must know I love her and did what I did so she could be free of the people in her life that were causing her grief and heartbreak. Men are so easily convinced that you need them. They lose interest so quick and then 'poof' - they're gone. We don't need them; they only complicate our lives.

Dermot, the loud American, called me needy and wouldn't answer any questions about Maddy - I wanted to know what she did to make him happy and all he could think of to say was that she made him feel like a regular guy...imagine...I wanted to make him scream in bed but he wouldn't betray Maddy...in the end, when he was being cruel to me, he said they had never slept together. Right. Who would believe that? I've seen his hungry eyes when he's looking at her. Of course Maddy would never tell...she wouldn't say anything negative, not even to me, her very best friend in the world...I thought girlfriends told each other everything. Wrong.

The Professor, beautiful Sam, wouldn't ever say a word against Maddy and that made him even more dangerous. There was no way I could come between them...he told me so.

Christian, so cool and aloof, but protective as a mama bear when it came to Maddy. I never really liked him. He was so...so...German. He wouldn't even humour me...

Sebastian, proper and levelheaded, was an easy mark right from the start. Inviting him to dinner with the children was brilliant on my part...especially when he was so upset about Maddy disappearing. I knew he wasn't right for her. The children were wonderful and it didn't take long to convince him Maddy would run away again if anything happened...she didn't want the stability of a family and being tied down. The month was good for us as we got into a routine with children and meals.

I did try to seduce him several times, but he was so untouchable it was exhausting. When he did find her and go to her I thought I might not be able to pull this off...but I knew when they got home the timing was right...Maddy wouldn't tell us where she'd been or what had happened. It was deliciously easy to convince Sebastian that she would leave again...she had so many secrets; so many other places to be; so many other people to care for.

Sebastian was so willing to believe that Maddy was leaving with Dermot, the American cad - when I showed him the bag she had packed, his face fell. Again, she wouldn't confide in me, her best friend, where she planned to take Sebastian for a romantic holiday. I watched her pack a bag for both of them...I only showed him her bag.

It turns out that sabotaging your best friends relationship isn't a great idea...Sebastian is still in love with her and will never betray her - how can you find success when the bloke won't give up on her. I thought I was so clever but he went back for her...I hope she turned him away.

Sadly, he wouldn't dance with me (he was always dancing with Maddy) and he wouldn't consider sleeping with me...it was hurtful when he said making love with Maddy didn't require a manual - it just came naturally. How would you feel if someone said that to you?

When we left the fundraiser Sebastian was so ornery and his driver, little Davi, was impertinent - he stopped the car and for a moment I thought they would make me get out and walk home. Sebastian said he had made a grave mistake and had to remedy the situation...right, situation...he called this a situation. I hope Maddy won't have him back...not now.

At home Jeffrey was panicking as he didn't know where I was. He and Davi had words at the door, and when he came upstairs Jeffrey was in a state.

He asked me why I was trying to hurt my friend, why I had gone to such lengths to disturb lives and how did I think he could leave the children alone with someone who was clearly unhinged. He slept in the guest bedroom after his tirade - he called me names like crazy, batty, unbelievably cruel...I just stopped listening. I fell asleep dreaming of Maddy alone on a deserted island, calling my name, pleading with me to be her friend.

Jeffrey visited last week, I think, it was last week. He is still angry at me and says this is for the best. The children are at boarding school - can you imagine? He doesn't want to bring them to this place - he says it will upset them to see me here. I know that is not true. My hair looks great and they help me with my make-up...I am fine.

Well, I try not to go to sleep, just in case this is the night Maddy comes for me. We will have a wonderful life together. I'll get the children back and we can live at the beach. I can make Maddy happy, happier than she has been - I won't break her heart like they did. I'll just wait for her to come, she'll get lonely enough and need to save me. She's probably wondering where I am and planning my escape right now...

Sam, The Professor

Reflecting thoughts

Since the success of the charity event my dance club, Decades, has been busier than ever...several offers have come in from unexpected corners - friends of Deirdre have expressed interest in buying the Club. It's flattering and I find myself thinking about what I would do away from the Club more and more.

Maddy has suggested I come to Villa Mirage and start a music program there. It's an interesting offer, to be sure. She pads the offer with promises of wonderful food and a balmy climate. It's tempting.

Several of my music contacts are anxious to purchase Bellmere - they love the house and the gardens, and they see potential in converting the garage into a sound studio. Grace and Daveesh live next door and they seem fine with that arrangement. I don't think they see much of Sebastian these days.

I guess Maddy cannot see herself ever going back to the house or returning to London. I'm not surprised, but I am sad that things turned out so badly for her. She really loved that bloke...I hope I see him again, just so I can punch his lights out. She did not deserve a public breakup, no one does.

I'm heading to Italy next week to look at some property near the Villa Mirage and to play guitar for the wedding. Who knows what will come of that visit? I am anxious to see Maddy and know she is doing alright. She is a survivor. She seems happy enough, certainly keeping busy. I miss her, gosh, I miss her more than I thought possible. It's true you don't know what you got, 'til it's gone.

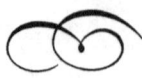 # Dermot

Reflecting thoughts

I've always been lucky. I'm a 'right place, right time' kinda guy. First, I got a great job out of college; then I got elected to a state position on my first attempt; then I got offered the plum assignment as U.S. Ambassador in London; my wife can't handle the English weather or the British way of life - so she returned to Washington to be with her friends, her well-connected family and to continue working as a lobbyist. London is cold and damp, just like the social requirements…and then I met Maddy, and she made London come alive for me.

We played tourists to the coast of France and Maddy brought D-Day alive for me. She included me in social functions and made every encounter more bearable. She has taught me the importance of friendship.

As it happens, I was right there when the stiff English guy dumped her at this amazing charity event - best event I've ever attended, by the way. Fortunately, I was there to pick up the pieces and hope she would turn to me for comfort, when she suddenly disappeared. I saw Sebastian come back to the Club and I made sure he didn't come in - he said he needed to talk to Maddy - too late, buddy. Sam and I sent him away - we wanted to punch his lights out, but Sam reminded me there were too many cameras around.

I should have warned Maddy about her loopy friend, Audrey. The woman was unnaturally fond of Maddy…weird about anyone else being near Maddy. I can't help but think I could have saved her from the pain. Not to brag, but I can easily negotiate with government officials, trade officers, corrupt police and corporate executives but I could not figure Audrey out. Still makes me shake my head.

No problem eventually finding Maddy - advantages of the job. I'm itching to get out of London and then, bingo...Maddy is in Italy and there's an opening as Acting Consul General in Florence. It could be seen as a demotion but I'm finally working on sorting out the worst marriage ever and need a change of pace, to prepare for my next move.

Maddy is less than an hour away and she agrees to come into the city for special occasions or Consular events. She's amazing at remembering everyone's name and something trivial about them...she feeds me intel as we walk through the event and I can honestly say I would not be able to do the cocktail patter without her. She even corrects my Italian pronunciation. My security detail enjoys having Maddy around - she's a good card player and she always follows protocol - she doesn't want any scandal or anything that would hurt my career. I feel blessed to have her in my life.

It was a stroke of good luck that we saw the 'cuccioli in vendita' (puppies for sale) sign on the way home last week. We stopped and Maddy fell in love with the pups. She turned around to speak with the owner and the cutest little pup followed her, sitting at her feet. How could I not buy that puppy for her? When she picked up the puppy and I told her it was a gift, she flashed me the most endearing smile - she was absolutely radiant, and I felt my heart skip. We decided to name the puppy Speranza, which means hope. Great name for the dog and for me. Anza, as she is known by the locals, is never far from Maddy. She is looking out for my girl when I'm not there.

I'm taking it slow because I think she's still hurting after that dumb-ass left her, but someday she'll see me as her 'knight in shining armour' and we'll choose the next posting together. It's rare to find a woman who enjoys football, American football, to be precise - rare enough. As a matter of fact, I heard there was a high-level post coming up in Washington. Great way to round out my career as a bureaucratic wonder - no campaigning required. I wasn't sure what to think when my old college roomie arrived and swept her off her feet... Oliver can be larger than life...I'll talk to her this weekend.

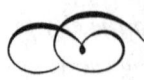 # Father Dominic

Reflecting thoughts

I never imagined the impact one person could have over a sleepy village with no prospects. I've spent my life teaching the word of God, trying to establish faith and love in my parishioners. Villa Mirage and namely, Maddy, have turned this village into a tourist mecca. Even the laziest sheep in my flock are now willingly working to make the village a better place to live and visit.

Maddy cajoles us, yes, myself included, to work the fields and then feeds us, creating a sense of camaraderie that is Moses-like. She just tells us what needs to be done and when she is going to be in the field, and we all show up. She plays music and makes the toil such fun that we all look forward to the next 'play date'. I now understand why they added a Spa at the Villa...I am feeling my age in tired muscles and a massage is, excuse the pun, heavenly.

I pray for Maddy, but I don't know how to lift her out of the doldrums - she has not confided in me, as a friend, or as a priest. She is pragmatic about what happened in London...I'm not sure what to make of the situation. I was disappointed to hear from the American, Dermot, that Sebastian had been so cruel to Maddy. I thought him a decent man and a friend. I quote the bible to Maddy and she tells me we can't know what people are thinking. We are at an impasse in this matter.

I must say, the puppy, Anza, has been a positive influence - Maddy is happier with the little puppy following her all day. They seem to need each other.

Villa Mirage has exceeded every expectation from a business level. Tourism to our little village is steady - the shops are doing well, and the locals are eager to produce goods for sale. We have never been so prosperous. The Church is fine, at long last, and although Maddy is not a regular at Mass she does encourage the villagers to seek my guidance. We are a good team. She has brought music back to my Church. She lights many candles.

The village is excited for the wedding next week - it will be a great celebration. The Contessa would have been proud of Maddy and her vision. I wonder what we will do if and when Sebastian returns to the Villa. To be truthful, I miss our friendship - I always enjoyed discussing world issues, drinking wine and playing cards with him. I have saved some exceptional Cohiba Robusto cigars for our next poker game.

Ah, it is time for prayers. My knees protest but Our Father awaits.

 # Giselle

Reflecting thoughts

Life throws us many opportunities and meeting Maddy has been a life changer for me. I was unhappy at the ski lodge in the French Alps, dealing with snooty rich people who demanded the most ridiculous standards from a mountain lodge. When Maddy invited me to visit Villa Mirage it was a work in progress - she included me in the plan and eventually our dream became a reality. Our guests are seeking refuge from the city and the madness of life…we offer local produce, quiet nights and spa services to get them ready for a return to the hustle and bustle. Our European guests return several times a year.

Father Dom is a wonderful resource and friend; he and Maddy discuss an idea and make it happen, with the help of the villagers. My Italian is improving, but thankfully Father has intervened many times for me in negotiations. Maddy is now quite fluent and I am delighted she is here - ideas flow from her and she is never idle. I see her in the fields, in the vineyard, in the lobby greeting guests - showing genuine interest and gathering feedback. She livens up a dinner party and is forever ready to take on a new challenge. I fear she is looking for something she has yet to find.

Sorento, the Italian designer and admirer of Maddy, begged us to include a boutique of his fashion designs - very lovely and affordable ensembles - Maddy insisted they be affordable - and the guests seem to enjoy taking home an exclusive Italian label. Sorento also sends Maddy a package each month for her approval or comments. She has many lovely outfits, mostly in blue, and when she walks through the dining area to chat with the guests, they inevitably ask about the outfit and voila - she sells a dress and a scarf. She is shameless. I guess that's why I love her to pieces. Sorento adores her - I don't know the story but Philippe tells me there was an incident involving Sorento, a yacht and PC from Texas - Maddy was able to negotiate a face-saving solution and they all became friends. It is typical Maddy.

My happiness is due to Maddy and right now I wish I could hug away her sorrow. She still laughs and pretends to be happy, but her eyes are not smiling. It's unbelievable that Sebastian would have done something so egregious, yet I feel she misses him. I saw them together and I can't believe they are apart.

Dermot is so American and blasé, yet he seems to offer a diversion that is healthy. His friend Oliver is attractive in so many ways, but I can't imagine he is the best choice for Maddy. Where Dermot really isn't likeable, this man Oliver is too charming and handsome to believe. I'm waiting for Sebastian to make his big move - if he doesn't do it soon, we will lose Maddy and I'm not sure we could ever forgive him. The handsome Marine will soon return, and I can tell Maddy is restless. Philippe says Maddy is strong - she will make the right decision when the time comes. He respects her judgment.

The puppy has certainly added an element of happiness to Maddy's life. That little dog follows her everywhere. Anza is very cute and smart - the guests are loving her - she adds a feeling of home to the Villa. It was a clever move on Dermot's part, I will give him that.

There are so many things to prepare for the wedding - thankfully Maddy is here. I don't know what I would do without her.

When Philippe calls me Gigi it sounds so sexy and personal. All of a sudden everyone is calling me Gigi…but I get goosebumps when I hear Philippe say my name. I adore him. Tsk tsk…am I too old to feel so foolish? Maddy says not at all.

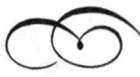 # Grace

Reflecting thoughts

We actually travelled to Italy for the wedding, transporting Chance and all his baby accessories. Davi is nervous of flying and I was reluctant to leave the coffee shop but Auntie and Uncle, and dear Mr Simpson, agreed we needed a break. The four-tiered wedding cake I have designed is certainly a labour of love. Maddy suggested a grape vine wound around the tiers…I'm sugaring the grapes…it will be spectacular, even if I say so myself.

I wasn't sure how the big move would work - selling my little coffee shop and moving to Maida Vale was intimidating but Mr Simpson has been wonderful to work with - he is a lovely grandfatherly figure and an asset in this neighbourhood. He trusted Maddy when she approached him to modernize the old bookstore - the children's reading room is a major hit, and we are selling more specialty coffees than I could ever imagine. Mr Simpson seems younger everyday - he and my beautiful little Chance have become quite close.

Moving to the new house, previously owned by Esme and Gordon - it's ever so big - was a scary affair for both Davi and myself. In the beginning we sat in one room, afraid to venture into the rest of the house, but now we are settled, and we laugh at how silly we were. I wish Maddy was still next door, but she hasn't returned since the charity event and her lovely garden is wild and overgrown these days. Sebastian doesn't leave the house much anymore - thankfully he and Audrey didn't end up together…no surprise. Jeffrey has sold the house across the boulevard and moved so we haven't seen the Buttons for some time. Poor little things.

More or Less Reckless

After many years of loyal service to Sebastian and his family, Davi toys with the idea of resigning. His life has been service to the family, and he cannot imagine abandoning Sebastian - I think he believes Maddy will return and he doesn't want to let her down. He has completed his studies and has taken the marketing challenges in stride, but he enjoys baking and I love to have him in the kitchen. We get along fine at work and at home. I know he misses Maddy as much as I do. It will be smashing to see her again.

The last time we spoke Maddy seemed to come to terms with her heartache. She said she probably didn't spend enough time or energy making Sebastian feel important. She had no thoughts on Audrey and the strange behaviour leading up to the breakup. It was still too soon to open that wound. Sebastian wanted Maddy to help Deirdre and when she did, giving it her all, as she always does, he left her for the first woman who cried wolf. I can't tell Maddy she's better off without him. She loves him.

I don't know what I will say to her when I see her - I want her to be happy, we all do. I cannot imagine how I would feel if Davi walked in one day and said he was leaving with my best friend…I wouldn't grieve, I would harm him…and her. Maddy would be angry if I felt sorry for her - she is always upbeat and so positive about Villa Mirage that only I feel her pain. Maybe seeing little Chance again will make her smile. We can only hope.

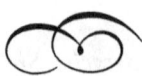 # Henry

Reflecting thoughts

Blimey, adults are hard to understand. TBH, I thought Sebastian was cracking over Maddy - she was always so happy to see him. I don't care for Audrey at all and I was gutted that she and Sebastian ever thought I would want to live with them. Audrey said Maddy couldn't offer stability so they wanted to adopt me. Can you even imagine? Audrey told me all about the plan but Sebastian never mentioned it. Good thing.

I mean, really…Maddy has encouraged me to bake, create, appreciate and participate in things I never dreamed I would be exposed to. She introduced me to Michael and sailing; she took me to the Mission, and I enjoy my weekly volunteer commitment. The Headmaster has agreed that I should continue - he sometimes comes with me. I'm pretty good at cooking for large groups and I enjoy the banter, but mostly I feel good about helping out. Sebastian hardly speaks anymore. Thankfully, I see Christian once a week and we talk about sailing and Maddy. Jolly good thing I don't have to pretend to like Maddy's friend Audrey anymore. She was narky at the best of times.

The train seems slow today and I am excited to see Maddy and the Villa. I would have contested the adoption, with the help of Christian. Now I spend the holidays with Maddy - she has agreed to let me sail the Destiny home with Christian when he retires. Maybe Maddy would come with us…that would be bloody rad.

We never talk about Michael Riley but I know Maddy misses him, so I try to be sensitive and not mention him. When he came to Australia and found me he always went on about her and I know if he was still around he would, obvi, kidnap her and make her happy. I would help him. Maddy cried when I told her that Michael had explained how things worked between girls and boys... he said he didn't want to leave that talk for Maddy or Sebastian because he had more experience. It was embarrassing but I'm glad that's over and I know what to expect, although you learn a lot about stuff like that on a sheep farm.

Florence is the next stop and Maddy is meeting me up at the station - lucky she didn't suggest I ride with Dermot. He makes me nervous. Maddy says we have to adapt in life, but honestly, I am tired of adapting to no parents, life on an Australian outback sheep farm with crazy aunts, back home to no Maddy...I just want to hang out with her and go sailing...enough adapting, already. I'm anxious to see how Anza has grown since my last visit...those two are inseparable. My screen shot is a photo I took of Anza looking up at Maddy...it's so adorable. It reminds me of how I look at Maddy, I guess I should be careful - I wouldn't want anyone to think I'm soft.

I can hardly wait to show Maddy my acceptance letters. She'll be so pleased for me and she'll be very objective about my decision. She understands that you have to do what you have to do. I may need her help in explaining why I want to do what I have planned. Maddy said you have a lifetime to make practical decisions...make one that makes you happy. I want to join the Navy...that would make me happy. I'm not sure Sebastian will agree.

Maddy better be ready for the biggest hug ever.

*TBH - to be honest
*cracking - crazy about
*gutted - upset
*narky - moody
*obvi - teenspeak for obviously

 # Philippe

Reflecting thoughts

Life is offering me another chance for happiness and my one regret is that my best friend, my schoolmate, my former business partner and the guy I call whenever I need brotherly advice, may not be here.

Sebastian and I have been through the frustrating high jinx of boarding school, the demands of university, the drama of marriages to two friends who both died in an accident where we lost our sons and our taste for domestic bliss. Sebastian was the only one who ever defended me and remained an ally when I was called 'Frenchy'.

I thought he was happy with Maddy, she was good for him...she made him come alive. I don't know what happened, but when Gigi told me he left her for someone else - I knew it couldn't be true. He hasn't mentioned anything to me, except that he is working towards retirement. We are due for a heart to heart talk which will require much wine, I expect.

The vineyards are looking promising - Maddy and Father Dom have done wonders with the farming aspect of things. I am experimenting with the grapes and although they are very different from my Bordeaux varietals, I find them pleasant enough. The wine will be easy to drink.

The sale of the vineyard in France was serendipitous, to say the least. My neighbour partnered with a franchise winery and offered a foolish amount for my land and operations. If I was a younger man, I might have negotiated for even more but at this point in my life I just want to be comfortable and enjoy time with this wonderful woman. Gigi, my pet name for Giselle, made me realize how lonely my existence has been…she is the opposite of Maddy, calm and soothing to be around…they make a good partnership, those two.

Ah, bon, it appears the crew is returning from the vineyard for lunch. They will be anxious to taste my barrel samples.

 # Sebastian

Reflecting thoughts

The last time I was at Villa Mirage, we stood on the balcony overlooking the courtyard - I proposed to Maddy and she proposed to me and then we got home, and she took on the charity event for Deirdre and we never got it done. I can't look at that window without feeling regretful. If only we had taken the time to marry before Audrey started her campaign to ruin Maddy…I am a fool. Deirdre says so.

That's all there is to it. I broke Maddy's heart, and in doing so, my own heart, for the ravings of a crazy woman who wanted to show Maddy how it felt to lose your best friend. It sounds insane but it was a grand performance by Audrey and the result changed everything. I'm thankful for the few days we had at Applecross.

My driver and friend Davi, has been civil but something has changed; my long- time assistant Lambert, has been efficient but aloof; Christian has resigned the very Committee we both established; Henry has taken sides and prefers not to dine at The Club anymore; the garden apartment at the house is rented out and I dare not visit the beach cottage as Rod, my childhood pal, has expressed his disappointment in our estrangement. It's a wonder I'm invited this weekend.

My palms are perspiring, my heart is beating a sporadic rhythm and my head is pounding. I haven't seen Maddy for three weeks, except on FaceTime. We speak daily but I can't wait to hold her. When I saw the dance video I couldn't breathe, It was disconcerting seeing her with someone else. She looked fantastic - there was no hint of sadness in her eyes. Am I too late?

We have been working on the plans for the cottage and I must say, as a collaborator, Maddy is a fantastic partner. She has fresh ideas and she has no problems expressing her vision. I would have enjoyed a working partnership with her. Why did I think my work was so important? It was Maddy who envisioned the transition in Bellmere - her thoughts on the remodel were astounding.

Sam, The Professor, contacted me about the house - he had a buyer who was willing to pay cash and move in immediately. The man is a sound engineer who says he met Maddy on a flight…he was sold on the house just from hearing her describe it. I haven't responded - I want to be sure Maddy doesn't want the house. It's awkward to hold off making decisions because you don't have the courage to speak to the person you hurt, the person you love.

My meetings are done and my work load has been reassigned. It's time for me to retire and spend more time with Maddy. I'm here for as long as Maddy wants to stay at the Villa. I'm not sure of my next move. For the first time in my life I don't have to be anywhere, for anything, other than Maddy.

I have completed all the paperwork on the charitable foundation so Maddy has complete control - she's more adept at making decisions on sensitive matters - she's naturally empathetic. I'm happy to spend my time researching her various projects.

I have committed to having the cottage ready for Philippe and Giselle - Maddy has handled the trims, the decor and the garden patio…I'm anxious to see the results.

The usual crowd will be gathered, no doubt. I can't imagine what sort of reception I will receive - it's unsettling at best.

All I want is a chance to dance in the moonlight with the woman I love… maybe I will hear her forgive me, maybe not. Just holding her would be enough. I never imagined I would care so much about a woman that I would dance and endure sitting in a bath. Is that love or infatuation?

Either way, she makes me happy. Indeed.

 Love Me Like You Do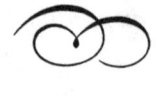

Sebastian saw Maddy across the courtyard. He had just arrived at Villa Mirage and was eager to be alone with her. Maddy was speaking with guests, gesturing towards the garden. She looked wonderful in her sundress and sandals, her skin bronzed by the sun, tendrils of hair loose on her neck. He was enjoying the view, biding his time, waiting to hold her.

Maddy turned and smiled, then realized it was Sebastian. She walked across the cobblestones, slowly, watching him. Deliberate in her steps. Her smile lit up her face, her dimples deep, her eyes dancing.

"I can't wait to hold you." Sebastian whispered as she neared.

Maddy placed her hand on his chest. "Not good enough. I need you to be naked, I want to wrap my legs around you, I want you to touch me and stroke every part of my body that no one else can see, I want…"

Sebastian pulled her towards him, his lips finding hers, hungry and passionate. "You win." He didn't need to hear any more…he just needed Maddy, all of her. In one movement he picked her up, cradling her in his arms. Maddy flung her arms around his neck, whispering in his ear, kissing him as he carried her across the courtyard.

Maddy wriggled free, standing next to him. "Save your strength. You're going to need it." She took his hand and led him up the stairs to their suite.

Sebastian quickly shed his clothes - Maddy turned so he could unzip her dress, which fell at her feet. He ran his hands down her body, removing her panties, lifting her onto the bed. His heart was pounding. He buried his face in her hair and again followed the lines of her body with his hand, finding pleasure points that made her arch her back and moan. Maddy pulled him close and he stopped thinking, his body responding to her touch.

Exhausted, but desperate to talk and touch each other, they saw the sun rise and herald a new day...a new day, together.

"I'm better when you're here with me. How long will you stay?" Maddy asked in a sleepy voice.

"Never leaving. Close your eyes and try to get some sleep." Sebastian held her close.

"That's lovely..." Maddy fell asleep, her head on his chest.

"Indeed."

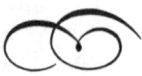 # Wedding Bells

Rays of sunshine danced on the courtyard walls, making long shadows, while the cypress trees rustled in the light breeze. The hum of the crowd filled the air, awaiting the arrival of the bride. Soft guitar music filled the spaces between the rows - Sam, The Professor, was playing Italian love songs…he looked up and smiled, changing his tune to announce the procession.

Maddy was slowly walking Giselle down the aisle; the folding chairs were lined with fresh autumn flowers tied with wide white ribbons. They made quite a picture - Giselle, small, raven-haired, radiant and lovely in her off-white sequined, fitted gown; Maddy, tanned, serene and breathtaking in the latest Sorento design of heavenly pale blue with flowers in her hair. The groom and his best man, Sebastian, watched them approach the arbour, both holding their breath and smiling their approval. Father Dom, waiting to officiate, gasped when he saw the two angels, who seemed to be floating down the aisle towards him. He said a silent prayer to focus.

The ceremony was touching - The Professor played beautiful ballads - the vows between Giselle and Philippe so personal and emotional; it was romantic and charming. The tastefully decorated outdoor tables were laden with food and wine; the noise level increased as the guests laughed and enjoyed the late afternoon festivities. The speeches were heartfelt and short. The dancing began as the sunset bathed the garden in a soft hue.

Dermot drank several glasses of wine before asking Maddy to dance. He was unsettled to see Sebastian and Maddy at the wedding party table. He watched as Maddy made her way to the dance floor with Sebastian,

Henry, Father Dom, The Professor, Philippe and several older men from the village. He hoped things would be back to normal after the wedding - everyone would leave, and he meant everyone, and he and Maddy would talk about the exciting lifestyle awaiting them in Washington. Dermot hoped Maddy would accept the job offer he had proposed - he hated the thought of leaving her behind when there were so many exciting opportunities in his new office.

When they finally met on the dance floor Maddy was interrupted by the housekeeper. She was needed immediately. Dermot was no stranger to urgent matters and interruptions but somehow the situation bothered him. He downed a glass of *limoncello,* wiping his mouth with the back of his hand, and then another, and as he was waiting, another. Heavy, dark clouds had rolled in, hiding the moon and sending a cool breeze across the festivities.

Finally, Maddy returned to the courtyard, her smile betraying the fact she was lost in thought - she was somewhere else right now. He swept her in his arms and stumbled, enough to realize he might have fallen with Maddy in his clutches. He moved back and released her, looking into her eyes, the eyes that always made his knees weak.

"Baby, I might have had too much of the *limoncello*. I better sit down." He sat heavily, the room spinning. He tried to take inventory of his consumption - he was normally so disciplined - a few Bellinis, a little Campari, the Negroni and more wine than he could imagine as well as the local *limoncello*…no wonder he couldn't stand. He was a lite beer man. "You go ahead and have a good time. I'll just sit here for a minute."

Maddy asked the waiter for water and coffee and gently moved his hair off his forehead, loosened his tie and kissed his cheek before walking away. He watched her nod at Father Dom and then she was gone…out of the courtyard, out of sight. He closed his eyes and held the cool glass of water to his forehead. If only the world would stop spinning.

The band had disappeared, the rain was falling in sheets, stinging his face, forcing him to sit up and look around. The courtyard was empty, the lights dimmed and swinging in the wind. He heard voices and walked unsteadily towards the sound of laughter and glasses clinking.

Dermot walked into the room and noticed Maddy was not there.

"Where's Maddy?" He asked no one in particular. He remembered she had been called away.

"I believe she is helping a friend." One of the women responded, off handedly.

"In this weather? Friend? Well, we all know she isn't the best judge of friends, don't we?" He hoped to sound cavalier, but the remark came out wrong. The room was deadly still.

Maddy had just entered the room, standing at the door, out of his line of vision. She was soaked to the bone, her hair hanging straight, dripping on her shoulders. She turned quickly, hoping no one would see her face; her disappointment. She walked towards the main door, not sure where to go…she had just come in from the vineyard, helping to secure the cover on the vines. Father Dom and the foreman had ordered her in - there was nothing more to be done tonight. They would have to wait out the storm and hope the damage was minimal.

She kept walking, the cold rain falling on her face, blinding her, stinging her cheeks. The night sky offered no light, not even a shadow. She felt tired; exhausted from the physical task of pulling the tarps over the vines. The rain and the cold wind made her shudder. The pain of the storm beating her body felt like punishment she was destined to endure. She stumbled forward, hearing someone call her name. She had to get away…

Suddenly there was a hand on her shoulder, and she was whipped around into someone's arms. A voice was yelling in the dark, barely audible over the strong wind and beating rain. She heard the words *"no more, no more running away"* as she tried to break free from the hold on her shoulders.

A raincoat was thrown over her head, her senses were assaulted by the smell of rubber; but the needles of rain had stopped. She felt soft kisses on her eyes, her cheeks, her upper lip. She tried desperately to move her head, but she was tired of fighting. Another kiss and as hard as she tried to pull away, her body gave in and she responded to the kiss, slowly at first and then as though she expected the kiss to save her - save her from the madness…from herself.

Suddenly, her mind in a fog, Maddy tried to push away, to escape the strong arms holding her. Months of misguided passion erupted, and she had to break away.

"No, no…let me go. You walked away. You left me…leave me alone." She was shouting into his chest, trying to beat him off.

"I'm not leaving you. I love you. I will always come back for you. I'm not leaving you." He was yelling against the rain and wind. His arms wrapping her tighter against his body, as if he were protecting her. He felt her hands pounding on his chest and then she fainted in his arms.

Maddy felt like she was floating, weightlessly hovering above the meadow. The sunlight was warm on her face and the grass was a lovely bright green; the sky was light blue, and the puffy clouds looked like soft marshmallows, calling to her. She was tired, so tired and the clouds were inviting. She needed to rest. She heard a voice reading from the book she had left at her bedside…she recognized the voice. She felt confused - why was she floating above the man reading her book - why couldn't she wake up and tell him she loved hearing his voice? Had she imagined that he had kissed her? Had he really come out in the storm to find her? Why did he come back into her life? Was she ready to let him go? She was so tired…someone was holding her hand, pulling her away from the clouds, bringing her back. She felt safe. She slept.

 # Save My Soul

"She's waking up. *Chiamo il dottore e Padre Dominic. Presto.*"

Maddy stretched and looked around the room. Her body felt stiff and her legs ached. She tried to sit up and fell back, no strength in her being.

"Gigi, aren't you supposed to be on your honeymoon?"

"Oh Maddy, we are on our honeymoon. We spent two nights in Paris and woke up to heavy rain, crowds and traffic noise...we both wanted to be back here, in our beautiful little cottage. It's amazing how this place gets under your skin." Giselle fluffed the pillows and helped Maddy sit up as she spoke.

"What about the damage to the vineyard?" Her head clearing, her thoughts on the results of the storm.

"Father Dom will be right here. He and Philippe are pleased with what you were able to salvage after the storm. You did a good job covering the vines. I'm sure they'll want to fill you in."

"What day is it? How long have I been lying here? What happened, anyway?" Maddy shook her head, not sure of anything.

"You had a few days of rest; rest you desperately needed. You were exhausted and you needed a break. Your fever is gone and I'm sure you are hungry - I'm going to get you a bowl of soup. Just stay put."

"Where is everyone?" Maddy asked, not sure she wanted to know.

Giselle hesitated before leaving the room. "Father Dom sent everyone away...everyone is gone. He said you needed time to regain your strength. It's been quiet here."

Maddy closed her eyes, swung her legs over the side of the bed and willed her legs to take her to the door. She slowly made her way across the room, grabbing at furniture and resting with every connection. She could feel her heartbeat pounding in her ears as she edged towards the exit. She stopped to catch her breath…frustrated at how weak she was. She somehow made it down the stairs, sitting on each step before sliding down to the next. She heard a familiar noise in the courtyard and changed direction, leaning into the wall as she made her way towards the clanking sounds. She would see the vineyards next.

She looked back, up towards the stairs, smiling at how far the distance seemed right now. The afternoon breeze in the courtyard was refreshing - like a soft blanket. She shivered, her silk nightdress moving against her legs. She crossed her arms and took a deep breath. Leaning against the doorframe she watched with wonder as Sebastian, kneeling by the motorcycle, his face smeared with grease, was oiling the chain of her BMW motorcycle. He must have had her bike brought here from Spain, where it had been left in storage. His black Triumph proudly displayed on the stand - the Triumph she had had restored for him. The Triumph he had ridden north to Applecross to be with her.

Sebastian sat back on his haunches, then stood up, wiping his hands on the stained cloth - a satisfied look on his face.

The movement of the nightdress caught his eye and he looked over to see Maddy watching him. They looked at each other for what seemed like an eternity, neither moving.

"Ah, you're finally up. The ride leaves in a week. Will you be ready?"

She tried to process what was happening and felt a smile sneaking up on her. She could hear Giselle calling her name. She nodded and turned, taking a deep breath, preparing for the long journey back to her bed. She felt her legs fold and then Sebastian was carrying her up the stairs. Maddy leaned into his chest, surrendering herself to the smell of his body, the warmth of his arms and the sound of his murmurs - telling her everything was going to be just fine. Indeed.

Moonlight Sonata

In her dream there was a full moon and soft music playing; it was magical. She could feel herself giving in to the music, moonlight and warm hands on her body. It was soothing and so familiar…….

She sat up, disappointed the dream was over. There was music playing; the moon was bright, and the light flooded into the room. She rubbed her eyes, wondering if she was still dreaming. A warm breeze caressed her face as it moved the voile curtains. She stepped onto the tile floor and in her bare feet, padded down the stairs to the courtyard. Her silk slip rippled as a soft zephyr moved against her forward motion.

Her hands behind her back, she slowly walked into the courtyard and embraced the moon; so close she felt she could reach out and touch it; caress its face. She closed her eyes for a moment and felt his presence behind her before he touched her shoulder. He wrapped his arms around her, pulling her into his body. She felt safe in his arms.

"Dance with me." He whispered into her ear as she moved her head to one side, snuggling into his neck.

She turned slowly, every nerve in her body alive with anticipation.

They danced in the moonlight, moving together as lovers do, not hesitating, vaguely aware of the music, the beauty of the night and the cool stones on their feet. They held each other, comforted by the familiar smell, the familiar movement of the other. His warm breath made her shiver. He tightened his embrace.

It was intoxicating; having her so near, the fragrance of her hair, the feel of her body next to his; he could feel her heartbeat.

"Will you ever be able to forgive me?" He whispered into her hair.

Maddy shivered in his arms and he tightened his embrace. She looked up at him and he moaned as he looked into her eyes.

There were no words, just a look, a shared smile - he lifted her hand to his lips, feeling her warmth and led her towards the stairs. At the bedroom door he turned and swooped her into his arms, carrying her across the room and gently laying her on the bed. His heart was beating fast and he wanted her; needed her - yet he stopped to admire the masterpiece before him - the woman he loved was softly bathed in moonlight.

She placed her hand on his chest, stopping him. "What will happen now? I won't let you hurt me again. If you plan to leave tomorrow because it's best for me, I can't do this, not again." Her eyes were moist with tears she was trying to hold back.

"I'm not going anywhere without you. I need you - I don't want to waste another minute of my life without you. Can you forgive me?" His heart was drumming against his chest, his desire for her so strong he couldn't catch his breath.

She raised her arms above her head, leaving herself vulnerable. "Can you forgive me?"

He sighed in relief. He moved his hands up her body, slowly, from her ankles, up her legs, to her thighs, to her hips, kissing her as he moved upwards towards her neck. She pulled him down and before their lips met they looked into each other's eyes and in that moment, they realized there was no going back…they were meant for each other.

Their lovemaking was intense; as though they were hungering for the familiar touch of that first embrace, that first real love they had shared.

Sebastian fell asleep with Maddy breathing softly on his shoulder, her arm across his chest, their legs entwined.

He slept soundly for the first time in months.

Can't Stop the Rain

"What are you doing?" Sebastian walked into the courtyard, surprised to see Maddy frantically taking the towels from the clothesline.

"It's going to rain, and I need to do something normal." She smiled.

"Normal?"

"Yes, taking in the laundry, smelling fresh linen, waiting for the rain to cool the cobblestones...you know, normal things people do. I feel I need some good, old fashioned normal moments." She continued folding the laundry into her basket.

"Let me help you. I'm very good at this. It reminds me of being a boy, standing by Belle, hoping she would let me bury my face into the sheets." He laughed.

The rain drops bounced off their faces as they hurried into the kitchen with the laundry basket.

"Just in time." Maddy took a deep breath. Sebastian stood beside her and placed his arm around her shoulders. He wondered why he found the smell of her hair so intoxicating, so comfortable. He rested his chin on her head and held her as they watched the rain wash over the courtyard.

"I'm making a pot of tea to enjoy with my freshly baked scones. Interested in taking a break?" Gisele's soft voice broke the spell.

Maddy and Sebastian glanced at each other, turned to Gisele and in unison they nodded with a happy "Indeed."

 # Someone Like You

"You have one new phone message."

"Hey Babe, missing you. How are you? Hope you're feeling up to a night out...did you get my basket? I personally chose items I thought would make you smile. You haven't forgotten about tonight, have you?" Dermot cancelled the speaker button and picked up the phone, lowering his voice. "It's a pretty big deal and I really hope you feel up to making it happen. Call me. I'm on my way to the airport to pick up the MuckyMucks...on my best behaviour. Did I tell you I miss you? Please call me. Later."

Maddy listened to the phone message and smiled wistfully. She had not seen Dermot since the wedding and this was his big night - he really wanted to impress the Secretary of State - he felt it was time to return to Washington and either move up or move out. Maddy had previously arranged the menu for approval, the guest list and the entertainment. If she left now, she would make the reception. She owed him that much.

"Giselle, whatever will I wear for this function tonight?" She called out as she ran by the office. "I've lost weight and everything hangs...help."

Giselle followed Maddy up the stairs, considering the options.

"How about the silk wraparound? It looks fresh and the paparazzi will love that you've chosen an Italian designer."

"Quick shower and I'm gone. Thank you."

When Maddy came out of the shower Giselle had laid out sandals, cloche, and matching scarf on the bed. The dress was hanging on the back of the door. Maddy smiled and gathered her outfit. She carefully placed the dress in the car and walked around the car to the driver's door.

"Shall I drive you?" Sebastian was standing in the doorway.

"No thank you. I have to do this on my own. I'll be back later this evening."

He wrapped his arms around her, hoping she would not sense his fear. What if she didn't return tonight? What if Dermot convinced her that life in Washington was more exciting and glamorous? What if she realized she was missing a wonderful opportunity?

Maddy looked up at him, her eyes bright, her cheeks flushed. "Don't worry, I know what I have to do, and I'll be back before you know it. Dermot is my friend and I owe him the courtesy. Anyway, we have plans, remember?"

She hugged Sebastian and bent down to rub Anza behind the ears. The dog jumped up to lick her face. Sebastian wondered once again why he hadn't insisted on having a dog - Maddy obviously loved the animal.

Sebastian and Anza watched the car fade into the horizon. Sebastian had whispered he loved her, now he wished he'd shouted it out.

"You look amazing. I've missed you so much Maddy. Are you feeling up to this? Do I have a tie to match your dress?" He felt nervous.

"You look very handsome. Be careful you don't overshadow the Secretary of State." She checked his tie and kissed his cheek.

"You look different somehow, everything alright with us?" Dermot asked, feeling insecure for a moment.

"This is a big night for you. Don't lose sight of the goal." She smiled and patted his buttocks. "Come on, Signor Acting-Counsel General, *Andiamo*."

He took her hand and lead her into the reception.

The Secretary of State departed for Rome after dinner, impressed with the evening and with Dermot. He also mentioned how much he was looking forward to seeing Maddy in Washington. Dermot watched Maddy easily handle the crowd, moving from cluster to cluster with a light touch on the arm, a quick smile and an attentive nod of the head. As he watched her, he realized what was different about her, other than the weight she had lost. Her eyes were bright, full of hope - she looked content. He leaned against the wall as he realized the look was not for him or a future with him.

"Washington is yours. You'll be amazing. I'm so proud of you." Maddy was beside him, touching his arm.

"Tonight was perfect. Thank you." He kissed her hand. "We make a great team, you and I." He waited for her to agree. He looked over the room, hoping she would lean into him.

"You're not coming with me, are you?" He wanted to ask so much more. He wanted to say so much more.

"You don't need me. You're on the fast track and I'll always be here, my friend - waiting to dance with you in the shadows. Your wife will be pleased to have you back in the country. She's been waiting for you to return and move forward. Promise me something."

"Anything, anything in my power." He gave her a crooked smile.

Whatever it is you do, wherever the opportunity takes you…just be brilliant. Be bloody brilliant." She kissed his cheek and walked away, forcing herself not to look back.

Dermot watched her walk out of his life and suddenly he knew he had to stop her.

"Signor, photo please." A journalist was standing in the way, two willowy models in tow.

"Of course." Dermot smiled, for a moment hating his position, his duty - arms around the women, as the camera clicked. They giggled and spoke but he excused himself and ran towards the foyer.

"*Hai visto Signorina Maddy?*" He called out to the doorman.

"*Ah scusate.* Signor, she drove off but a moment ago."

Dermot leaned against the marble column, feeling sad and empty. Slowly, he walked back into the reception area, muttering to himself. "*You want me to be bloody brilliant…I'll be so bloody brilliant you'll wish you were there with me.*"

The traffic was remarkably light, allowing Maddy to drive out of Florence quickly. When she saw the lights of the city in her rearview mirror she pulled over. She stepped out of the car, throwing her shoes into the back seat. She realized she was crying. Dermot had been there for her when she needed a friend; she hoped they would meet again and that his estranged wife would join him on his journey to the top.

"*Ci revedremo, amico mio…*" she whispered.

She wasn't sure how long she had been leaning against the car, watching the lights of the city, thinking about the choices she had made in her life - had she actually made the choices, or had she let life and everyone else around her make the decisions? A cool breeze made her shudder and she reluctantly got in the car. She drove the rest of the way home singing with the radio.

Sebastian, Father Dom and *Anza* were waiting for Maddy when she arrived at Villa Mirage. She smiled at the looks of relief they exchanged. *Anza* was excited and ran circles around Maddy.

"Did I miss curfew?" She asked as she touched both men on the shoulder.

The men folded their cards and touched her hand, realizing too late they had both reached for her hand.

Father Dom stood, announcing it was time to go. He turned to Maddy, "You are part of my flock and I am pleased to see you safely home."

He bowed, waved and slowly made his way down the path, feeling the effects of the wine.

"Everything alright?" Sebastian asked, anxious to hear how the evening had turned out.

"It was a lovely event, and everything is fine. Dermot is sure to get the Washington job. I'm tired."

Sebastian took Maddy into his arms, holding her tight. He couldn't say why he felt better knowing Dermot would be an ocean away.

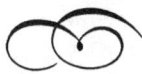 # Sebastian

Reflecting thoughts

I could not have imagined a more wonderful way to see the beauty of Europe. I was taken by the freedom of riding our motorcycles off the main roads and every day I appreciated Maddy even more...she was a great travelling companion - I wondered how we would settle for the same view each day when we returned home - wherever that might be.

After a few days on the road we developed an easy routine - breakfast, ride the best part of the day, find a suitable pension, Maddy usually did the laundry in the sink or bathtub as our choice of clothing was limited. Then she would sit in the sun reading or writing in a journal; while I planned the next day of travel - Maddy graciously left the planning to me. We would head for cocktails, usually in a busy local bar so Maddy could learn about the area and make new friends. We would have a quiet dinner, based on recommendations, then we would dance before settling into a welcome sleep, in each other's arms.

Most mornings I would outline my plan for the day and Maddy would either agree or suggest we take a side trip - she never hinted at what we were to see, only that we would be delighted if we made the time. When she smiles at me with those blue eyes, of course we change the routing - only to be rewarded with unique dining experiences, lovely ruins or beautiful relics.

In Prague, for example, Maddy suggested we have lunch at Velkoprevorsky Mlyn. We walked across the Charles Bridge into Mala Strana and saw the John Lennon Wall, taking photos and reading the graffiti. Maddy had been to the Wall in the late '80's and wanted to see if the tribute was still an icon.

Anne Marshall

The restaurant was indeed charming - we sat in the garden on the sheepskin covered chairs and watched the tourists paying homage to the Wall. Maddy ordered potato pancakes, schnitzel and duck for us to share and of course, apfel strudel. It was just one of her many detours and it proved to be a delightful experience.

We were headed to Strasbourg, near the border of France and Germany, when Maddy suggested we stop in Colmar, Alsace. We walked the cobblestone streets and enjoyed the sandstone and timber architecture in the old town. It is known as La Petite Venice with a picturesque canal wandering through the town, and as the home of Bartholdi, the designer of the Statue of Liberty. I would not have included Colmar in our routing, because I had so little knowledge of the history and beauty of the town, but it was a gem, indeed, and we certainly enjoyed the wine.

At the Dunes of Pilat, as we drove through Bordeaux, Maddy suggested we have a picnic overlooking Arcachon Bay. The view was spectacular as we arrived on a clear day - an experience not to be missed, although the climb was arduous.

I could go on with spirited stories of our finds along the way, but I will leave the telling to Maddy - she is sure to want a dinner party on our return and her recollections will be more animated than mine.

This time together has been cathartic for both of us...we have talked and laughed about our best times, realizing the happy memories far outweighed the sad moments. My British reserve has taken a beating, not from Maddy but from myself. I resolve to be more open and let this wonderful woman know how much I need her.

We were making our way back along the beach to the little inn on the Greek Island of Ios...Maddy decided we should go for a late-night swim. I'm sure I mentioned how dangerous that might be, but moments later we were naked, enjoying the cool breeze and the moonlight. I held Maddy close, to keep her warm. When she wrapped her legs around me I was ready for her... it was glorious...why had we never made love in the ocean before, I wondered. I whispered I loved her and suddenly, there were floodlights on us. The beach police shouting at us to come out of the water. Maddy stood up and started yelling at them...it was surreal...we were going to be charged and fined and Maddy was shouting at them. It occurred to me she might be crying and here I was, naked, no handkerchief to offer her. Suddenly there were several officers in the water with us, shining their lights into the water. I rushed to the beach to struggle into my clothes while Maddy had the police looking for her ring. She told them I had proposed and she had thrown the ring in the water... they were helping her find the ring. It seems everyone is a romantic. Needless to say, we were not charged but we were admonished and told not to swim in the ocean at night. Maddy wrapped her shawl around her and hugged each of the officers. They left us on the beach, apologizing for not finding the ring and wishing us a good life together; shaking their heads and feeling sorry for me, discussing how volatile women were.

It was difficult to keep a straight face and not laugh out loud, especially when I saw the contrite look on Maddy's face. Somehow we made it back to the inn, stumbling up the hill, in silence. When we burst into our room we fell on the bed, laughing, rolling back and forth in each others arms. Just another adventure with Maddy.

The days are getting shorter and sadly, it's time to make our way back to the Villa Mirage. This morning the sun crept into our room, turning everything to gold. I watched the dust in the air dance over her face while she slept. I knew she would soon stretch and move her leg up my leg, knowing I was ready for her. It was the best part of the morning.

Maddy stretched, her arms over her head, purring softly. Slowly she opened her eyes, smiling up at me. She turned towards me, her hand tracing my face, softly rubbing my chin, down my neck, to my shoulder, across my chest to my hip, my thigh and then, when I didn't think I could stand much more, in one swift movement she straddled me, her hair falling on my chest. She looked like a gold goddess in the sun - I pulled her towards me and rolled her under me. She giggled as I kissed her neck and shoulders. She wrapped her legs around me, lifting her hips to meet me and I was lost to her.

"Let's spend the day in bed, it's so beautiful here in the mountains, I don't want to go anywhere today." She whispered as she lay beside me.

"As enticing as that sounds, we should do the mountain pass today, the weather isn't looking good for the rest of the week. Shower with me, we'll have a big breakfast and get over the pass and I promise you an early evening."

She sighed but we did leave that luxurious bed.

We headed for the mountain pass, it was going to be a hard day of riding the serpentine turns up the mountain and down the other side. Snow was forecast so many riders were anxious to get over the pass.

As we climbed, I knew Maddy was feeling taxed with the steep uphill turns, she was quiet in our communicators, concentrating on the turns. At one point she must have looked down the valley because she made a comment about imagining heaven looking just like this. I laughed and told her I loved her just as I saw the grill of the truck in my face shield; the sound of metal connecting to the scant guardrail, blood curling screams - and then I was sliding on the pavement...then nothing...

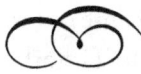 # End of a Chapter

Sebastian woke and realized he could not move. His eyes took a moment to focus. There was a nurse in a crisp white uniform beside the machine on the wall. A beeping sound echoed in his head. His arms were heavy, and his mind was foggy.

"Where is Maddy? Is she alright? Where is she?" His voice sounded thick in his ears.

The young nurse turned in alarm. She pressed the call button to summon the doctor or a more senior colleague. Her English was not the best.

"Signor Walker, you are in hospital. Your friend is here ah, before. She go. Today, funeral London. I find *el doctore* for you." The nurse quickly left the room.

Sebastian tried to process her words - Maddy had been here but now she was gone. The funeral was in London. Was Maddy dead? He hadn't spoken to her since the crash. He cried out in agony. When the doctor arrived he was concerned the patient would hurt himself - his reaction of grief was inconsolable. A sedative was given to calm the patient.

The black hearse made its way slowly through the cemetery to the gravesite, followed by a small procession. Black umbrellas opened and formed a cocoon around the coffin. The Vicar was sniffling as he stood waiting to begin, not too pleased to be out in the rain. He looked around at the mourners gathered and raised his eyebrows, glanced at his watch and hoped he would get a nod from the impatient couple on his right.

"We have to wait, just a moment longer, please. We can't start yet." Henry cried out, looking down the winding road.

The car approached the gravesite; the woman walked slowly towards them, leaning on her cane as Christian held her arm and tried to position the umbrella over their heads.

All eyes were on Maddy. It was the first time they had seen her since the wedding in Italy.

The vicar cleared his throat and welcomed everyone who came out to pay tribute to a great man. "Roger Ewan Simpson was a father to Timothy and a friend of many. You are here today because he touched your life. Timothy?" He motioned towards his right.

"Well, I didn't really know my father. He spent so much of his time teaching and sitting amongst his old books. He was absent for most of the father/son moments in my life. He did attend my wedding, but he left early because he met someone who had an original manuscript. I can't wait to hear all the wonderful, heartfelt stories about him." Timothy shuffled his feet and looked at the vicar. The mourners exchanged looks, confused by his lack of empathy for the kindly older man.

"Mr Simpson was kind, generous to a fault, always willing to help his neighbours. He was intelligent and certainly knew his authors. He was a mentor and a great friend, and he will be missed." Maddy spoke from across the coffin, her voice quavering.

"Mr Simpson, I have a china teacup here for you, I know you love having tea in a proper cup and I'm also leaving you my copy of *The Portable Dorothy Parker* - you have time to read her now, you always refused to acknowledge her work - no more excuses. We will discuss when we meet again, dear Mr Simpson. Rest in peace." She leaned over and placed the cup and the book on the coffin.

Grace and Davi, The Professor, Christian and Henry smiled as they imagined Mr Simpson and Maddy discussing the book. They knew Maddy would miss having tea and talking with her friend.

Appropriate bible passages were read and Mr Simpson was laid to rest. The group waited to speak with Maddy before heading back to their vehicles. Grace suggested they meet at the Coffee House in the Bookstore rather than stand in the rain.

Inside the Coffee House everyone was anxious to see Maddy. The ramp had been completed just weeks ago so access was seamless. Maddy felt a twinge of loneliness as she looked up at their worried faces.

"We are fine, really we are. Sebastian is still in the hospital - his back is broken but he will walk again and I'm sure his spirits will lift when we get him out of the ward. I'm just broken but, on the mend, as you can see. We had a glorious trip." She felt her throat tighten. "I miss you all. Tell me what's happening." She looked around at her dear friends, wanting to hear good news, needing to hear good news.

Sebastian was still in the hospital. They had been flown by air ambulance to Milan, awaiting the medical assessment. The attendant reported that Sebastian had asked for Maddy all the way to the hospital, between passing out. He told the attendant it was his fault; she had not wanted to ride that day. Maddy had been able to sit by his bedside for two days, watching him sleep, as he was heavily sedated. She was anxious to get back and assure him she was fine. They were lucky to survive the collision - other riders on the turn were not so fortunate.

"Maddy, what will happen now? I miss having you nearby. We have such a steady business and I know Mr Simpson said repeatedly his son Timothy did not want the bookstore." Grace looked concerned." She looked over at Davi and Chance. "We are so settled here; I hate to start over again."

Maddy smiled and wondered how much she should tell Grace. "Do you remember the episode with the man in the car who wanted, no, insisted, on my showing him the house?"

Grace nodded. She and Lambert exchanged glances. "We were so worried he was going to kidnap you."

"He was a friend of my father - it's a long story but he was assigned to take care of me, and he kept all the money my father had given him in a Swiss Bank Account. Christian and I went to Geneva to see what was in the bank and there were rolls of foreign currency, rare coins and photos. I gave the currency to Mr Simpson - he loved to trade and sell anything old and rare - and he amassed quite an account for me. When we had enough to pay Timothy for the building, we bought it out and he signed off on his inheritance. I own half of the real estate and the will should tell us how

Mr Simpson wants to divide his half. It seemed like the right thing to do at the time." Maddy laughed.

"I believe Mr Simpson wanted Maddy to have the building…he felt she was the only one who understood how important it was to him." Christian smiled, recalling the transaction.

"Oh Maddy, you're always saving me…it's a big relief. You know, our revenues are beating projections and we have a viable business model… here's Henry, he'll want to have a word. We'll talk later." Grace moved away, mouthing *thank you.*

Henry, Christian and Sam/The Professor crowded around Maddy, offering assistance. They realized she was tiring and made arrangements to visit during her stay. Sebastian was to be transferred to Villa Mirage by the end of the week, so she hoped to see her friends before heading back to Italy. To their credit no one mentioned Audrey or questioned why she and Sebastian had been travelling. No one was surprised - they belonged together.

There was much laughter and many tears before Maddy returned to Villa Mirage. Maddy had stayed in the Mayfair apartment Sebastian had purchased for their occasional visits to London. Bellmere was being sold and she wondered why she had no desire to visit the house one last time. Their possessions had been moved to the flat - Sebastian and Lambert had taken care of the decorating. The apartment was pleasant and grand and held no memories. It was perfect.

Maddy lay in bed each night wondering how to deal with the future.

She had to make Sebastian understand the accident was not his fault - they had to move forward - she was tired of taking one step forward, two steps back.

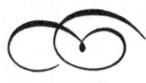 I Want To Know Where Love Is

Sebastian heard Anza barking in the courtyard, a deep voice was calming her down. He sat up as he realized someone had arrived to see Maddy. He could hear the laughter and the comfortable way they spoke to each other. For a moment he felt he shouldn't listen, it was personal…but he was caught up in the excitement of their voices.

"I survived six months in Cyprus thanks to your letters and postcards. It's wonderful to see you. You look great - are you feeling any pain? Come here, you are a sight for my weary eyes."

Maddy laughed at how protective Anza was acting. "Your uniform is intimidating my dog."

"Call your dog off. Tell the dog I adore you. Tell the dog I have always adored you."

"It's so good to see you Oliver. Cyprus was good for you. You look very fit. I'm fine - all healed. How long can you stay?" Maddy sounded happy.

"Just a quick visit. I'm flying out of Milan in two days. Dermot asked me to stop by and make sure you were okay. No hardship for me." He laughed. "How would you like to spend some time in Milan?"

"How is Dermot? I heard he was replaced, and I haven't ventured into Florence for a few months to meet the new Consul General."

"He's setting up his team. Washington loves him. I'm on his personal staff, no surprise. He'll do well. He is expecting to be named to a high-level position right after the inauguration."

"Wonderful news. Please give him my best. You can tell him I think he's bloody brilliant. He'll know what you mean. Come on, we need to get you a drink…*Dai* Anza."

The couple moved away from the courtyard and Sebastian laid his head back on the pillow and closed his eyes, trying to block out the sound of their laughter.

He could lose her…

 ## Stand By Me

Maddy flung the heavy drapes open, blinking as the bright sunshine filled the room. She heard a groan from the bed.

"Get up. It's time to face the world. Today, you are going for a walk. Get up. I need you to get up." She tried to sound stern. Enough was enough. Sebastian could not spend another day in bed, feeling sorry for himself.

"Leave me alone. I'm tired."

"No, get up. You need a shower. You haven't spoken or ventured out of this bed for days, they tell me."

"That's not true. I'm doing my exercises and I've got my strength back and I haven't seen you for days...I thought you left with the American... your childhood sweetheart."

"It's not too late...if I'd known you were going to stay in bed feeling sorry for yourself I might have gone with Oliver...his offer was genuinely appealing. A few days in Milan would be nice. I guess I need to move on if you've given up."

"Oh please Maddy, don't say that."

She turned to go. *Anza,* no longer a puppy, close at her heels.

"Maddy?" He sat up and looked around the room, afraid she was gone.

Maddy stopped at the door, waiting to hear that he was ready to shower.

"Maddy, don't go. I'll get up, I'll dance with you and if you lie here beside me you never know what will happen." He tried to laugh.

"What's wrong with you? Sebastian, you're not this bedridden old man I see. Tell me what's wrong?" Maddy moved into the room.

"I don't know how to ask for your forgiveness - the accident….."

"Stop. It was an accident Sebastian. An accident. We were incredibly lucky. It wasn't your fault the brakes failed on the truck - you actually saved me - you told me you loved me, and I didn't panic, I let my bike fall and I rolled out of the way. You were pushed back, and the truck was wedged in between the rocks. You fell and slid down the asphalt on your back. Our helmets saved us from any head injuries. The bikes are junk but we're okay. The riders ahead of you were thrown over the guardrail and the riders behind us had nowhere to go. We were the lucky ones, all because you said you loved me." Maddy had moved towards the bed.

"Maddy, I hurt you and I got a second chance with you, another second chance. You wanted to stay in bed that morning…"

"Stop. We can't do this anymore. I can't do this anymore. We have to believe in the future, not keep dragging up the past. I'm tired, I don't want to keep defending what happened. I just want to be happy…" She walked over to the window and looked out over the garden, recalling her first visit and her first look at the gardens. So much had happened since then. For a moment she was lost in her thoughts.

She felt his arms around her and leaned her head back into his neck. It was comforting.

"I thought you might not come back. I thought you would leave with the American." He whispered, enjoying the feel of her in his arms.

"It was tempting. He made a compelling offer." Maddy sighed and moved away.

"Why did you come back?" Sebastian asked, cautiously.

"I never left. Father Dom and I went to Rome for the day to deliver some wine. It gave me time to think."

"Why didn't you go to Milan? Why didn't you go to America?" He didn't want to know, yet he felt he had to know.

"It's silly really. You'll laugh if I tell you."

"Try me."

Maddy turned to face him. She looked up shyly, blinked and closed her eyes, afraid to say what she had been dwelling on for the past day. She turned away, looking out the window, concentrating on some far-off object.

"Oliver proposed with such a lovely speech - he's retiring and wants to settle down. He wanted to start a life together, if I would have him. He asked me to come and find a home in Washington. He said he was willing to be patient and give me time to make my decision - what was another week after all these years. Then he kissed me..." Maddy wrinkled her nose and shrugged her shoulders, "and I couldn't..."

Sebastian felt his heart racing. He stepped forward. "Maddy, look at me." He was jubilant as he registered the impact of her words...Maddy had always told him *a kiss never lies...*

Maddy took a deep breath and looked up at him. Her eyes moist, her expression tentative. "Besides, I'm in love with someone else."

His body moved before he knew what was happening...his hands searching for her hands...his cheek touching hers...his lips hungry for hers, his body responding to her, holding her tighter. He had to fight for her...he had to let her know he wanted her more than anything. He couldn't let her go...this is where she belonged.

He tasted the salt of her tears and pulled away to see why she was crying.

Maddy was smiling at him; her most mischievous smile, her moist blue eyes dancing - she looked happy, not sad.

Sebastian started to speak...

She touched his lips with her finger, shaking her head, letting him know words were not necessary. She didn't need time to make a decision, the kiss had clearly said everything there was to say.

"Welcome home, my darling. Welcome home." He whispered into her hair.

 Truly, Madly, Deeply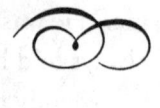

Sebastian absently reached over and stroked Maddy's arm as she lay sleeping beside him. His mind was as foggy as London was this morning - they had enjoyed a rather late night at the Club - everyone was delighted to see Maddy and hear of their adventures. They may have consumed a few more drinks than usual...it was difficult to leave once word got out that Maddy was back in London. Sebastian had been worried about the reception he might receive but any malice towards him was quickly overcome by the sheer joy at seeing Maddy. She had not been back to London since the fundraiser and his less- than-cavalier move.

They had flown back to London for the final signatures on the sale of Bellmere House. Saying goodbye to the garden apartment where they had first declared their love was sad; although leaving the family home was easier than Sebastian had expected. They had checked into The Savoy, enjoyed Afternoon Tea and then ventured over to the Club for dinner. They both wanted to save the arrival at the new Mayfair apartment for later - to start a new chapter in London together.

Maddy stirred and Sebastian marvelled at her resilience. She already had luncheons and events planned for the upcoming month. He kissed her nose and she stretched, rubbing her face. She turned towards him and he knew when she touched his thigh there was no turning back. He was wide awake now - he would take it slow and enjoy every moment of having her, all of her, before they left this luxurious bed.

"Hmmmm." Maddy smiled and let her body respond to his kisses and caresses. Every nerve in her body was alive, even if her eyes had not yet opened. She called out, arching her back, delirious with his touch. She reached out for him, wanting him.

Sebastian fell back on the bed, his breathing heavy, his body limp. Maddy reached over and touched his chest.

"Let's stay in bed today. There's nothing else I want to do…" she whispered in a husky voice, keeping her eyes shut, hoping to fall asleep on his chest.

"I want to get married today. I need to do right by you. We keep talking about getting married, but something always gets in the way. Our deadline is today - we've given our notice twice and the year is up today." Sebastian pulled her close.

"We are married. We don't need the paper. I really don't want to move. This is lovely. Just stay in bed with me."

"Maddy, please. You know I need things to be in order. I want to be your husband and I want the world to know it. Please. Davi and Grace are meeting us at 11:00 a.m. at the Registry Office. Christian is driving us - he wants to celebrate with us. Henry will join us as soon as his exam is over. You have forty minutes to get ready after I take you to the shower."

"Oh Sebastian, why can't we sleep in and do this later? You haven't had a bachelor party and I shouldn't be seeing you right now. Isn't that tradition?"

"We aren't traditional Maddy. Let's get married and live happily ever after. Come on…shower time." He was surprised at how spry he felt, leaping out of bed. He leaned over and gathered Maddy in his arms. He was sure she would come around once she had a warm shower and a cup of tea. Today was their wedding day.

Christian whistled when he saw Maddy in her blue dress, adorned only with her pearls. Her shoes matched her dress. Her hair was swept up, begging for a flower adornment. Standing in the sunlight she looked like a shy teenager, her head leaning on her raised shoulder. She was indeed a blushing bride.

Sebastian stood beside Christian and admired the woman he loved. His morning suit was impeccable; he looked every inch a fine gentleman.

Maddy smiled and walked towards the men, feeling more confident with each step. She and Sebastian were going to get married…the idea had never been important before this moment.

Grace had thoughtfully sent a bouquet of garden flowers wrapped with ribbons for Maddy and a single white rose boutonniere for Sebastian. Christian handed Maddy a hair pin with diamonds and an antique comb… something new, something old, he said as he kissed her cheek. It seemed everyone was ready for this wedding.

The Registry Office was dark with wood panelled walls, but the sun was peeking through a high window, lighting the couple with a prism of colour and disturbed dust. Vows were not required in a civil service, but Sebastian vowed to love and protect Maddy all the days of his life. Maddy vowed to spend the rest of her life adoring and loving him. They kissed as their witnesses applauded and sighed with relief… these two were destined to be together and now they would be joined by law as well as divine powers. Grace and Davi exchanged smiles and held hands.

The happy group headed for the large glass doors, anxious to celebrate lunch with a toast to the newlyweds. Sebastian, laughing at the promise Maddy whispered in his ear, pushed the heavy door and stepped out on the landing as shots rang out. He reached for Maddy and folded his arms around her as more shots rang out.

Maddy cried out as Grace and Davi rushed to pull the door closed. Christian had been behind Maddy - he was surprised to see blood on his jacket.

Oh my, too late for a shotgun wedding. Maddy thought, giddy with happiness. In that instant she realized something mad, something crazy, something unthinkable, had just happened. She could see a woman lying on the ground out on the landing. A man had fallen beside her. There were screams, more shots. Someone was rushing up the stairs - it looked as though they tripped. Her mind was racing…what just happened? "Is everyone alright?" She called out.

Sebastian was leaning heavily on her. She felt herself falling backwards with his weight. He was whispering in her hair. "I love you Maddy. I love you…" His voice was weak. She tried to stand upright, alarmed at the weight of his body, his whispers. Sebastian was clutching the marriage certificate and a note in his hand. Maddy tucked them in her bra.

"Help me. Sebastian, are you alright?" Her voice panicky. She wanted to scream. "Answer me, Sebastian, please, sweetheart, answer me."

Davi and Grace tried to pry Sebastian away from Maddy. He was staggering forward - dead weight. They were able to gently lower him to the ground as Christian held Maddy back.

Maddy fell to her knees, kissing Sebastian's face, her hands desperately feeling for a pulse. Her hands were covered in blood. Guards surrounded them, weapons drawn, anxious to curtail any further mayhem.

One of the guards shouted, "There's a gunman outside, he's shooting at the couple on the landing, stay down everyone. Don't move until I tell you. We've called the ambulance and our men are taking the gunman now. He's shot himself." His voice did nothing to calm the frightened group huddled on the marble floor.

Maddy was holding Sebastian in her arms, crying softly. There was activity all around her but she was concentrating on the man she loved. A paramedic asked her if she was injured. She didn't know.

She heard Christian explain what happened to the paramedic attending to the flesh wound on his arm. Sebastian had stepped out, holding the door for Maddy, when the shots rang out. He had turned to protect Maddy, taking the bullet in the back. The bullet had gone through him and grazed Christian's arm.

The ambulance attendants tried to pry Maddy away from the body, but she stubbornly hung on, hoping he would open his eyes and wink at her. It took several guards to remove her and sit her down nearby. The body was covered with a white sheet and moved away, down the steps to the ambulance. Grace was speaking to Maddy, but she was oblivious to anything around her - she only heard the last words he had whispered... over and over and over...what if he hadn't whispered to her, would he still be alive? She shuddered, wrapping her arms around her. At that moment Maddy wondered if she would ever feel warm again. She pulled the note from her bra, recognizing the neat handwriting. She opened it slowly, blinking back tears.

My darling Maddy,

You are truly the best thing in my life. The doctors tell me I haven't much time - they can't say if it will be swift or painfully laboured - all they know for certain is they cannot mend my broken heart. I am determined to spend every living moment with you. Your smile is the best medicine available. No tears, no sadness. You are my compass.

All my love
Your Sebastian

The late edition news reported the bizarre shooting - a lone gunman had killed four people and injured two others on the steps of the Registry Office before turning the gun on himself. His ex-wife and her newly married husband had been shot as well as two innocent victims. One of the victims was identified as Sebastian Walker, a prominent London design architect. His accomplishments on various committees and design sites were mentioned. He was survived by his wife, Madison Davis Walker. The other victim, a young man, was shot in the back as he ran up the steps. He was yet to be identified.

One year later……..

The sails were billowing, the snap of the fabric in the wind cutting through the air. The sun was bright and the sky dotted with fluffy clouds, the kind you can see images in as they pass. The boat moved effortlessly through the waves. The Captain tipped his cap to the Harbour Master and smiled as Maddy came up from the cabin, holding a coffee mug, her short hair tousled, her denim shirt flapping in the breeze. She handed him the mug and looked back at the shore. He reached out for her and pulled her close. She closed her eyes and leaned into his body. The salt air filled her lungs as tears rained down her cheeks.

"It's a beautiful day for sailing. Let's see where the wind takes us, shall we?" He held her tight as they ventured into the Mediterranean.

How will a grieving Maddy cope with the loss of Sebastian?

How will she handle the choices before her?

How will she move on with her life during a pandemic?

Will she find romance once again?

Her story continues in Reasonably Reckless.

Coming soon.

 About The Author

Anne Marshall is an adventure seeker. She and her partner have travelled the world by small aircraft, motorcycle, by foot and more recently in a camper van. Her career in Hospitality has offered wonderful opportunities for lasting friendships and signature experiences. She calls rural Ontario, Canada, her home.

CPSIA information can be obtained
at www.ICGtesting.com
Printed in the USA
BVHW030555270421
605907BV00001B/2